The Solutionist

A Novel by: Sam Ofman

EyeScream Media Fine Arts Production

Sam Ofman grew up in Chicago's north suburbs. He developed an interest in literature during his undergraduate years and went on to earn a Masters in Creative Writing from Northwestern University. Since completing his degree Sam has published work in the *Carbon Culture Review*, the *Solipsist Arts Journal*, and *Scribe Base*. *The Solutionist* is Sam's first novel. He works for a sports publishing company in Chicago.

EyeScream Media Book

Published by EyeScream Media Fine Arts

EyeScream Media (USA) Inc., 300 W Briarcliff Rd, Bolingbrook IL

CreateSpace independent publishing ®

Amazon

Kindle

Kindle Direct Publishing

CIP data available.

ISBN: 978-0692670644

Printed in the United States of America

Set in Baskerville Old Face

Graphic design by Alpha Sadcopen

Photography by Joshua Mcwan

Edits by All Staff

Head Publisher: Ebonie (Elise) May

All members listed above as EyeScream employees

Sky Eyes
Monday, May 8th, 1989

The Solutionist had gone silent, nobody had seen Eddie Mondo since the previous Friday, and the woman who exited the black sedan outside my trailer looked to be expecting answers that I either didn't have, or wouldn't want to give. She knocked with metronomic precision, attuning me to the wakefulness of my no longer resting heart rate. I peered through the slatted windows to size her up. Pegged her at thirty, but if I had to guess I'd have said twenty-nine. I'm not stupid. Thin lips, high cheekbones, her chestnut brown hair pulled back into a professional, athletic ponytail. She had better posture than the Washington Monument and I got the feeling she'd be just as much fun to talk to. Her Aviator sunglasses covered most of her squirrelly-cute face, and in the lenses I couldn't see her eyes, only the reflected image of the scattered tents and lean-tos set up by the zealots, wanderers, and hippies that congregated around the Solutionist's hut. The sheen of her jacket zipped to the collar blocked the diluted warmth of springtime in Chilton, Illinois. Whether she wore it to keep cold out and warmth in, or cold in and warmth out was impossible to tell. In her motionless stance she had a robotic, mechanical grace. Her body was a feat of modern engineering and proper nutrition, a sleek device that only emitted heat as a practical function to efficiently cool its internal gears and engines; unlike my own body which gave off heat because it was alive and didn't know any better.

I've traipsed over a lot of the earth's surface area in my line of work and everywhere I've been I've seen t-shirts that say "FBI," but spying on her from the safety of my sedentary mobile home I got the feeling the capital letters on her jacket were more sanctioned than souvenir. Seeing as I hadn't taken a contract since the front end of Reagan's second go around commanding and chiefing I doubted she arrived to put me away. Might explain why Ed skipped town though. Either way, I opened the door armed with nothing but a smile.

"Can I help you, Miss?" I raised my palm for a handshake, she raised an eyebrow and shook her head.

"Agent Ignatz Xidas, I'm with the FBI." If memory serves, she had Aviators on in the photo staring back from the laminate she flashed inches from my face. I measured about a Q-Tip over six feet, and as the trailer rested a few feet over the ground a toddler could have stood on her shoulders and still not met my eye line. Yet despite this psychological edge I found myself shifting my weight, even shaking a bit. I rubbed my neck and found it beading with sweat.

I take great pride in being a man of principle. Please don't confuse my utter lack of principles as taking away from that. My lack of principles is exactly what allows me to remain principled. A man who believes in one code of ethics cannot adjust to variables or circumstances. From time to time, complications compel this man to break his code and abandon his principles, which leads him to lose faith in himself and question his entrenched ideas of right and wrong. Men like this excel in two highly correlated fields: Scared Talk and Frightened Shouting. Men of principle without principles can act in the moment, can call a moral audible on the fly, and always do what they believe is best while trusting whatever principle they've adopted in the moment. When Agent Xidas first spoke to me, I adopted a principle regarding my respect for women.

I'm a man of principle. I respect women. My mother, who I see more as an anthropomorphized hybrid of a pterodactyl and a steam engine than a God fearing member of her church's *Ladies of Heaven* book club, made sure I was raised to treat the fairer sex more than fair. As an eight-year-old I gained a reputation for holding doors and pulling out chairs in public, eliciting many a 'isn't he an angel' and remarks of its kin. I'm also a red-blooded man who at that moment wasn't so much knocking on the door of forty as I was convincing myself it was locked. Meanwhile, I languished in an unwanted period of sexual dormancy, and Agent Xidas stood in my doorway armed with an exotic name, tight jeans, and presumably a firearm. That's a tri-fecta for a shameless, self-proclaimed man of principle who happens to be a non-governmentally designated pervert such as myself. Although, if the government knew I existed in the first place they may have slapped a few labels on me, "sexual predator" far from the most dubious.

I didn't normally receive many Federal Agents at my quiet residence, so the arrival of this one disconcerted me more than a tad. But how could that name not warrant the initial reaction?

"Agent what now?" I half laughed.

"Sir, tell me about Eduardo Mondo." Agent Xidas, as uninterested in discussing her ancestry as she was in discussing mine, wound her head like an owl, watching the believers tend to their fires and swap their stories. I kept my eyes on her, having had more than my fill of the Solutionist's followers. "I found your name..." she addressed me indirectly, peering over her left shoulder as a pack of followers inspected her fresh off the assembly line 1989 Cadillac Sedan de Ville, "on several documents..." she continued over her right towards the hut. Professionalism proved difficult to maintain amidst my front yard Hooverville. Finally finding my face, she concluded, "Mr. Frogg."

"Agent...?" The time had come to shake off some rust. I ran down the old mantras to get myself back in the game. *Don't be too forward, but not too relaxed either. There's a thin line between being a fool and being aloof.*

"Xidas." She didn't so much speak the name as allow it to seep from her mouth, such were the depths of her exasperation. If I knew anything about the feds it was that Agent Xidas wouldn't give up on her most promising lead just because he was hitting on her.

"Now is that spelled with an X or an E?" I smiled. She didn't. I liked to think of myself as a Tom Selleck type, only without the upper lip carpeting. Leaning against the doorjamb I hoped to put out the vibe, let on a little that I had the testosterone and will power to grow that mustache by noon the next day if I had to. I carried the body of a man who had once been in shape, but had expanded into shapes. I could still throw a right a hook, but the prospect of bobbing and weaving for even one round in the ring left me out of breath. I shaved, sometimes. When the planets of my toiletry solar system aligned and I remembered to shave, wanted to shave, could locate a razor and happened to have some Barbasol in the trailer. I hoped Agent Xidas saw my cut off sweatpants and sleeveless mesh shirt as signs of my needing a feminine touch instead of signs of late onset

3

adolescence, though I was living proof that the two aren't mutually exclusive. Washed up single men pushing forty often inhabit such a lifestyle.

"Mr. Frogg," Agent Xidas said from the base of the steps, "Do NOT waste my time. I'm here on behalf of the United States Federal Government. I don't *have* to ask for cooperation."

"I'm sorry, miss." I straightened up, nodded with mock severity, and looked out over her head at the Solutionist's hut. His followers had grown as adept at ignoring me as I had grown at abhorring them. "Tell me again, why are you asking about Ed? You wouldn't happen to know where he is?"

"All I know is that Eduardo Mondo has a file the size of a porterhouse. It's my job to find him and you can help me finish that job."

"Well I don't know where the old man went. Haven't seen him in days."

"Shit." Agent Xidas peeled her sunglasses off like a Band-Aid and held them by the bridge between the mechanical vise grip of her thumb and forefinger beside her hip. She pouted like a girl who just dropped her ice cream and while bending to pick it up lost her place in line at the pony rides, composed herself with a deep, snorting exhale, and looked skywards for some sort of answer. She stared up at me without squinting despite the bright gleam of a cloudless day.

There they were. Her eyes were the same tinged chartreuse color as the sky the morning the Solutionist arrived, as though she were looking at the world through a vintage coke bottle. Once in my life I've interacted with the Solutionist, and although I recall being unable to recall the amount of beverages consumed that evening, I do remember the phrase "sky eyes" and how the idea of coming out of retirement arose in our brief chat. My muscles tightened, my knees locked, I didn't breathe for longer than a healthy person should go without breathing, and I retched at the thought of going back to work. No way would I be sleeping that night. But still, damned if she wasn't the loveliest officer of justice I'd ever unexpectedly found at my doorstep. Every ounce as pretty as she was serious. God's recipe for this one must've called for equal parts cinderblock and Cinderella. I could worry about the Solutionist's prophecy later. Agent Xidas commanded my full attention. Looking left and right, then up to me she said, "Then let me ask you this. What the hell is going on in this town?"

I stood aside, and, feeling a bit of that late onset adolescence kicking in, squeaked out a voice crack that would've made a rubber duck proud. "Cof-fee?"

"Mr. Frogg, this is very serious. It's a matter of-"

"Agent Xidas," I cleared my throat with an overly husky baritone and cut her off. Based on the widening of her eyes and the not so subtle drop of her jaw, I believe I'm the first person ever to do so. "First off, drop the Mister." I gestured with an open palm towards the dank interior of my trailer and stood to the side. "Why don't you come inside, we'll have some coffee, I'll tell you what's going on around here and you can tell me what's so important about an old man that he's got the prettiest FBI agent in the country looking for him?" She was not flattered. She was not blushing. But she did take on the makeshift wooden steps I'd built and walk past me out of the rural Illinois air into the trailer. *This could be the last day of my life*, I thought, trying to smell her hair as she moved by me.

"I take mine black." She said.

"Good," I answered, closing the door. "Because I don't have cream, sugar, or a spoon. Make yourself at home."

Scotchlogic
Sunday October 25th, 1987

"You didn't need to do this," I said, accepting the scotch. Ed had already produced two plastic cups from the grocery bag.

"Just a housewarming gift." I poured a few ounces into the cups Ed held out. His fingers were bonier than his otherwise stubby and fleshy build, and between their rough, dimpled skin and their hourglass shape they reminded me of three chambered peanuts. The cups shook in his hand, though I don't know if it was a symptom of his old age or his youthful anticipation. We touched glasses. "You know Carl," his paternal tone burst with undue pride as he thrust an authoritative finger at me, as though even in congratulating me he felt it necessary to imbue some reprimand or life lesson. "It's not every day you become a homeowner." The warm tawny liquid lied to my throat, first claiming it would soothe, only seconds later revealing its more sinister plan, the one where it takes a jackhammer to my esophagus.

"Hardly a homeowner," I sputtered out the words, suppressing a cough and wiping a shameful tear from my eye under the guise of scratching an itch. "It's just a piece of junk trailer."

"You living in it?"

"Yeah."

"Own it?"

"Yes, sir."

"Then you're a homeowner." Ed turned and waddled away to deflate onto the couch, slowly lifting his feet up so he could lay across it with his head on a stolen airline pillow. A short couch, even for a trailer, it fit his stocky frame without so much as an inch to spare on either side of his head or feet. Ed massaged the sides of his forehead with his thumb and pinkie finger, his Mediterranean skin as wrinkled and crusty as uncooked rotini.

Ed represented the quintessential coot. He had old man strength. The type of strength born from experience and efficiency. Sure, his muscles sagged and drooped, but when he needed them he knew how to best manipulate his tendons and ligaments to get the most strength from the least effort. Nothing wasted. The same could be said of his beard. His face knew which follicles could still grow full and strong and concentrated on getting those particular whiskers out in the open, leaving the lesser hairs behind. Sparse spikes of white hairs shot out like icicles along his jaw line. If I hadn't of known better I'd have thought him a madman. In fact, having known his as well as I did, I never could be certain of his sanity.

The couch ran the width of the trailer against the far wall like a poor man's banquette, with a depressing pair of unpadded armrests. The kitchen table folded down from the wall in front of the couch, but at the time remained locked in its upright position, which really opened the place up when guests popped in.

"Damn it, Carl." Ed barked from the couch without looking at me, "I need something new. The same old just isn't doing it for me anymore." Ed enjoyed his frequent stopovers. First when I was living with Anne, then when I wasn't, then when I was again. That he didn't waste time visiting the trailer was no surprise. The only surprise would have been if he didn't have a bottle of the hard stuff on him. He had a talent for talking about the old days without talking about his past. All I knew was that those were better days, they involved better scotch, and they were occasionally spent in Italy for "much needed vacation."

For Eddie, the "same old" meant his job at the hardware store. He took it the day he arrived in Chilton and he'd been at it ever since. I don't remember a single citizen from town that didn't like him, granted it's not much of a sample size. I didn't know many people's names, but they all knew mine. *That Neanderthal in the trailer.* Chilton didn't quite match the religious fervor of the town in Footloose, but it had a similar distrust of outsiders. As far as I could tell, Eddie and I, and I suppose the flocks of Solution-Seekers camping around the hut, were the only out-of-towners that had danced their way into town and kicked off their Sunday shoes. That being the case I developed a principle: You leave me alone, I'll leave you alone. Living on the outskirts in a trailer, outside of shouting distance of any neighbor that wasn't an omnipotent deity, afforded me a quiet life. Eddie needed more interaction. He lived a few blocks from the bustling thoroughfare of First Street, whose ordinal title always got a rise out of me, seeing as there was only one "downtown" street and thus no Second Avenue or Third Boulevard. He became the town's mascot, an adopted novelty act for the farmers and bible thumpers. He was the splash of Sistine Chapel reflected on the acrylic varnish covering Chilton's American Gothic landscape. On bingo night the Old McDonalds shed their E-I-E-I-O work flannel and threw on their evening plaid to swap stories of their latest run in with Good Old Eddie Mondo. "Last week he switched to Italian mid-sentence!" "I heard him yell 'Ciao Bella' to the Anderson girl last weekend." "I saw him checking out at the Meijer with nothing but Olive Oil." Farm Country doesn't appreciate the hick stereotype but I've found they don't mind dishing out the generalizations when it comes to their European cousins.

While Eddie endeared himself and grew close to the close knit community, I either safe guarded myself in Anne Land, or later, sulked in the trailer. She put up with the stigma of dating me, going as far as to take me in, but I'm guessing she got tired of sticking up for me. I hoped exiling myself to the trailer would lessen people's disdain, but the arrival of the Solutionist and his followers, and all the fanfare that accompanied them blocked me out even further. I was poor as a pariah, sorry as a shut in. Not so much a recluse as a loose wreck. But hey, at least I wasn't getting in anyone's way.

The town itself didn't command much attention. The buildings rarely eclipsed one story and if their walls could talk they'd offer about the same. There was a hardware store that usually ordered whatever customers needed from catalogues and one barber who wasn't any good but monopolized the industry nonetheless. Not exactly the fashion capital of the Midwest. Folks didn't just know everything that went on in their neighbors' lives, but their neighbors' dogs' lives too. And everybody was your neighbor in Chilton. Except me. I was a fish out of water. A Frogg out of pond.

I met Eddie by chance when I needed an Allen wrench to fix Anne's disposal, for some reason he took a shine to me, and we were close from then on. He had an illicit quality, something in the way he carried himself, like he could see you without looking. I'm guessing he saw me in a similar light. As they say, it takes one to know one. Who would have thought small town Chilton would be such a hotbed for the disenfranchised criminal subculture? At least it was quiet.

"Yes sir," Ed said, toes pointing to the ceiling at the end of his uncrossed, stumpy legs. "This piss water couldn't hold a candle to what I was drinking at your age. Oh well, Remember the Alamo!" After spouting his favorite American toast Ed gulped the last of the liquid without sitting up or spilling a drop. He drained a glass of scotch the way kids drain milkshakes, guaranteeing an immediate headache and finishing so quickly he had no choice but to ask for another.

"Doesn't seem to bother you." I pointed to his empty cup from across the trailer.

"Filler up." I poured two more glasses and set up my folding chair beside him, scratching the back of my neck hoping I'd uncover the right words to broach a new subject. No words turned up so I just dove in.

"I spoke to my mother today," I said, resting my elbows on my knees and watching my fingers turn my scotch glass in a slow counterclockwise motion. Eddie kept quiet. He understood how to listen, which meant he knew how not to talk. My distaste for my mother was no secret to Eddie, or anyone else who'd spent ten minutes with me in the last handful of years. So, Eddie *and* Anne. He knew she lived only a few hours' drive and that she had no idea I'd settled so close to home. For all she knew I could be in Italy mocking stereotypical Middle American farm culture. But, like what I knew of Ed's life, what he knew of mine was vague and cloudy. There were no reasons, only outcomes. We were in Chilton, and we only had each other. That was all that needed to be said. The old man sat up in his chair and cleaned his glasses on his shirt.

"Did she ask about me?" He winked.

I delivered a verbatim oral transcript of our phone conversation. Presented here with authorial notation for the reader's further understanding.

Eileen Frogg: Hello? *She has aged.*

Carl Frogg: Hi....*Shit, I've aged too.*

EF: Carl! Oh Carl baby. How are you? Where have you been? I've been worried half to death. *Note the rehearsed quality. Saying exactly what she wants to say, like she* knew *I'd be calling.*

CF: I'm fine, Mother.

EF: Fine he says. *Who says?* My son disappears from the face of the earth and finally calls his poor mother to tell her that he's fine. *Would she rather I not be fine?*

CF: I am fine. How are things by you? *Now that's a reasonable comment, no?*

EF: Well, besides the fact that my only child abandoned me, life is just swell. Please tell me you're calling to say you're coming home. I heard awful rumors. Tell me they aren't true. *This is the point of the phone call where I realize I had not planned out what I would say, I had forgotten why I was calling in the first place, and the realization that I was speaking to Mother sends pinpricks down my spine. Best case scenario...is still a bad scenario.*

CF: Home? *This is the point of the phone call where I sound like a moron.*

EF: Yes, Honey. Whatever it is that made you take off, God will forgive you for it. Lord knows I already have. I just miss my baby. Please. *All expenses paid trip to Guilt.*

I hear the grandfather clock in her living room ticking in slow motion.

EF: Carl, darling. I miss you so much...

Even a man of principle has to hang up on his mother sometimes.

Ed nodded his head and started to open his mouth, presumably to ask, "Why exactly did the tadpole leave Mommy Frogg?" But he doesn't. He doesn't have to. The fact that I did is enough.

"Sometimes you stumble on the first step back to life." He looked serious, for all of six seconds, before exploding into giddiness. We got on with the housewarming party, Ed derided the inferior quality of the women in Chilton, including Anne, a favorite target, and we laughed together until the bottle ran dry. I staggered into my miniature new bedroom and left Ed dozing beneath the hum of the still running uncovered light bulb. He'll sleep well, I thought, knowing that I wouldn't. How were we supposed to know we'd wake up with a Solutionist on our hands?

When I woke the time on the clock radio read 37:88, which, using scotchlogic, I registered as meaning I could afford to swipe the damn thing across the room and continue sleeping for a minimum of two decades. I never really needed an alarm. I've always relied on my internal clock and natural proclivity for circadian rhythms. I owe this to my mother and her symphony orchestra aspirations, and subsequent piano lessons.

I managed an impressive four and half hours that night and when I opened my eyes I discovered my brain cells enthusiastically engaged in the second round of an air hockey tournament hosted in my frontal lobe. I licked my chops but my mouth was dryer than an un-oaked chardonnay in the Sahara. I got up for a glass of water. Yesterday's scotch cups constituted my entire collection of kitchen goods, and I soon found out that tap water from a trailer with the strong scent of blended scotch whiskey does not make for an effective hangover cure.

I slaked down a glass, heaved some much-needed oxygen, and slaked down another. Ed had left the door open on his way out and the morning sun trespassed undeterred into the trailer. Going to shut the door I discovered Ed standing with his back to me, staring up at a green tinged sky that looked like no time of day I'd ever beheld. It wasn't a dawn sky, or a morning sky. Not twilight. Not dusk. Just a timeless green sky framing a strange old man and a stranger red hut. There was no precedent in my varying sets of principles for what to make of it, at least not without succumbing to scotchlogic. But I was stone cold sober, and that morning's sky just wasn't from this world.

"Ed," I walked up and stood staring beside him, a light breeze furrowing my plaid boxer shorts. "You see this yesterday?"

"No, son, I do not recall it."

"What do you reckon?"

11

"Worth a look." We walked up to the hut, finding no way in, no signs of construction, no tire tracks, no indications in the earth of any disturbance at all. Nothing but an odd little hut in front of my new trailer. Ed smiled, "Good fences make good neighbors."

We circled the structure, me to the left, Ed to the right, until we met again in the front and shared matching shrugs. The hut stood about eight feet high and no more than three feet deep or wide. Its walls were solid oak boards, painted a beautiful, bright red and connected in horizontal slabs. It had a corrugated sheet metal roof that slanted down to each side. No doors, only a small window in the front like a confessional booth. Beneath the window a slot had been cut and beside it a small cubby held sheets of scrap paper. A security ball chain pen dangled in the breeze.

Eddie liked mysteries, liked to be involved in the unknown, so it's fitting that he took up the pen, instinctually knowing how to best interact with the tools at hand. Ed scribbled, "What's all this?"

The slip dropped through the slot. Within seconds it came dancing back to the grass, displaying, in a typewriter's precise print, the first of what would prove to be a series of undeniably true responses: "This is the Solutionist."

Ed read it aloud, paused, looked back at me with a closed mouth smile meant to assure me of his control, but instead gave me the willies. "Solutionist..." Ed whispered again and again, staring at the note. He shook his head and pressed on with his investigation, writing: "The what?"

Another irrefutable answer. "The Solutionist."

"What's a solutionist?"

"A provider of solutions." On it went, a back and forth between the two, like a chess match between a grand master and a young challenger. Ed tried all the tactics he could. He wrote, "I don't believe you," but the Solutionist called his bluff, not bothering to respond. I didn't know what to make of it either, but that didn't stop me from believing what the guy in the hut said.

Ed upped the ante, writing, "Ok Smart Guy. What should I do now that you're here?" Ed's old fingers tapped against his forearms as he waited for the response with crossed arms, avoiding my concerned stare. The slip flitted back through the slot, landing softly in front of us. Ed scooped it up like a hawk. Unfolding it, Ed reeled back several steps. He screamed, "Who are you? Who sent you?" The old man pounded the red walls with tiny, withered fists, threatening to crack open his peanut shell fingers against the solid oak. "Tell me Goddammit." I had never seen him like that, enraged to the point of violence. He wore his fury with practiced confidence, as comfortable in his anger as he'd be in his favorite, stretched-out old sweater. "Who do you think you are?" He'd dropped the note. Ed's hair, in defiance of the decaying organism beneath it, maintained a fullness and thickness. Whiter than a polar bear's fur it bounced atop his body like whitecaps on an ocean wave as he berated the hut. Bending for the note, I read: "There are many things you should do. You have a complicated life. You should maintain a low profile. You should quit drinking. You should leave town before someone catches up to you. Until then, stay close to me, and listen to me. Also, a colonoscopy would be wise. Meet me, alone, for consultation in exactly 19 hours."

It was almost always quiet in the trailer, but that night it contained the added density of unasked questions. Ed sat leaning forward with his elbows on his knees, his head propped up between his thumb and pinkie finger, which forcibly massaged his forehead and threatened to test the malleability of the fully developed human skull. I sat at the foldout kitchen table keeping my eyes on the hut through the slatted window. We had until 3:30 in the morning to wait for Ed's appointment. I wanted to know why Ed was so upset, but, as I previously explained, I'm a man of principle. Just then, one of these principles revolved around the idea that the past is the past. If Ed wanted to tell me why someone was, according to a slip of paper that came out of a magical hut, hunting for him, then he could do so in his own good time. Similarly, Ed had never asked how I ended up in this town, or why he found a 9mm taped under the couch at Anne's house while looking for an AWOL tortilla chip. We sat like this for an hour or so before Ed broke the silence. "Why didn't you ask it anything?"

I offered a half hummed, half breathed noise of utter futility and considered the questions I may have chosen. Why did Anne end things between us? I already knew that. How did you get here? Didn't matter, he was there and that was all there was to it. What is Ed running from? I'd rather have heard it from Ed.

"Well Eddie," I leaned back and rested an ankle on my opposite knee, interlocking my fingers behind my head. "I guess the only solutions I'm after are the ones I come up with on my own."

"Ha!" Ed looked me in the eye and it was like I'd never met the man. "Carl Frogg," his voice became less friendly but significantly more earnest, "*Signor Rannochio*, you really are a sunnuvabitch."

The Solutionist Keeps Odd Hours
Monday May 8th, 1989

The air in the trailer doubled the effects of gravity, like sitting inside an emptied out can of Manhattan clam chowder, each breath infused with the taste and weight of a dense, maritime broth. The Feds must train for this type of habitat because Agent Xidas adapted to the trailer's climate with ease. "What's going on in this town," I said, "is nothing. Not anymore. Just a Solutionist that stopped working."

"Mr. Frogg." Agent Xidas began as she placed her chipped ceramic mug down on the foldout kitchen table. She crossed her legs, made an overt double take at the reading material on the floor beside the couch, and grimaced with an incredulous shake of her head. *The Prince, Siddhartha, All the King's Men*, a dog-eared library copy of Rushdie's new *Satanic Verses* which made me appreciate that Ignatz wasn't a popular name in Iran, an extremely worn copy of *Finnegans Wake* that I'd never actually opened, and naturally the latest Victoria's Secret catalogue, which I had. Unfortunately, the latter topped the pile.

"Call me Ted." I said, distracting her from my leisure reading and setting a trap.

"Mr. Frogg, perhaps this is an inappropriate question, but could you please explain what you mean by Solutionist. And also, your name is Carl, not Ted."

I rose and checked the pocket of my sweat shorts for my trailer key. I learned never to leave it unlocked with the vagabonds encamped around me. "Follow me outside and I'll do you one better." As she stood up I conceded, "And you're right, may as well call me Carl, then. Or at the least, just Frogg." I like to think she smiled, but more likely she bit her lip to suppress an all too appropriate reference to the second plague of Exodus. I held the door open, just like my maniacal, devil-horned maternal overlord trained me to do, and followed Agent Xidas out of my soup can.

Outside I pointed to the structure about fifty yards away from the trailer, straight down a path of trampled yellow grass that was so beaten into the earth it had taken on a blended, smeared appearance reminiscent of a Monet. "The outhouse?" Agent Xidas asked, zipping her jacket and gesturing towards the Solutionist's hut with the point of her chin.

"Not exactly, Iggy. That's the Solutionist. He's in there 24 hours a day, seven days a week. Never leaves." She marched ahead of me down the path, ignoring the stares of the dust-caked, disheveled believers lining the way. I let her go on ahead, telling myself she's better off experiencing it on her own, but knowing I just wanted to observe the ebb and flow of her hips. She stopped short in front to take it all in. I followed and stood a few feet behind her, waiting for the inevitable questions. Who is he? What is he? How does it work?

"Frogg."

"Yes?"

"I carry a gun, Frogg. Do not call me Iggy."

"Sorry, Sir." She lifted her glasses and let her eyes do the shooting. "Agent Xidas, it is."

She asked the inevitable questions. "Who is he? How does it work?" Her eyes fixed on the hut, instantly drawn to the mysterious entity I had all but forgotten until seeing her take off those sunglasses.

"Why don't you go up and see for yourself? The Solutionist doesn't bite. Hell, the Solutionist may not even have teeth."

She gave me a sideways look and timidly approached the hut, like a puppy suspiciously sniffing an unknown houseguest, jutting its nose forward while keeping its weight back. "What's with the window?" She asked.

"He slides it open for consultations. If the light catches it just right you can see a sort of silhouetted hooded figure, but it never moves. Most solutions come back in writing." I approached the hut and indicated the essential components, miming the elementary acts of scribbling questions, placing them in the slot, even checking my wrist for a nonexistent watch to demonstrate how to note the passage of time while waiting for a response, then picked up the phantom response paper and unfolded it, furrowing my brow in mock concentration as I deciphered the message. "It's pretty simple," I said. "Easier than a deposit slip at the bank, and usually a shorter line."

Agent Xidas slowly circumnavigated the hut, an unpainted fingernail tracing an invisible equator across the red oak, sky eyes narrowed to pierce the exterior. "From what I hear, the solutions aren't all that cryptic. My ex-girlfriend, who's out of the picture completely in case you were curious, got a note saying 'Buy a dog' after we broke up. I don't know what she asked." I'm a man of principle. I don't see two women at the same time. Not my style. Throwing an ex under the bus or using an ex to showcase my abilities to a prospective future ex, however, doesn't rattle the magnetic fields of my moral compass. I'm not thinking about Anne these days. For all I care Anne and my mother could get together and roast marshmallows with their demonic fire breath, wouldn't bother me a bit.

"Other times, though," I went on, "for the real big problems, the Solutionist will hold a consultation. Usually late at night, like two or three in the morning." Agent Xidas kept circling the hut, always keeping some form of physical contact with it. She didn't ask me to keep talking, but she didn't ask me to stop either. "I've heard of times he's scheduled for 'first snow' or 'when wind hits 16 mph with western heading.' Needless to say, the Solutionist keeps odd hours. But the advice is good." I rubbed my neck, looked up at the sky, and released a long, steady exhale. The only advice I ever received felt more like a sentencing. Not an undeserved sentencing either. "I asked him something once. Can't say its lead me wrong. Yet."

"So," she rejoined me, standing at my side watching the motionless structure with its quiet inhabitant, a pimple on the otherwise smooth grassy face of the Midwest. "He's just a guy in a hut who gives advice, like some sort of circus act meets pseudo-therapist?"

I raised my hands to the sky with upturned palms, as though pleading for manna, and slowly brought them down to the hut as I spoke. "I like to think of him more as a cosmic sorcerer sent down from Heaven to help our small town solve its small problems."

"Wicked." The appearance of the heretofore disguised Boston accent signified the first crack in Agent Ignatz Xidas's personal privacy armor. In other words, I thought I was that much

17

closer to sleeping with her. "That's very poetic for a guy named Frogg. Used that line before?"

"He appeared in my yard, Agent Xidas." I figured she liked this new side of me so I hammed it up for her. "I think of him constantly." Here I placed two hands against my heart. "When I lie down to sleep and when I rise in the morning. Even in my dreams." Subtly mentioning my bedroom, I hoped, would plant some subconscious seeds in her mind. Although I lied about the sleeping and dreaming, as I hadn't been doing much of either for years. I pried, "Probably the way you think of your husband?"

"Don't have one." Her fascination with the hut distracted her, letting her forget she was on the clock, and that she was talking to a six-foot three-inch slob, roughly a generation older than her, in a small field of disheveled, mostly homeless lunatics. Naturally, I pressed my advantage.

"Boyfriend?"

"Nope."

"Larry Bird?" This brought her back to reality, if not back to business.

"I wish." The pretty G-Man smiled.

"So it just appeared from nowhere?" Agent Xidas, almost human in her growing interest, led the way back into my trailer, uninvited but certainly not unwelcome, and sat on the sofa. Those damn sky eyes glowed like fireflies in the dank air, eager to hear more about the Solutionist's origins.

"That's right," I said, shutting the door and doing my damnedest not to notice the hint of cleavage peering out from the freshly unzipped FBI jacket.

"And when did all these people come?"

"You mean these people?" I did my best Vanna White and presented to her the horde of unwanted visitors camped around my home. "It didn't take long for word to get out on the Solutionist. I'm surprised you didn't hear about it. Made some national headlines."

Her fiery stare told me she had better things to keep tabs on than our small town's small problems. I wasn't offended; after all,

18

that's part of the reason I picked the place to settle down. No news, no history. And up until that day, no threat of multiple life sentences.

Iggy was too beautiful to be a fed. I could hardly bare to look at her, especially with her shades dangling from the sensual perch of her V-neck, mocking me with their reflections of a washed up, trailer bound bum that looked an awful lot like Carl Frogg.

I filled her in with a lecture from Solutionizing 101 as I paced back and forth in the confines of my soup can, explaining how he hadn't been around much lately. How he wasn't answering all week. Going a few days without a response wasn't unprecedented for the Solutionist. Especially right after the spotlight came down. For a while, in the beginning, people didn't really know what they were dealing with. They asked for miracles, pleading with post-its for the paraplegic to again become bipedal, beseeching with a billet-doux for the man in the hut to make their beaux fall bum-backwards in love. They'd show up by the hundred and crowd around the hut, shoving their way to the slot with questions written in advance, trying to force open the window. It amazed me they never tore the place down. I'd watch from my doorstep, sometimes. I didn't have a television.

One night, a particularly hectic night, Old Eddie intervened on the Solutionist's behalf. He barged in, straight from the hardware store with shovel and hammer in hand. Pounding away at the spade he bellowed like a town crier, demanding attention as he spoke out for one who couldn't speak for himself. Like Dr. Seuss's Lorax, a stumpy bearded figure standing up for a silent friend, only with a tendency to liberally sprinkle Italian cuss words into his rants and raves. I helped raise him up onto the trailer and he began to chide and preach from above.

Ed, with hammer and shovel clutched in his hands, positioned himself against the wall of the trailer as though about to be frisked. I bent to lift him by his feet. As the distance between us shrunk the temperature rose. It felt like Ed could double as a space heater. The moment I made contact with Ed I felt a surge of heat. Not like reaching into a fire, but more like a hot tub. It enveloped my fingers and forearm, clinging to my skin. In that moment of hoisting the old man up onto the trailer I grew confident in his plan despite not being at all sure what he was planning. By the time he scurried over the top the warm sensation had dissipated and all I had left was a new source of confusion. At least I had a crowd of lunatics on my lawn to distract me. When I yelled up to Ed to see what he'd do next he'd started his sermon.

"People! People! This man...this, Solutionist." The crowd turned to face the red-cheeked demagogue as he paced atop the trailer, banging his tools together. "He is not a god. He is not a miracle worker. Do not ask more of him than he is willing to give." The old man pointed his shovel at the faces below him, milking his silences like a highly trained, albeit overly sentimental politician. His words seemed to come from some source other than himself, his language not his own. "He offers solutions." Ed looked to the wheelchair bound and her family. "Do not ask him to validate the invalid, but instead, how to enrich the lives of those who suffer." Next, to the young girl languishing in unrequited love. "Do not demand he shoot cupid's arrows. Ask how to better yourself, ask how to be confident and beautiful so that that special person will fall in love without the aid of miracles." Eddie paced with posture, or maybe it just felt that way because of my view from below, but I remember thinking that I'd never seen the old man stand so tall. He moved with fluidity and spoke with fluency, as though performing a scripted, painfully rehearsed scene from a play. The audience formed a semi-circle around him, enchanted by his series of reprimands, as poetic as they were painful to hear. Behind them the Solutionist, if such a man truly existed, enjoyed a rare moment out of the spotlight. I didn't like the idea that half of Chilton was eyeing my trailer, considering in all the hubbub most of them hadn't even noticed my residence so near at hand, but looking up at Eddie surrounded by a starlight that could only shine in the pastoral fields of Illinois, I couldn't feel upset, couldn't feel anything but pride and wonderment. Ed picked apart the foolish whims of the mob for more than an hour. All the while brandishing his hardware store inventory like scepters and batons, leading the kingdom and conducting the band. "That's all you can do, for it's all he can do. His existence here in this lot is miracle enough, is it not? Christ people! He's not Jesus. Give him a break." The sermon finished, the faces in the crowd traded sheepish grins, acknowledging their foolishness, agreeing to take their share of the responsibility for past mistakes and future behaviors. With his work finished Ed caught his breath and tossed the hammer and shovel to the ground. He looked from side to side with limp arms and said, "Rannochio, you down there?"

"Yeah," I said, surprised to find my throat dry and my words choked back. "You got a ladder?" Ed called down and I smiled, relieved to hear his crusty voice.

Later, I asked him about his speech, and if he felt feverish or hot. He scratched his white head, put on an empty expression, and avoiding my eye by staring out the slatted window at the Solutionist's hut, coolly inquired as to what the hell I was talking about.

Two things changed after that night. First, they did give the Solutionist a break. No longer did the masses demand of him or praise him, but instead utilized him for what he was capable of. The obese asked for guidance on weight loss without eating into too much of his time. The philosophical asked for a pathway to enlightenment without lighting candles under the hut's eaves. The high school girls' tennis team asked how they could win state ("Practice," the Solutionist advised). From my makeshift stoop I watched them all leave satisfied, their curiosity sated and their countenances contented.

As for Ed, his fiery sermon established him as a sort of liaison. For months he planted himself in a folding beach chair beside the hut. Part security guard, part ambassador. Though he often failed in his self-appointed responsibilities. As a man of principle I whole-heartedly oppose unfair judgments, be it based on race, gender, and in Eddie's case, age. I've never been one to behave differently in personal or professional settings when dealing with people of different backgrounds, tendencies, or whatever it may be (to be fair, my professional way of dealing with people usually left the judgment to St. Peter). I am not saying that old people are incompetent, or that no old person should take up the role of ambassador/security guard for anyone, be it a political leader, country music sensation, or, as is our case, a Solutionist. However, Ed spent most of his time 'on duty' with his brilliantly coifed head slouched forward, mumbling in heavy

21

Italian and dangling a bottle of scotch an inch above the ground.

I related these tales to the lovely Agent Xidas, who maintained her robotic posture in what seemed less like listening to my history of the Solutionist than downloading it to her hard drive. I just couldn't get a rise out of this one. At least with a brick wall you don't have expectations for human interaction.

"And you don't find it odd that the person who has the closest relationship to the Solutionist disappeared at the same time that the answers stopped coming?" Her point was hard to ignore. Unfortunately for her, I had a hard point of my own that I couldn't ignore, thanks to the hint of aforementioned cleavage showing between the unzipped portion her metallic jacket.

"What I find odd, Agent Xidas," here I delivered the coyest, most boyishly charming grin I could muster at my ripe, tender age, "is that you have a boy's name. You've got as much explaining to do as anyone in this case, Ignatz."

She sighed, one of those uniquely feminine, earthquake inducing exhales of surrender that significantly alter the air currents of the tri-state area. "Here's what I know, Frogg. You're Ed Mondo's best friend. His only friend. What I don't know is why you are so eager to sell him out to me?"

Agent Xidas didn't waste time reminding me who was the one asking questions. She just asked the questions, and that was the one I'd been looking forward to as much as I'd been dreading. The answer as liable to remove the weight from my chest as it was to shackle my wrists. The first step in taking the advice of the faceless spirit inhabiting my lawn. Why would I help Agent Xidas track down Ed Mondo? "Well, Iggy," Moments like that made me wish I were a smoker, just for the timely pause and dramatic ring of slowly dispersing vapor that would punch up these memories with a little more theatrics, "it's like this." A tattered folding chair rested along the trailer's wall, and, to show my earnestness, I unfolded it and positioned myself across from her. I stared into her eyes, fixing her fierce lemon-lime 7 Up irises with my standard issue RC Cola browns in an effort to assure her of the gravity and sincerity of the moment. I pressed on. "Remember how I said the Solutionist only ever told me one thing? Well," my fingers formed a tepee of flesh and bone around my mouth and nose, and if Agent Xidas expected a letdown, as her expression portended, then she had another thing coming.

Why, as a man of principle, did I struggle to be straightforward with this woman? I had known this moment would arrive, had practiced this speech during sleepless nights. *Screw this*, I thought, *Let the chips fall where they will. I'm already way past the average life span for a frog.*

"Iggy, before I moved to Chilton I killed seventeen people. For money. The Solutionist wrote to me that to live with myself I'd have to help the woman with sky eyes find the missing man, and in the process make it an even twenty." I looked at the ground between us and exhaled before meeting her gaze. "And Iggy, you've got sky eyes."

The Slaughter Rule
Saturday, July 23rd, 1983

The first kill was a distance kill. Sniped the poor son of a bitch from the top of the suburban community's youth services center. A guy named Mark Hilson. There was no way in Hell, let alone God's green Earth, that anybody could have wanted this guy dead. At least not badly enough to pay top dollar to see it through. I read the file and the whole thing stank. Hilson's entire life revolved around umpiring little league games, for Solutionist's sake. Still, when the envelope arrived, only two days after I signed on, Mark became my very first mark.

A few marks (note the lowercase) later I recognized what had happened. Mark wasn't a client's mark, rather, something a bit more remarkable. The Agency picked him out as a test run, a casualty of protecting the bottom line interests of their investment in me as a long-term employee with the unquestioned loyalties expected from a man of principle. The higher ups—if the Agency even had higher ups—weren't bound by law, be it constitution or commandment. Their business model involved a biblical amount of cold-blooded murder and enough unreported quarterly revenue to wallpaper the Jefferson Memorial (including the columns). This isn't to say an organization like the CIA isn't wont to bend the rules, but the Agency didn't suffer the same bureaucratic sidestepping and spin doctoring that the "official unofficial" gunslingers had to wrestle with. My boss, who probably never actually existed in the way I knew him, had no qualms with dispatching a man of principle to put a .243 Winchester half way through an innocent Mark Hilson's skull.

The Agency, whose name probably wasn't the Agency, if it had a name at all, was a particularly tricky organization to pin down. They had no headquarters, no company logo, no vertical integration, and no mission statement. Faceless, placeless, and traceless. That'd be their motto, if they had one. I had enough brains not to try to find out. I didn't know how people found them, how they performed their reconnaissance, or how the government let it happen. I didn't have to know. Knowing wasn't in my job description (If I even had a job description).

I was an anonymous cog in a fictitious machine. We didn't exist. But the results were concrete. When you don't exist you don't have to follow too many rules. If the Agency did one thing right, it was giving their employees agency. It didn't matter how much swashbuckling and ragtagging it took, as long as I produced results they left me to my own devices.

In the years I spent in their employ there wasn't a single voice or face that I could point to as a superior or colleague. The company newsletter was seventeen syllables short of a haiku and in all my years I never received an invitation to a single Christmas party. But the envelopes kept coming. And more importantly, so did the paychecks. They recruited me at just the right time. Two weeks into a six-month stint for an amateur criminal effort and already thoughts of Steve McQueen's motorcycle popped up in my incarcerated imagination. Wrong place, wrong time, helping the wrong people sell the wrong stolen merchandise to the wrong buyers. In retrospect, all those wrongs would have made a right, tight sum of dough, had those wrong buyers not ended up being cops. In my ensuing fourteen day sabbatical from freedom I managed to keep word of my situation from reaching Mother's innocent ears. Though I kept things mum with the mother hen, I opened up to a little chickadee that reached out through the Illinois Prison System Pen Pal Program. Enter: Anne. At seventeen she wrote to the prison as part of a church based initiative to help teach teens the power of forgiveness. I was thirty-three.

Dear ???, I guess I don't know your name yet! Sorry! Mine's Anne. I'm 17 and I live in Chilton, Illinois.

Anne doesn't know this, but I stopped reading for a minute to do a little number crunching. As a man of principle, even as a prisoner of principle, I had some qualms about the age gap. Of course, she wasn't reaching out with the intent of meeting a sexual partner, but I was in prison, what else would I have on my mind (besides Steve McQueen)? I subscribed to the mathematical principle of "divide by two, add seven." If a woman had been on earth for half as long as me, plus seven years, then it was mating season for Frogg. Using this heuristic, at thirty-three I could date a woman, without social ridicule, of twenty-three years (note my chivalrous rounding *down*). By this rule, Anne, my coquettish correspondent, wouldn't enter the picture until I was forty-six (46/2=23, 23+7=30. 17+13=30). It added up, all but the part where I wait thirteen years for a chance at a thirty-year-old woman.

Young, teenaged Anne saved my soul. We kept in touch after the Agency liberated me from the justice system and released me into the wild to mete out some justice of my own. I never told her I was out of prison. I never told her I was a contract killer. I told her about my road to redemption. I told her about my recovery, my remorse, and how her letters mended a broken man's heart.

If a man of principle doesn't need principles, then a man of truth doesn't need honesty. The encouraging words of an innocent seventeen-year-old girl from small town Chilton soothed me. Sure, it was all based on lies and deceit, and the letters didn't make me feel innocent, but they sure made me feel less guilty. As I read them, I realized that somewhere, in a parallel universe, things could have been different. The possibility existed, if only in her mind, that I was a good man. A man of principle.

It's a lame town. Nobody here does anything fun at all. I can't wait to get out of here one day. I'm thinking of running off to Chicago but I don't know what I'd do when I got there. Have you ever been to a big city? I hope you'll write back. I'd love to hear from you! Chilton is pretty boring. The other girls in my high school and church didn't want to participate in the pen pal thing. They'd rather plan the pep rally for Friday. But I was like, whatever, at least it'll be interesting? Right? Anyway, if you want to write back go ahead, if not I understand. I'd at least like to find out your name!

Sincerely,

Anne

She dotted her i's with hearts. She sounded like a sweet girl to me. She was the light that kept my life from total shadow.

Once you get used to it killing another person isn't all that hard, but because of the taboo nature of the act people shy away from doing it themselves. Beyond that, they're willing to pay heavily inflated prices, exponentially above the actual value of the tools, labor, and various expenses of the job. Consider this: I received *two hundred thousand United States dollars* for my third job (And remember, we're talking the '80s here, when a gallon of gas cost less than a dollar and a pack of cigarettes ran you about the same, except of course back then you could smoke them in a Burger King without fear of legal consequences). I flew roundtrip, strangled the guy in his kitchen, and splurged on the in-flight headset for a total cost of about $400. I ate for free, finding a sandwich in Mark's (after one I found it easier to call them all Mark) fridge, and got home that same night. Easy as pie, which, generously, Mark's unprotected refrigerator was kind enough to also afford me a slice of.

The Agency didn't offer retirement counseling. They provided AK47s not 401Ks. Being a man of principle I thought I could assuage my guilt by cracking open my nest eggs and making a charity omelet. I threw all my money into philanthropy, and I mean *all* of it, even contributing six figures to Hands Across America. But I still couldn't sleep.

The original Mark, Hilson, of course, never saw it coming. I watched the game from a safe distance, admiring the innocence of the scene from beneath an overhanging canopy of leaves. The overzealous fathers coaching third base, the disinterested space cadet hugging his knees and practicing his cursive in the infield dirt, the fact that it, baseball, had been and always will be played right there on the dinky small town field somewhere in central Iowa.

Like all American boys, from Charlie Brown to Charles Manson, I played baseball as a kid. Though it was different for me, seeing as most nine-year-old boys aren't coached by their domineering, shark-toothed mothers whose competitive bloodlust and overbearing nature come together to ruin recreational athletics for their child's remaining years of eligibility. Tyrannosaurus Mom, a carnivorous mammal that subsisted on a diet of meaty little leaguers' hopes of beating her team, demonstrated her species' stubborn nature by refusing to accept that her offspring, the previously mentioned boy of principle relating this tale, lacked the preternatural gifts of an all-star destined to lead his team to glory. Each game she had us boys kneel before her as she ran down the roster in her holier-than-thou white sneakers that never seemed to collect any of the dirt that always stuck to us players' faces. And each game she granted me the privileged position of pitcher. And each game I faulted, failed, flopped, and fled the field following another unfortunate display of ineptitude. I was miserable, both in mind and talent, but the fact didn't stop Mom from stranding me out there on the mound for the next game, and the one after that, until finally my teammates, tired of losing on account of my batting practice fastball, took to a habitual post game pile on that, while the parents mistook it for a sarcastic bit of celebration, was in reality a regularly scheduled prepubescent beat down. Still, I have a soft spot in my heart for the sport, though it may be less nostalgia than the lasting effects of those torso tenderizing team meetings.

Not so fond memories aside, the game I watched the day I shot Mark Hilson recalls a better time in my life. It was, after all, the last day for a long, long while in which I felt the youthful bounce, the undeniably vivid state of body and mind that accompanies a good old-fashioned American eight hours of sleep. The last night my mind's nocturnal cycles included REM instead of R-U-M. The last time my nights were sheepless instead of sleepless.

I watched from my personal bleacher seat as Hilson's gangly frame loomed behind the catcher, scratching my head wondering how such a simple man could have made an enemy willing to go as far as the Agency to handle him. He stood like a giant when he rose between pitches, all six feet five inches of his bony frame casting shadows over the children. If he turned sideways he'd disappear. The man carried no more than 165 pounds on a skeleton that wouldn't fit in a studio apartment closet. I took out Hilson's file, hoping to catch something I'd missed that could explain his imminent doom. I flipped the pages over rapidly, scanning for a reason to pull the trigger. Nothing. He lived one of those lives that appeared long and richly imbued with experiences, only it wasn't. The file contained zilch regarding his early life, nothing about growing up or family. It said he lived alone in a rare apartment complex amid the suburban family landscape, and not much else. Nobody remembered ever seeing him outside of the baseball diamond, let alone out of town. His was a life of balls and strikes. These were a different variety than others of his generation encountered. Not formal balls, the ones with gowns and zakuska toting tuxedo drones, and certainly not airstrikes dropping Agent Orange on Vietcong, just baseballs lobbed too high, outside, or in the dirt.

His adventure free existence afforded him the opportunity to hone his specific skill. Bending awkwardly with each pitch he'd reach into his bottomless bag of baseball banter to produce another of his cherished calls. "Ball 2, he watched it through," "3 and 1, this'll be fun," "Strike 3! Close, but Adios," and my personal favorite, "2-2 like a train." You got the sense he'd been doing this for generations. The local dads sat in their folding chairs along the outfield chalk lines and smiled, picturing how they endured the same shtick with their sepia toned eye rolling twenty years earlier. A beloved, though never truly loved figure in the community, Hilson was the man you'd be sorry to hear passed away, but wouldn't bother to inquire about the time and place of the funeral service. A living legend in a small town. At least he would be for another hour or so.

The game ended early on account of the colloquially apt "slaughter rule." This rule involves a merciful concept of not letting the dominant team run up the score, thus crushing the souls of the youngsters on the losing team, though simultaneously removes the losers' chances of experiencing a come from behind win, thus crushing the spirit of the underdog. I found it unfair to the trailing team. Ten runners in the last inning are just as likely, if not more likely, to round the bases than ten in the first. Why teach these kids to give up while there's still fight left in them? On the other hand, I wasn't entirely opposed to finishing up early.

The game ended and the divorced dads helped their boys hop the passenger doors of their midlife crisis convertibles as the moms loaded up the jealous son's of traditional nuclear families into their wood paneled Dodge Caravan carpool clown cars, leaving only the umpire and a fledgling assassin to inhabit the sacred space of the baseball diamond. Hilson bird-dogged his way through the dugouts, snatching up every last candy wrapper and recently caved in juice box advertising the latest Teenage Mutant Ninja Turtle cartoon. Tossing the debris in the city trashcan he next moved to pick up the bases and lock them in the storage container until the next game. I had him in my crosshairs as he made first base, contorting his lanky limbs and picking up the rubber square. My finger trembled on the trigger and I pulled away to take a few quick breaths. Hilson moved to second and I zeroed in again, still trembling, and wiped my forehead with the sleeve of my non-trigger arm. I saw Hilson whistling in the scope. I drew in a long breath and released a longer exhale, and then pulled the trigger on a bullet from the cheap seats of deep, deep left center field.

The bullet whizzed past his ear and collided with the earth by the foundation of the home team's dugout. Hilson hit the ground, cowering his spindly extremities into a ball that resembled a pile of rolled up dark blue string. He looked back in my direction. He couldn't have seen me, but the threat of being seen provided as good a reason as any to finish him off. Hilson tried crawling for cover, shuffling through the dirt towards third base. A man of principle doesn't leave a job unfinished. *But does a man of principle murder for money?* I winced in anticipation, drew another deep breath, swallowed the acrid fluid that sloshed in my mouth, and gunned the runner down in a bang-bang play at third. Mark ought to have known the unwritten rule of base running, having led a life surrounded by the game, never to make the first, or in his case, last out trying to reach for third base.

I fled the scene, leaving nothing but an innocent corpse on the field and a small mound of shameful vomit on the roof of the youth services center. The Agency got word of my ability to pull the trigger and execute a job well done. They could rest easy knowing their newest asset to be reliable. A real man of principle, they'd probably thought.

That night, lying awake in bed, I kept hearing the whistle of distant trains and the voice of a friendly old man. "2-2 like a train!"

The Bombtiger
Monday May 8th, 1989

The sedan's air-conditioning tasted stale and inauthentic, but even after smacking my chops in protest Agent Xidas refused to switch to windows. I couldn't tell you if she came around to my advances much by that point. I registered mixed signals. Sure, she put me in handcuffs (perhaps hinting towards becoming the old ball and chain), but at the same time she *did* let me sit in the front seat. My soup can and its neighboring hut had long since vanished from the rearview and she still refused to disclose our destination. She had her jacket zipped again, and in her shades I saw the perpetual band of unbending Illinois highway extending to the horizon. I made a mental note not to tell women I'm interested in, especially those in the business of arresting contract killers, that I have dabbled in contract killing. In fact, that became a principle of mine.

I liked the Cadillac de Ville. Black, sleek, and enormous, we didn't occupy a car so much as we sat in the cockpit of a plane or hull of an America's Cup sailboat. The thing had fuselage. The Solutionist's hut would have fit in the trunk.

I'm haunted by the similarity of Agent Xidas and my mother's driving styles, sharing the same West Point posture and unfailing adherence to speed limits. Agent Xidas remained silent and stoic as an oaken kitchen table from the moment we started driving, only if a table were driving we'd probably have made better time. Her silence didn't reflect her feelings on arresting me as much as it did the immediate aftermath, which, I'll admit, seemed to go a lot better while it was happening than it did in hindsight.

If forced to give a rough estimate on the amount of time she considered my confession before reacting, I'd say a rather quick 1.5 seconds. After 1.5 seconds my folding chair had folded, somehow with my body flat atop it, and I found myself staring up the barrel of a firearm, which brought about an odd relief after staring down so many in the past. It seemed I had lost a step. I groaned and squeaked on the floor, the pain reaching a level that restricted my breathing. Originally, I attributed this to a fractured ego and sprained sense of

31

manhood, only to realize the true source was Agent Xidas's heel firmly pressed down and threatening to fracture the physical manifestation of my manhood.

"On your stomach. Now. Hands behind your back." I complied, no resistance. As I inhaled the specific stench of my soup can's thin layer of carpeting (old fast food marinated in stale scotch) I caught sight of my reading material beside the couch and smiled, realizing I had finally discovered a scenario in which reading *Finnegans Wake* represented a less painful alternative to what I endured at the time. Unfortunately, this Frogg had bigger fish to fry, and I needed to keep my head on my shoulders to get out of this mess with my head on my shoulders. Slowly, I got back on my feet and played the good behavior card.

"Agent Xidas," I said as she jammed an elbow into my back, reminding me of a recent Chuck Norris flick I'd fallen asleep watching in Eddie's living room. "You'd agree I've made no effort to inhibit this arrest, and I've been very accommodating in coming forward with my confession, correct?"

She started me towards the door with ease. She must have studied some Eastern martial arts discipline, controlling my entire bulk by applying slight force to various pressure points. I felt like a hand puppet at her every whim. Kermit the Frogg. I'm glad I chose not to fight back. I don't know if I could have taken her, with or without the cuffs on. She huffed, "Yeah. Sure."

"Enough so to have earned a small favor?"

"I guess so," she huffed again, pulling the strings on my limbs without worrying about knocking my head into the wall. Despite the circumstances the fact that a woman was touching me set my synapses ablaze. The Solutionist's followers probably got the wrong idea. If this trailer's a-rockin', don't come-a-knockin'.

"Do you think," here her handling of me became rather rough, "you know, I'd really like to change into jeans. You wouldn't have me go through due process in cut off sweats, would you?" And to my great surprise, she relented. Of course, there was no way in hell she would un-cuff me, knowing I was a practiced killer with what she believed to be, though I no longer was certain of, a sizeable advantage in physical strength. Likewise, there was no way in Hell she was going to let me out of her sight, as practiced killers and men of principle such as myself likely keep their trailers loaded with secret stashes of killing tools. This left one option for Agent Xidas: Help change the pants of the slovenly contract killer, who, she was about to discover, was one of the lucky ones in the realm of male endowment.

"Quickly," she said, retaking the reins and leading me towards the little dresser that housed the handful of tattered boxer shorts, mismatched socks, and various sleeveless garments that constituted the saddest thirty-nine-year-old's wardrobe east of the Mississippi. "And quietly. For the love of God, Frogg. Quietly."

I pulled down the sweats from behind, wriggling my ankles free with my hands still chained behind my back. "Say hi to Little Carl," I told her, the outline of my member protruding flaccidly, though no less heroically, from behind its thin cotton integument.
"You're disgusting," She said, sliding one foot through the length of the pants leg at a time.

"Actually," I said, looking down and catching just a flicker of cleavage finding her windbreaker's zipper dropped during the preceding scuffle, "I'm Little Carl. That," I nodded at myself, "is Big Carl." With this she slipped her fingers in the side belt loops and yanked the jeans up with the authority and force of Old Faithful, slapped me across the face, and puppeteered me out the door of the trailer, once more "accidentally" knocking my head into the wall as I waddled bowlegged trying to keep my unfastened button fly from succumbing to gravity.

"I wish you'd have grabbed any other pair." I tried to lighten the mood in the sedan but breaking into the Big and Little Carl routine weighed things down. "Honestly, these are my worst jeans. I can't stand the button fly." I flopped around in the passenger seat trying to gesticulate despite having my hands cuffed behind my back. "If you're in a bathroom emergency and need to act fast a button fly could cost you a pair of-"

"-For the love of God, Shut Up!" She'd had enough. Her massive Aviator sunglasses bounced atop the summit of the precarious perch of her girlish nose as she reprimanded me. Agent Xidas clenched her thin lips, only prying them apart enough to explain, "I need to think of what I'm going to do with you." Continuing on the road in silence I watched the clouds hang lazily, thinking about where Ed may be and what the Solutionist was thinking (does the Solutionist think?) tasking me with helping this ice queen, more and more like my demon mother with each passing minute—both in appearance and distaste for my childish antics—in her quest to find him.

The sedan rolled on, flanked by small ditches on either side of the two-lane rural route 40, beyond which Elysian acres of corn stood with ears that heard not a peep from our silent car. Agent Xidas put on the radio to drown out the residual sound waves of my voice. Phil Collins' "Two Hearts" came on and I wondered if mine still worked. And if Agent Xidas even had one. We passed the homemade road signs, the private billboard soapboxes of rightwing farmers who populated the area. "GOD IS MY SOLUTION," "PRAY TO HEAVEN NOT TO A BOX," "SOLUTIONS FROM SATAN!" Bright letters, if not a bright outlook. Who would have thought the Solutionist would inspire a modern day Burma-Shave campaign? Soon the signs gave way and after forty-five minutes we'd made it out of range of the Solutionist's immediate sphere of influence.

I glanced at Agent Xidas, wondering how she planned for me to help her find Eddie Mondo with cuffs on. She sat with her seat adjusted for lumbar support, high and close to the wheel. Meanwhile, across the center console I had to stare up, and a bit forwards, from the reclined position that just barely gave me the necessary legroom. The way the light bounced off the hood of the sedan accentuated her freckles. In profile, her face had a sharpness to it, not a single aspect out of place. Each freckle located with purpose, each line augmenting some lovely element of her lips or eyebrows. Nothing was wasted. Nothing was by accident. Hers was a face of harmony and traditional beauty, the type better captured by calligraphy than photography.

She caught me staring and, without moving her hands from the wheel, turned her head with such subtlety as to offend an owl. She spoke over the low whistle of the A/C, "What now Frogg?"

"Where are we going?"

Her eyes back to the road. Not a word.

For all the easy listening that came out of the sound system there wasn't all that much to be done by my ears. Debbie Gibson sang the all too appropriate "Lost in your Eyes."

"Will you at least tell me what you want with Eddie?"

Nothing. What was I to her? A bum? A murderer? The sedan retained the last traces of new car smell. The car didn't belong to the Feds, the plates were civilian, the mileage barely off the lot, and if Vegas placed the over/under on cassette tapes in the center console at .5 I'd have bet heavy on the under. She must have flown in from Washington and rented it for the duration of the case. The dashboard flashed 3:59 in rigid green lines. Time for a new approach.

"You're very pretty, Iggy."

Nothing. Nothing verbal at least. But a man of principle picks up on a woman's body language. She tightened her grip on the wheel as though trying to wring out some saturated liquid, or possibly reduce the leather-wrapped band to dust. I spoke up before she got the chance.

"Did you know that the ancient Greeks associated the frog with fertility? Talk about an advanced culture."

Her knuckles turned whiter than Ed's hair.

"I have an itch." I did have an itch, though not the kind managed by typical scratching of nails over skin so much as the type satisfied through passionate, violent digging of nails across my back. She must have picked up on my suggestive tone because the car screeched to a halt and I found myself lying with my cheek pressed to the asphalt, feeling the now familiar sensation of Agent Xidas's heel boring into me. I don't even remember being yanked from the passenger seat.

Just as I became acquainted with the road she hauled my torso up so that I rested on my knees, wavering a bit at first, and then wavering a lot after the butt of her pistol larruped the side of my skull.

Ow, I thought, *why am I enjoying this?* The thrill of violence, after such a prolonged absence, was surprisingly welcome to me, even if I was absorbing it instead of doling it out. Like Ed Mondo drinking scotch, we quickly entered into round two.

She pulled me up again and I rubbed the blood off of my face using my shoulder, in the process dislodging a few chunks of my new friend, the road, that had implanted themselves in my cheek. The door to the sedan hadn't closed and the repetitive *ding* it produced acted as the ringside bell to keep Agent Xidas on schedule with the pistol pounding. For a moment, I forgot about Ed Mondo. It no longer mattered what would happen with the Solutionist. As I lay bleeding on the asphalt, again and again, I smiled with a sense of euphoria. Of well-deserved comeuppance. Finally, after seventeen Marks and a million sleepless moments, the world meted out fair punishment. The Law beat the crap out of the lawless. That's something a man of principle approves of. *Bring it on, Iggy. Let me have another. Remember the Alamo!*

Lift. Larrup Repeat. She'd send me crashing to the road, I'd wriggle myself up for more. I couldn't make out what she said, the ringing in my ears pounded too loud for that, but I picked up a few choice words about "criminals," "pain," and "what you deserve." As she walloped away I engaged in the endless struggle between gravity and the foolhardy male reproductive instinct, trapped in a fundamental battle between two of the relentless pressures of our universe. Knocked senseless from the left and right, smiling maniacally throughout, I grew partially aware of a figure down the road. As did Agent Xidas, who, panting heavily, glasses askance, jacket sleeves rolled over the elbows and slightly bloodstained, seemed to have had enough as she leaned forward with her hands on her knees.

I spat out two tablespoons of blood, a pinch of chipped tooth, and completed the recipe with a snot rocket big enough to make any gold rushing forty-niner jump out of his boots. The figure coming towards us, now easily identifiable as a local policeman enjoying a bicycle powered patrol of the rarely driven rural route, coasted closer in his head-to-toe taupe about to face the most severe, savage moment in his pedestrian career. No amount of noise complaints and parking citations could prepare a cop like this for a bludgeoning Federal Agent and a blood drenched serial killer. Poor guy was only a couple hours short of finishing another mundane 9-5 shift.

I judged him about one day from retirement and made the only play I could with the hand I'd been dealt. A bluff. "Agent Xidas," I said, letting loose an unexpected expectorate, less bloody than the last, but still rather bloody. "He looks old; I'll grant you that. But he also looks like a man of principle, believe me, it takes one to know one. I'm guessing he's read the book cover to cover and plans to go by it. What he sees here is a Federal Agent beating a cuffed prisoner senseless as that prisoner makes no effort to retaliate or resist.

"Iggy, I like you. I want to help you find Ed. Even after all this. I don't think this guy likes you so much as I do. I don't want to see your career vanish on account of me, but I'm guessing he won't mind the attention." It sounded clear in my head, but I have no way of knowing if my mangled mouth managed to follow my mind's commands.

"Here's what I propose. You take off these handcuffs, turn your pretty little sky eyes over towards that beautiful horizon behind us, and I'll make this guy go away for good. How's that sound?"

The officer, now but a mere 100 yards off, squinted against his myopia, leaning over the handlebars to make out the scene ahead. Agent Xidas emitted a slight grumble. "Iggy we need to act fast." Still on my knees I recognized that if I wasn't un-cuffed before this man reached for his firearm I wouldn't be liable to survive the next few minutes. "Iggy!" As I called out my new favorite term of endearment the shackles clicked and my arms broke free.

"Hey!" The officer called, alighting his two-wheeled ride.

"Afternoon Sir," I rose to my feet, gingerly, though knowing I needed to sell it. "Beautiful day we got, ain't it?"

Living a lie is different than telling a lie. Living a lie, as I'd been doing for years, is like having a housecat. It's always there, though it takes care of itself, it isn't dangerous or exciting, it allows for relaxation, comfort. Telling a lie, as I did in speaking to Officer Taupe, is like being chased by a Bengal tiger that's rigged with C4. At any time it may consume you in fiery bite marks if you aren't careful or stop outrunning it.

"Officer, don't be alarmed, this is merely a federal training exercise." He wasn't buying it yet, but his hands were still empty and he was almost within range. The adrenaline. The sweet, sweet adrenaline. How I'd missed it. I'd been all housecat and no bombtiger for too long. It gave my legs strength and my voice authority. I stood tall, wore my mask of blood with confidence. He needed to retain faith that I wasn't, in fact, on the verge of blacking out.

"What kind of training exercise? Let me see some ID." He crossed his hirsute forearms over his paunch like two resting river otters atop a boulder.

"Of course Officer," I took this window to step forward as I reached into the pocket of my still unfastened button flies pretending to search for a license or badge. "You see, we're in from the county offices (a place I hoped existed) giving my new apprentice here a chance to see some field work." Only a yard separated us, as soon as my empty hand came out of the pocket the game would begin. Up until that day I had been undefeated in this game, but my confidence dwindled with each run in I'd had with the sole of Ignatz Xidas's shoe.

"County, huh? Typical of them fellas to leave Colt City out of the loop," he said. "Hendricks still hanging around up there?"

"You better believe he is." I brought my hand out fast and sidestepped behind him. Both reaching for his gun it dislodged from the holster and clanked onto the road. I swung an arm around the officer's neck as he feebly attempted to disengage by jabbing a withered, atrophied elbow into my side. I firmed my grip, locked my hands, and used my knee to cave in his legs. I looked up at Agent Xidas as I broke his neck, and it broke my heart. *Snap. Gargle. Drop.* The officer's body on the road looked like an ecru comforter piled up on an unmade mattress of concrete. Agent Xidas stood silent, sunglasses dangling from her fingertips and eyes boring into me with equal parts confused terror and reluctant acceptance. I hoped she wouldn't faint watching as I dragged the body off the road into a slight depression of tall grass. Then I did the same with his bicycle. I hopped back and forth on the pavement gathering my kill and his bonus materials with the same exhilaration as my arcade counterpart. Frogg doing his best Frogger.

"Iggy we gotta go NOW!" I ran for the passenger seat as the Federal Agent remained rooted to the road. Knowing there was no time to waste when cops get murdered and my blood covers the scene I rushed to her side, snatched the keys from her fist, tossed her into the sedan and took the wheel. We peeled out. My mind worked in ways it hadn't had to in years. Contingencies, plans, alibis, escape routes, potential contacts all ran through my head to the point I barely heard the woman speak.

"He was right," she said with a muffled voice, staring but not seeing out the passenger window. "He said you'd kill for me and you did."

"We should keep going east," I said.

"No." She looked at me in a new way, recovering her wherewithal. I hunched forward with my head above the wheel, my frame contorted by the ergonomic positioning of what used to be her seat as the vacuous space of what used to be my seat enveloped Agent Xidas's womanly form. I put pedal to the metal but she didn't say a word. She just sat with her legs drawn in against the leather interior, creating a massive chasm between her feet and the glove compartment. She cupped her hands in her lap and knocked her knees together with tiny shakes before looking up at me with wide sky eyes. Not with gratitude, but at the very minimum they twinkled with appreciation. "No, not east." She said, shaking her head and extending her arm out to grip my wrist. "Take me back. I have a question for the Solutionist."

Cold Pizza and the Subconscious Mind
Wednesday, December 14th, 1983

The second kill was close. Way too close. This time, Mark was a fresh out of graduate school associate professor of philosophy for a small liberal arts college in upstate New York. That's about all the Agency told me about him, though the envelope included a key to an all-wheel drive pickup truck placed outside my apartment. Perfect for the pre-Christmas break blizzard that brought about more than its share of grounded flights and delayed buses. In Vietnam, the folklore states that when a frog grinds its teeth, one should expect rain. In upstate New York, a Frogg grinded his teeth a bit too hard, and the sky reacted in kind.

I kept Mark's photo on the dash during the drive up. Like Hilson, he looked innocent. A little chunky, he had round, rosy cheeks and the type of thick black curls usually reserved for less visibly accessible parts of the body. In the photo, he wore a stupid grin and seemed as though he'd be not only unwilling, but also physically unable to hurt a fly. Still, someone wanted him dead and I wanted to get paid. Circle of Life.

Next to his photo, I taped my most recent communiqué from young Anne.

Poor Baby! She'd said in response to my latest report from behind imaginary bars. I didn't make life in the clink sound all that miserable, but I did relate to her some of my childhood baseball memories.

That Bitch! She'd said in response to my mother's actions. *How could she be so cruel! Forcing you to pitch against your will is just, like, so uncool. And inviting the umpire over after the game for coffee? Who does she think she is? Jesus? No wonder the other boys were so hard on you. You sound like you could use a hug!*

Anyway, Xmas break is coming up and I'm supposed to help organize the holiday cakewalk for the church. Ugh! I know I shouldn't complain to you, especially because your mom is so terrible, but I can't stand having my mom watch over my shoulder when I'm mixing batter. She's such a control freak. Last year the cakewalk raised $250!

40

That was the town's personal record! And the brownies I made were really, like, super popular. I think we sent it to a missionary someplace exotic like San Juan or San Antonio or something. Stay strong in the slammer! Bye!

Finally, someone who understood. She hadn't included a picture, and I wasn't about to be the convict who requested one. I couldn't run the risk of cutting off the sole source of human normalcy I had left. Besides, she could never match my sweet imagination. Photo or no photo, I'd made progress. Her salutation selection sidled up from "sincerely" to the less professional, borderline intimate, "Your friend." Baby steps.

I pulled into campus amid flurries of snowflakes that pinballed against invisible bumpers, rushing in all directions like an overwhelmed waitress, the flakes never reaching a destination and demonstrating no adherence to gravity and a complete commitment to entropy. It felt like Mother Nature had been snorting her own mythical brand of cocaine, only to sneeze it back out across the Northeast. Unfortunately, the Agency didn't grant snow days, so for me and my silenced Fabrique Nationale, attendance was mandatory.

Along with the weather and myself, a foul temperament descended on the student body as the young minds attempted to buoy themselves with knowledge and stay afloat while waves of finals season stress crashed down around them. The campus libraries, for months abandoned in favor of light beer and homemade bongs, found themselves brimming with life as students hopped up on $5 a pill prescription amphetamines, finally got around to stocking up their just-in-time inventory of theories and formulae. This left the student bars all but deserted for poor old Frogg and his fantasies of co-eds with daddy issues. As it turned out, I didn't get a chance to sample that aspect of the college experience.

Professor Mark, yet to achieve, or rather, sink to the jaded state of his tenured colleagues, decided on an essay format for his inaugural final exam, accepting with it the responsibility of thoughtful analysis in grading. Sure, he'd spend Christmas Eve beneath the mistletoe kissing his dried out red pen beside a stack of exam forms. And sure, the other teachers would be three fingers deep into their eggnog at the department holiday shindig after two minutes of grading their multiple choice tests, but at least Mark's students would retain some semblance of the course material beyond their first celebratory post-exam puff puff pass.

My original plan fell in line with one of my principles of the era: Keep it simple. I figured I'd wait for him to work late, setting up for the big day, straightening papers, sharpening pencils or whatever associate professors do before they give a test. He'd be all set to leave the classroom in an otherwise evacuated building, and then, BANG! I shoot him the night before the test and leave town thinking how there's at least one kid who forgot to study and secretly, with immense shame, is grateful for the heinous crime I'd committed. Keep it simple.

Young, energetic Professor Mark was so invested in his student's learning that he had taken it upon himself to host a last minute review session for the course. Optional, on account of the weather, yet still almost every student braved the elements with the reward of free pizza and the potential for inside info on what the essay questions might focus on. Imagine my surprise when I opened the door, halfway to removing a pistol from the back of my waistline, and instead of one set of eyes horrified by the threat of death, I encountered twenty-three sets of eyes even more terrified at the ideas of Nietzsche.

"Can I help you?" The lucky son of a bitch asked.

"Um," I stalled. Not for time, but more in the way of an engine, sputtering guttural winter phlegm and trying not to scan the room for cute nineteen-year-old women. Keeping it simple no longer seemed appropriate, but because I'm a man of principle without principles, I ditched the simple plan and adopted a new philosophy: Keep it complicated.

Judging by the web of indecipherable hieroglyphics on the chalkboard I could tell Mark didn't care for blank slates, and seeing the look on my face he took it upon himself to fill in the empty space. "Picking up a student for break, huh? Lost in the cold?"

42

"Yes!" I said far too loudly, proceeding to ask the name of the building. "That's it, picking up a nephew." The students' collective interest in the strange man standing in the back of the room faded with the invented fact that I was an adult. They had me all figured out at that point.

"Well, feel free to take a seat and listen in until the snow calms down. And help yourself." The first-year teacher indicated a card table with a stack of half eaten pizzas and scattered cans of soda along the sidewall. Mark bounced on his toes, pacing from one end of the chalkboard to the other, calling on students by their nicknames and occasionally putting on voices to quote ancient Greeks. He wore pressed khakis, brown penny loafers (I don't recall if these lived up to the name and housed a miniature minting of the great emancipator, but looking back I like to think they did) and a sweater vest over a plaid button down. I could tell his cheeks remained rosy well past reindeer season. He had a harmless clumsy quality, the students adored him for it, and I assumed he must have been having an affair with one or two of the girls only because he was the last person in the world I'd expect to be involved in scandal. I liked the guy, which I hoped wouldn't make it harder to kill him after class. A few minutes passed and I decided free pizza is free pizza, so why not? Without a word I left my seat in the back row (where the cool kids sit) and went to the buffet while Mark fed the kids a healthy dose of Diderot. Nobody bothered to turn around.

The discussion played on in the background as I scrutinized the options at hand. I held a slice of pepperoni, its base cool and hard by the crust and drooping towards the acute angle of its focal point. When Mark first opened the box and exposed its cherished contents to the hungry Hyppolites in training, a perfect circle of bubbling grease and cheese welcomed them with the warm scent of the oven. Amazing how only an hour later I opened the same box to find one lonely, stale, stagnant slice of depressing, expressionless pizza. No longer part of a whole, no longer bubbling with life and inviting aromas, the piece I held in my hand looked painted on, the remnants of absorbed grease acting as a layer of varnish. I adopted a popular principle of the era: Avoid the Noid. I dropped the slice onto the

43

cardboard, grabbed a can of Coke and retook my seat as Mark opened the floor to a discussion of the subconscious.

"That's an interesting thought, Amanda." Mark leaned back against the front of his desk with straight legs and crossed ankles, left arm against his chest supporting the elbow of his right as he scratched his chin. "This could be fun, why don't we go around the room and see what we come up with?"

The room lacked the austerity of the Hollywood studio classroom. Just a box shaped room in the basement of a box shaped building. I didn't see any gray bearded, pince-nez wearing elderly professors, no floor to ceiling bookshelves, no amphitheater seating, no commemorative plaques for alumni and no smell of old books. It smelled like cheap, cold pizza. The girls wore skintight black leggings with Greek letters over their asses. "Gamma Phi Beta" may as well read "Getta Loada This" to the frat boys. They parked their lettered keisters in small chairs that slid across the floor over the slurry tracked in by winter boots. Like swirled soft serve ice cream, it coated the linoleum in light brown mush. Each chair had an armrest attachment that swung up and down, squeaked when an elbow leaned on it, and offered students a surface to write on (whether they employed a pen and paper or not. The saturation of graffiti and lewd drawings on the desktops made me wonder if the small liberal arts college acquired their desks from a Bronx public school yard sale). A handful of forward thinking music fans had headphones sticking out of their backpacks. A bulletin board hung beside the chalkboard covered in flyers for fundraisers and leaflets encouraging students to join business fraternities. Fluorescent lights shone down equally over every inch of the room, and wouldn't shut up about it. Mark's classroom hardly felt like an environment conducive to higher learning, yet here they were, two full soccer teams worth of young minds who braved the elements to discuss the subconscious mind and hang on every centuries-old musing Professor Mark had to offer.

"Like a basketball court, you know? It's like, a high school gym. Sometimes it's really quiet, but like, even then you know that it could get really loud. Does that make sense Professor Adler?" The speaker was built out of wet noodles. A freshman on the basketball team who ate 4,000 calories a day but still couldn't fill out or put on weight. He sat in the front row for the legroom, not for his interest in introductory philosophy. Intro level courses have a beauty in their diversity. By the time students pick majors they're in the same courses with the same peers. That first semester of general education credits forces intermingling of the various campus species. It allows the philosophy junkie to discuss the subconscious mind of the fledgling basketball star, to feel intellectually superior to the soon to be organic chemist struggling to make sense of the non-microscopic world, and to Getta Loada This from the Gamma Phi Beta design student.

"It does, and it's fascinating. Who else?" Mark wanted to keep the back and forth going with the students, but college kids know when the material runs dry, and by that time in the night, things had wrapped up. "Nobody else?"

The hum of the fluorescents droned on above as the kids shifted their weight in their seats, anticipating their release back into the tundra. This brief period of silence proved the wrong time for the supposedly inconspicuous killer to pop the tab of his soda. Instantly, I had two-dozen eyes on me, as well as another blank expression.

"How about you then, friend?" Mark asked. "How do you imagine your subconscious would look in the real world? How would it manifest as a physical place in reality?"

As a man of principle, I rarely missed an opportunity to address a crowd of fresh-faced academics eager to learn the ways of the world. Having the audience handed to me that night, I prepared to clear my throat and wax philosophic in a way only a man of principle such as myself truly could. I figured if I preached long enough it might just kill Professor Mark with boredom and avoid any violence. I went to sip from my soda, dropped the can, and while fumbling to pick it up Mark dismissed the class, knowing he'd never win them back from the fit of laughter I'd provoked.

Once the room cleared, Mark took his seat behind the desk and, as I predicted, straightened his papers, sharpened his pencils, and did whatever else associate professors do. Still in the back row, I watched him, waiting several minutes for the slow moving students to clear the building.

"Sorry for putting you on the spot like that," Mark said without looking up from the paper work. "I hope I didn't embarrass you." I stood and walked through the misaligned field of desks, splashing through occasional mounds of slush. "So what does your nephew study?"

"Huh?" I furrowed my brow and tilted my head. I didn't have a nephew.

"Your nephew? That you're picking up for break? Do you live around here?"

"Oh, right." I pulled the closest student desk up directly in front of Mark and took the seat, leaned back and released a sigh.

"History, I suppose. It's all history, really."

"Got that right." Mark still hadn't looked up. He rose from his desk and started erasing the chalkboard with broad, exaggerated strokes. Twice he coughed as the chalky residue filled his lungs. He bumped into his chair as he passed his desk at the center of the board and his non-erasing hand knocked a piece of chalk to the ground. It splintered in two with a soft tinkling sound against the tile. "Fiddlesticks," he said. I'm not kidding. He said Fiddlesticks. How the hell do you kill a guy who says Fiddlesticks? I leaned forward to scrutinize his clumsy fumblings. *Who would want him dead?*

"Professor," I cleared my throat and rested my chin on my knuckles, "do you think there's anybody out there who would pay to have you killed?"

The chalk fell from his fingers with another light clinking. This time he didn't bend to pick it up. The fluorescent hum grew in a perpetual crescendo as the man's cheeks faded like a dried out peppermint sucking candy, from rosy, to pink, to white. "Does somebody want you dead?" is the type of question that either receives an immediate "No" with a chuckle or otherwise requires a complicated "Yes." Mark's hesitation signaled complication. He hung his head and shook it twice, hard, before sinking into his desk chair. He swallowed as he noticed the firearm resting in my lap and panted like a St. Bernard. Grimacing, he plowed his fingers through the thick crop of his hair and tried to compose himself.

"I wish I could say that I can't believe it, but I can. My father."

I leaned back and rested an ankle on my opposite knee while scratching the bottom of my chin with the loaded handgun. He gave me a "What are you waiting for, you know the drill" look with expectant, sad puppy eyes. I motioned with the firearm for the young philosopher to go on.

"You really want to know? Well, we've never exactly seen eye to eye in terms of his business policies and things got heated at Thanksgiving. I threatened to go to the press with some of my qualms about employees' rights. That didn't sit well with him. 'What do you know about rights? About people suffering?' He said. Still, I didn't like the idea of doing nothing. His company has thousands of employees and relies on a family oriented brand image. All smiles at the restaurant; that was the family rule growing up. I'm sure you've seen the advertising. It wouldn't help to have his own son attack him in the media." Professor Mark sniffed back a tear and rubbed his eye. "I never thought he'd stoop this low. Although," the young educator drew a long, slow breath, "I can't really say I'm all that surprised."

"That's rough, Professor," I said. "I'll make this quick for you now." I felt guiltier watching him suffer than I'd feel after the deed. I lifted the weapon and pointed at his rosy cheeks.

"Wait." He held up a hand, "I'll go first." He put his feet up on the corner of the desk, the scratched penny loafers of a penniless professor. He recognized this would be his final lecture, kicking a stack of paperclipped homework assignments to the ground with no regard to the consequences, like an impassioned lover in the heat of the moment, only instead of making a move on a perky TA he chose to engage in a masturbatory philosophical soliloquy. "My subconscious, I mean. Neither of us got a chance to share with the class." Still with his feet up he interlocked his hands behind his head and, slightly teary-eyed, collected his thoughts. He breathed through his nose. A discarded overhead projector watched us from the corner, its swanlike neck supporting the unblinking eye of its lens. I watched him over the cool aluminum rim of my Coke can. Professor Mark addressed the class.

"My brain is like a city without doors." He began, his voice steady. "My conscious mind floats through the city, absorbing stimuli as it passes along the streets, aware of what's in front of it, accessing whatever it wishes. The streets connect the neighborhoods of past and present, happy and sad, and all of the buildings in the city seem familiar, whether connected by rarely used highways to places where old acquaintances live, or in the bustling downtown where my mind goes to work, attends routine meals with family, or drinks beers with my friends.

"There is one door in the city, and behind it lives my subconscious mind. I've floated there, on rare occasions, but can never recall the route I took to the building, or what it looked like on the outside. I merely stand outside the door in a hallway of clean, bright lights and shimmering white tiles. There are no pictures on the walls. The door is gray and locked. A loud silence emits from beyond the door, as though whatever typically happens in that space has been shut down until I exit the building. The unknown world beyond it holds its breath when I get too close. Unseen eyes penetrate through unknown barriers, all fixed on me. I feel I shouldn't be there, but it's my mind, it should belong to me. I grow tense.

"When the door opens I'm greeted by a boy of roughly eight years, always dressed shabbily in the clothes of an adult. Loosened tie, dress shirt half untucked, possibly missing a shoe. He is not me, does not look anything like me, and is not happy to have been interrupted. He says nothing but communicates nonetheless effectively. I imagine he is in charge, or at least high ranking in the hierarchy established beyond the door. Behind him the darkness doesn't allow me to see much, just shadows. The door closes and I hear the workings of unattended children start up again.

"That is how I see my subconscious: an eternal, unrestrained school recess. The laws are implicit, unspoken and enforced by majority rule. The politics and consequences are real but only to those inside and could never be comprehended by an outsider, let alone my conscious self. All of the children play a role, some actively aware and others swaying on swing sets, waiting to be spurred to action. Some have bruised shins, some are lonely, and they are all secretly in love, deeply afraid, and capable of so much more than they realize."

Mark and I sat on either side of the desk. He kept his eyes open but didn't pay much attention to me, or the gun in my hand. I took another long sip of soda and offered an obnoxious expression of refreshment to break the silence. He still didn't look up. Reaching forward, I tapped the desk with the butt of the weapon. "Professor, are you going to tell me why I'm about to kill you?" This brought him back.

Staring down the barrel gave him a reckless confidence. I recognized in him a "Nothing to Lose" principle and admired him for it. One more hurdle in the imminent murder, but I told myself I'd jump it. "You first," he said, loosening the top button of his sweat-stained plaid just above the V-neck sweater vest's collar and revealing to me the mystery of the associate professor's chest hair density. "Tell me about your subconscious."

"I haven't had the time to think it over, prof."

"Give it a minute. Think about my recess, or Michael's gym." He brought his feet down and sat up straight. "To me, it's a place like that. A place like a public pool, or a crowded restaurant, or the dance floor at a big wedding. A place where different types of people behave at different speeds in a controlled chaos, wear strange clothing, interact in ways that wouldn't make sense anywhere else."

He watched me with big eyes, looked right at me, right in the subconscious. With two minutes to live he wanted nothing more than to hear about the inner workings of my inner workings. What could I do but humor the man?

"I don't see mine that way," I said.

"How do you see it?"

"I don't know."

"Is it light or dark?"

"Dark."

"Inside?"

"It's a forest." I couldn't believe how readily the image came to me. I looked at Mark's chubby, smiling face.

"Tell me more," he said. "Close your eyes, dig deeper."

I shut my eyes, leaned my head back, and gripped the Fabrique Nationale a little tighter. "It's a forest at night. The sky is deep purple, but I can't see the damn thing. I just know it's there. I'm riding on a carriage, driving it. There's a horse pulling it, but the horse has no throat, and pieces of its flesh are missing all around its body. They hang and flap back and forth as the beast trots forwards." The image came so quickly, so effortlessly to my mind I couldn't help myself. I just described it as I saw it, like it had been uploaded to my brain years ago, waiting for me to access the file. "There's a train moving beyond the forest somewhere. It's always behind me. I want to catch the train but no matter how the horse gallops and turns the whistle of the train still comes from behind me. It feels like my face has been cut by tiny whips, but I can't tend to it because my hands won't release the reins. The whistle gets louder and louder. It's maddening. It's always night. Deep, purple, night. The train's whistle blows louder and faster. I feel blood collecting at my chin but it doesn't drip..."

I paused. The handle of the gun slid in my sweaty palm. I found myself out of breath. Opening my eyes, I noticed a strange absence of Professor Mark.

"Fuck!" I thought.

"Fuck!" I yelled.

The door to the classroom made a slight clicking noise as Mark sidled out and closed it. I hurled my soda can at the chalkboard, catalyzing a fizzing reaction between the dust and the carbonated liquid, and raced across the room. Two strides later I slipped on the winter slush and slammed my nose into the tile. My conscious mind had no trouble feeling for the blood, and it flowed out something awful. I got up, made it out the door, and chased down the hall in time to hear Professor Mark pushing through the heavy double doors to the blustery beyond. I took three stairs at a time getting out of the basement and rushed to the exit.

Outside, the changing winds whipsawed hunks of falling snow from side to side like windshield wipers. I stared into the distance trying to make out a figure among the dynamically static atmosphere.

Nothing. "Fuck!" I thought, being a man of principle, if not upper diction. I sat on the top step leading down the path to the campus quad. The Agency would have no choice but to fire me, and if there was ever a company that might take "getting the ax" too literally, it was the Agency.

As I sat imagining the horrors of the Agency's human resources protocols, I heard a groan from the great white flurry. It came from behind the sign marking the name of the campus building. I looked up just in time to see a shoe disappear behind the sign. A penny loafer. Lucky for me, Professor Mark had suffered a fall of his own chugging his way down the steps and twisted his ankle. I rose and leaned into the wind as I walked to the opposite side of the sign, pointed my Fabrique Nationale, and said to the heaving mound of doomed flesh at my feet, "Fiddlesticks."

Snowflakes whipped in all directions, and through the rushing whoosh of the winds I heard behind me the whistle of a distant train.

Buffalo, Mozzarella
Friday, April 24th, 1987

The bell above the entrance to the hardware store hung tenuously, affixed by a threadbare string. The poor construction worked as an intentional set up for failure, with all of Chilton's handiest men congregated around the contraption, awaiting the day they could gather closer and argue as one of them attempted to fix it. Each customer that pushed through the door tinkled the bell, and like Pavlov's dogs the regulars would turn their heads and salivate at the chance to perform an odd job.

After purchasing the Allen wrench for Anne's disposal, I got to talking with the new employee behind the counter. He smiled with his entire body. Hearing his voice gave me peace of mind, as though he absolved me of my life of sins. Maybe it was his resemblance to a pope. Maybe he was just a nice guy. Either way, we were friends at first sight. But a man of principle doesn't just shake hands and leave it at that. When I first met Eddie Mondo at the hardware store I, being the unprincipled sort of principled man, knew then and there that truly principled, gracious folks like myself always insist upon hosting new friends and neighbors for dinner. At the time I held a principle regarding my willingness to take no for an answer, and thus Eddie had no choice but to accept. "Scotch, ok?" Ed said as I walked to the exit. I pulled the door, it shook the bell, but the sucker held on for another day. Over my shoulder, I delivered a nod of principle.

"Aren't you the one always saying I need to be more sociable?"

"Yeah," Anne huffed, "But I meant with *my* friends, not with old guys you meet at the hardware store." She moved about the kitchen with her back to me. The folds of her skin crimping around her neck, which I had known her long enough to take as a sign of oncoming frustration. I sat at the breakfast nook table, admiring her curvature and nursing a domestic bottle. She wanted to yell at me again, but instead kept scrubbing away in front of the sink. Anne didn't take company lightly, so until Ed left she'd be too busy scouring to get started with the scowling. "I don't know what I'll wear; I haven't done laundry yet. And what I am supposed to make? I was planning to shop tomorrow after work. Honestly, Frogg. You're really screwing me on this." She sped through the dishes, arms fluttering at her sides in a blur like Road Runner's legs prior to "meep meep." Her body tilted as she leaned to her right to reach for a drawer, standing on one leg with the other extending outwards for balance. Hers was a body for balance, with a center of gravity about the same elevation as my patellas. Hers was not, however, a body made for stretching.

I walked up behind her and put my hands over her ample hips. "Calm down, babe." I traced her Rubenesque figure up and down the slopes of her torso with my palms. The top of her head didn't reach my chin. She had on a blue tank top and red pajama pants, the official warm-up outfit of the Harlem Globetrotters, though she'd have an easier time passing as the mascot.

We never talked about marriage and kids. No, we did. We never talked about *us* getting married or having kids. She wanted both, but she had enough brains to realize that no matter how many times she kissed this Frogg, I wasn't going to transform into a prince. However, I wasn't without my talents. I reached for the drawer and handed her a fresh hunk of steel wool, demonstrating a well-honed sense of kitchen wherewithal learned as sous chef in a trial by fire upbringing with my dear mother.

I wasn't the only one keeping secrets back in the days of our postal prison romance. Neither of us claimed to be supermodels, but neither of us was quite prepared for the day I arrived at her doorstep. She opened the door and we did a simultaneous sizing up, moving from the feet on up to the eyes. I was a world-weary thirty-six. She was an independent woman, and a wide-eyed twenty. We shared a moment of flawed, imperfect wonder, seeing the disappointed look on each other's faces and recognizing right away that we mirrored one another, that even though I stood a foot taller and she looked like a Botero painting, it somehow felt right. I stepped inside without a word. She stood aside, tacitly agreeing upon a new life together.

"He's not the president. He's Italian. We'll throw some pasta in a pot. The guy's old; he probably couldn't tell if you had makeup on if he were three inches from your face. Just relax. It'll be fun, babe." I let my fingers crawl around to her belly and slowly creep southward to the elastic of the pajamas.

Slap on the wrist. Denied.

"Jesus, Frogg." She whipped off her rubber gloves and stormed out of the kitchen. I guess she wasn't in the mood.

"Remember the Alamo!" Ed toasted from the end of the dining room table, indicating my scotch glass with a series of rickety gestures often made by old men with old joints. He took a long sip. "How do you like it, Ranocchio?"

"Very good, Eddie." I was under-qualified for the quaff, coughed, and sputtered an epexegesis, "Very smooth."

A lifetime with the surname and a complicated history of international travel, however discrete, had filled me in on several translations for the tailless amphibian that happened to be my personal homophone. I preferred Ranocchio (like Pinocchio), to say, its Russian equivalent. I don't know if I could have survived that dinner, let alone Ed's friendship being addressed in guttural, Siberian tones as *Lyagushka*.

Ed took another sip and released a voluminous "Ah." Anne and our guest sat on the ends while I mediated from the middle of the table. This meal marked my first visit to the good oak table in the dining room, which Anne's father had had shipped just before he and his wife passed away and left the house to Anne. I felt like Gulliver in Lilliput looking down on my fellow diners, neither of which topped five foot two inches. Michelangelo might've composed the scene. Me, playing the Adonis figure in the center of the canvas, extending my merciful arms to either side where a rosy faced cherub doted upon me.

Before uncorking the scotch Ed moped through the front door, slumped forward and scowling. His beloved countrymen had lost to France that afternoon. Italy's elimination from the '86 World Cup affected the man, and even months later when the teams played again in a friendly the defeat stung him deeply. Deeply, but briefly, for once the scotch met his lips he stopped holding my loose association as a French soccer apologist (on account of my being loosely associated with frogs) against me and changed into a smile. I tried to explain to the old man, who looked ten times more frog-like than I ever have, that I didn't support the 9th century campaign to overtake England and had never raised the frog-featuring coat of arms of the time. Ed dismissed my history lesson on the Charlemagne Empire in favor of the Charle-main event. He came for dinner, not lectures, he mumbled into his scotch.

He wore a red turtleneck beneath a straw-colored dinner jacket. His slicked back hair shimmered like a pool cue against the lavender walls of the dining room. "Anne," he said across the table as she set down her white zinfandel to offer her full attention. "I admire the way you don't feel the need to wear cosmetics when guests arrive." I heard her swallow but couldn't bring myself to look at her. Ed added, "It's refreshing in a modern woman." I swung my head around in time to witness my lady open her mouth in a half-surprised, half-murderous smile and manage a minute "heh" before subtly training her eyes on me. Her expression did not change, but I'd looked in the mirror enough to recognize the frozen countenance of a wrathful glare. To my right, Ed suppressed a giggle behind the guise of scratching his nose.

"I'll check on the ravioli." She left us boys to ourselves and scurried out of the room. I turned my palms up and bit my lip as though holding back a tongue-lashing.

"So you like them a little more zaftig, Mr. Ranocchio? Something to grab hold of?" I pointed and shook my head, but the effort was forced. Truth be told, I sided with Eddie. The moment I shook his hand I had sided with Eddie. He had a way about him that spoke to me. He didn't judge. Even if he knew about my past I don't think his opinion of me would have changed. I didn't have many friends growing up, and had even less in my working days. Eddie just showed up in my life acting like the two of us were thick as thieves. Being a man of principle doesn't mean I can't also be a narcissist, and the fact that Eddie liked *me* so quickly was one of my favorite traits in him, and because of that I liked him right back. So I sat there in silence, feigning frustration but secretly enjoying the show as he poked fun at my girl. My eyes did the smiling, but for Anne's sake I kept it to that.

Anne returned, a light layer of foundation sloppily applied to her cute, piggish face. I never thought of her as overweight, but Ed called it like he saw it, and she didn't lack for places to grab onto when the time came (though that night I wasn't too confident that time would be coming any time soon). She placed a towel in front of her plate and set the steaming ziggurat of ravioli atop it, still simmering in the pot. Through the rising steam Anne glared at a smiling Eddie as he extended his plate without a word, his stubby limb only extending about a quarter of the way to where she stood across the bare wooden landscape. I took the plate and passed it along, careful not to knock it into the plastic sunflower centerpiece. Handing it to Anne, I felt her hand shaking and looked up to see her lip trembling. Every ounce of appreciation I had for Eddie's antics, Anne matched with a pound of disdain.

Through open windows we heard the repetitive creaking of crickets, which made the absence of dinner music all the more glaring an oversight. *Creeeeak Creeeeak Creeeeak*, like the sound of a basement stair slowly having pressure applied by a hesitant character in a horror film. I wouldn't have been surprised if someone yelled from the front yard, "No! Don't go down there Frogg! She'll never let you hear the end of it this time!"

Anne globbed a pile of ravioli onto the ceramic china and sent it back down the assembly line. I had to avert my eyes to keep from snickering like an eleven-year-old in sex education. If I looked up at this woman's body, I'd surely lose control. Ed snatched his plate back with a boyish smile and I played a light chuckle off as clearing my throat.

"Like Mamma used to make, right Ranocchio?"

Anne sighed. "Don't get him started on his mother." I leaned back in my chair, innocent as an eleven-year-old boy in sex education, and watched Anne fix herself a plate.

"I didn't say a word." I put my hands up. *Creeeeak.*

Ed put his head down in focus and separated a ravioli square from the pile. We watched him work beneath his manicured swatch of wet, cottony hair as he used his knife to carefully bisect the chosen ravioli down its Y-axis. He rotated the plate 90 degrees and repeated the process, creating four congruent morsels. Before taking the inaugural bite he raised his head, exposing Anne and myself to a toothless, closed-mouth grin and a slight nod. My head made another pendulum swing from Ed to Anne. The whole night I felt like a spectator at Wimbledon.

I held out my plate but the recipient made quite a show of not noticing, admiring her nails, looking over her shoulder, and undergoing a pre-meal neck stretching routine. I waited two *Creeeeaks* before rising a few inches off my chair to reach for the ladle, a sigh of defeat forcing its way through my teeth.

"So Mr. Frogg doesn't care for his mother," Ed spoke once the plates all filled up. "Why is that?"

"The usual reasons." I waved a hand in nonchalance, hoping to shoo the subject away. My reasons couldn't have been more unusual, or cruel for that matter. I drank from my scotch glass and let the booze calm me down, hoping if I'd turned red I could blame it on the alcohol.

"Does she live far from here?"

"Only a few hours. But believe me, that's plenty close enough."

Ed nodded. He had enough tact not to press the issue, though his interest seemed sincere. Several *Creeeeaks* bounded through the window before he continued.

"How about you my dear? Tell me about your family." Ed didn't scoop up his utensils but sat with his fingers interlocked above his food, elbows up on the table as though prepared to say grace. I stabbed a full ravioli into my mouth but didn't chew. The ball had been sent back to Anne's half of the court and I needed to see how she'd volley this one back. Her eyes widened and she sat up straighter, took a sip of her wine, and set the glass down lightly.

"Well," she smiled and patted the corners of her mouth with the fancy cloth napkins she'd never used before. I crunched my teeth, once, warily, over the soft lump of pasta and cheese. As a man of principle, I tried to see the situation from her point of view. Halfway between a girl and woman, she retained the warm soft body of youth, but lately she'd wised up; experience had piled up in her piggy little head, and I scrutinized her every move, seeing how she'd handle herself against two men well beyond her years. "My parents both passed a few years ago. They were born and raised here in Illinois, but my grandparents from my dad's side moved here from Buffalo."

"Mozzarella!" Eddie cheered. He picked up his fork and daintily scooped the first quadrant of his surgically prepped ravioli onto the tines of his fork.

Anne's face twisted up, unsure of what to make of the exclamation. I saw the gears churning in her mind as she deemed it harmless, honked a nervous laugh, and went on. "Right. And Mom's folks came over from Germany back in-"

Ed dropped his fork against the plate, a soft metallic clinking rang out, like sleigh bells. He coughed and gagged, slapping himself in the chest. I sprang to my feet. Anne yelled "Oh God!" But Eddie waved me off. He pushed his chair back from the table and leaned forward, coughing between *Creeeeaks* and holding a hand up to ward off any assistance. Anne stood across the table with both hands over her mouth. The coughing subsided, Ed caught his breath, and he pulled himself back to the table, forcing a too-wide smile that displayed each of his well-worn molars.

"I'm sorry. Wrong pipe." Ed tapped his chest with his fist. "You were saying, my dear?"

Anne took her seat and appealed to me with a worried glance. I made a show of not noticing, admiring my nails, looking over my shoulder, and undergoing a mid-meal neck stretching routine. She gulped the last of her zin.

"My Mom's folks came over from Germany, and my grandfather found work in Chicago in meat packing but didn't care for it and ended up moving down here as a farmhand."

Ed Mondo finished his ravioli sections and begun operating on his next pasta patient, surgically crafting four more identical bites. Without looking up from his work he asked, "Do you know what part of Germany, by chance?"

"No," Anne said, "I always forget, but I think it was pretty far west. Why? Have you been to Germany?"

Ed stopped cutting, placed his knife down beside his plate and ran his fingers through his hair. I noticed my feet sweating in my shoes, like I had wool socks on, only I didn't. "Yes and no," he said.

I'm a man of principle. Back then I was a man of principle too. Same man, different principles. That night, I believed that a person had either been somewhere or they hadn't. I knew I had never been to Germany. No, not no and yes. Just no. I wanted my guest to adhere to my principles.

"Hold the phone Eddie. What do you mean? You've either been there or you haven't?"

Creeeeaks measured the growing silence. Ed stared at me. Normally, I can hold a man's gaze and stand my ground, but this little old man's stare cast a spell on me. My knees wobbled under the table. I looked to Anne for support but, oblivious, she turned her glass in circles, studying its emptiness. Ed's eyebrows cinched inwards and I felt a warm tingle in my feet. I tried to move my toes but couldn't. The sensation flowed upwards to my ankles and I relaxed, unable to move. The warmth continued climbing, reaching just below my knee when suddenly it disappeared at the moment Ed spoke.

"Frogg," he nodded to me. "Yes and no. It's a long story. You'll hear it one day."

He took up his fork and knife and went back to the operating table of his plate. I looked at him, wondering if he knew what I had felt. *Creeeeak*s came through the window. Anne ate quietly, Ed ate carefully, and I wiggled my toes trying to recapture the strange sensation. Again, Ed resurrected the conversation.

"And you, Ranocchio, how did you end up here in our little town?" This dinner occurred prior to me and Ed establishing our "The Past is The Past" principle. However, I did hold to a principle of not revealing the details of my criminal background to new friends and current cohabitants.

"I used to work for the government," I lied. "They don't like me talking about it and I left for complicated reasons." I offered some vague nonsense hoping it'd satisfy him. "They agreed to set me up in the middle of nowhere with a pretty decent severance if I kept my mouth shut. This was a part of the country I'd grown up in, so here I am. Luckily, I found someone to take care of me." No time like the present to start mending the domestic situation.

Ed placed another ravioli square in his mouth and slowly slid the fork from between closed teeth. He smacked his lips and repeated, "So here you are."

Creeeeak Creeeeak Creeeeak.

"Is that the whole story, then?" He asked. Anne excused herself with her empty wine glass. When she had cleared the room, Ed went on. "Frogg, you don't need to lie to me." I knew he was right.

"Eddie," I leaned closer and whispered to the old man. "It's a long story. You'll hear it one day."

Ed reeled back in laughter as Anne came back to the room with another glass of zinfandel. "What's so funny?" She asked, putting on a coy maternal tone. "You boys look guilty."

"You're right, my dear." Ed threw up his arms. "Perhaps I should call it a night, yes?" He rose from the table and bowed to the hostess. Turning to me, he winked. "We'll save the scotch for next time, Mr. Ranocchio Pinocchio." Before I could get up, he had slipped out the door into the twilight.

Anne and I shrugged to one another.

Creeeeek Creeeeek Creeeeek.

Just Enough Cat Butt
Monday, May 8th, 1989

"You're driving too fast." Agent Xidas reverted to her earlier mechanical state. Blood-stained jacket zipped to the chin, Aviators denying her face the chance to betray her façade by demonstrating the slightest hint of humanity. She had sex hair, though, and while tempted to reach over and touch the frizzled poofs on either side of the ponytail's node, my desire to maintain the connective integrity of my arm and shoulder outweighed my primitive lust. I kept my hands glued to ten and two. With me behind the wheel we'd make it back to Chilton before the sun went down, instead of letting her drive and hoping to make it back before it came up the next morning. The radio, still working as my wingman played Sheriff's "When I'm With You" until Iggy shut it down, leaving me with just her.

"You have to drive fast when bombtigers are chasing you." I mumbled.

"What?"

"Nothing," I said, remembering that Agent Xidas didn't approve of nor share in my years of experience meting out untimely death. She had never tamed a bombtiger before. "It's time to get straight with me. What's the FBI really want with Ed Mondo?" I asked, hoping her work would bring her back to the world.

"Answers, mostly."

"What kind of answers?" Like my mother taught me when she trained me as a volunteer designated driver the day I got my license, you got to keep them engaged if you don't want them to pass out or vomit. I needed to keep Agent Xidas talking, for her benefit as much as my own.

"It's strange," Agent Xidas adjusted the passenger seat forwards and returned her seat back to its upright position. "Nobody in D.C. could give me a consistent history on him. I've heard he worked as a CI, some say he used to traffic arms, some say art thief. The only point of agreement is that he had a big job for someone, possibly even the CIA or FBI, then he disappeared. He was just gone until we got wind of him living out here."

"Hold on." The sedan was coasting on the two-lane road, heading back west on rural route 40 to Chilton and the Solutionist's hut. The rearview showed no bombtigers and the windshield only open road. Evening had set in, the spring sky layered with wisps of orange clouds like strips of tangerine peels. I liked to play a game where I'd blink in rhythm as I passed each blurred yellow dividing line between the lanes. I blinked a lot trying to piece together Ed's history with the FBI. "How'd you find out he was in Chilton?"

Agent Xidas sighed and bit her lower lip. I sensed the wheels spinning in her mind. What sort of confidence had I earned by snapping that cop's neck? Already that felt like ages ago. Another murder, but this time, I did it for me. For her. I heard the *Pop!* Of the neck snapping and smiled. Sure, the cop's innocence couldn't be questioned, but this one didn't feel all that bad. Iggy probably worried I'd do the same to her.

"I haven't been completely honest with you," She said. "I knew about the Solutionist before I met you. This was recently brought to my attention." She unlatched the glove compartment, revealing a creased, yellowed sheet of grocery store journalism. She held it up for me to see the headline, adding, "The FBI keeps up with your small town's small problems, after all."

SOLUTION OR ILLUSION?

Small Town Prophet Offers Answers, Raises Questions

CHILTON, IL – Following reports of a supernatural being, hundreds have made the pilgrimage to the small Illinois town of Chilton this week, seeking the wisdom of a mysterious figure known to locals as the Solutionist.

"The Solutionist doesn't do interviews," said Ed Mondo, an elderly man who acts as sentry beside the Solutionist's small, doorless abode. "These lunatics don't know what they're talking about," Mondo said, referring to the hordes of followers and knowledge

seekers who believe the mysterious character's origins could be alien, heavenly, or simply fraudulent.

 Those who believe in the omnipotence of the Solutionist come from all walks of life. Men and women of all ages, races, and backgrounds have flocked to the field, pitching tents and swapping stories of their brief, written communications with the figure inside the hut. "There's a sense of unity here," said one woman who had driven from Texas with her boyfriend. "Just yesterday the Solutionist told my boyfriend to propose, and last night we were married by a priest from Toronto who was camped beside us."

 The only permanent structure within shouting distance of the Solutionist is a small trailer whose owner refused to comment. This reporter finds it unlikely that there wouldn't exist some relationship between the two strange figures living in such isolated proximity, and many of the encamped followers agree. "We see about as much of him as we do the Solutionist," said one member of the makeshift community. Many of the people surrounding this mystery remain skeptical, believing the whole thing a hoax. True followers insist it's not. "I used to question the whole thing too, until I asked something and heard back," one man said of his newfound faith. "Whatever it is, it's a miracle. And it's beyond this plane of existence."

 Whatever forces are at work in the farmlands of Central Illinois, be it phony or fantastic, the mystery of the Solutionist remains a mystery. The only thing we know for sure, however, is that some strange being, human or otherwise, is here to answer your questions."

 I remembered the article from its original publication. Most of it was misinformed, but it still beat the industry average for tabloid integrity by a substantial margin. It appeared not long after Eddie's soup can sermon. Even though he'd calmed the locals down, the out of town crowd still made the pilgrimage from time to time in the first year of the Solutionism craze. Dozens of articles just like it popped up in similar periodicals, until the next UFO sighting or achievement in celebrity weight gain photography took its place. The news stopped, but the Solutionist didn't, and the fanatics kept on trickling in and out of my yard.

"So you were playing dumb with the hut earlier?" I said. Every aspect of my body sparked to life since notching number eighteen. I carried on with Iggy with total focus as my eyes consulted with the rearview mirror, scanning for cops and my throat swallowed small sips of blood without knowing whether it originated from cracked lips, a busted nose, or if I'd bit my tongue. The rest of my attention split between thoughts of Ed and trying to determine what else Agent Xidas might be less than honest about in all this mess.

"A little." She returned the article to the glove compartment and took off her glasses. I could feel those frostbit jungle eyes on me, but I couldn't turn to face her. "Do you think the Solutionist will be there?"

I heard her but thought only about Eddie. He disappeared from the Feds and wound up joining me in rural open hiding. Where had he been? What clues could he have left about his history? I'd have to piece it together later, as a man of principle doesn't leave a lady's question unanswered, especially if the lady asking has the physique of Agent Xidas and happens to owe you a favor following a monumental, strangely arousing ass whooping.

"I'll drop you off and let you find out. I'm going to take a look around Ed's place."

Agent Xidas laughed. I could see why she didn't do it often. Laughter, as a general rule, enlivens the atmosphere with a contagious, convivial quality. Her laughter produced a fight or flight reaction in my internal organs that nearly caused me to pull over and make a break for the security of the cornfields on foot. It reminded me of my mother. Composing herself, she said, "You may not remember this Frogg, but you're under arrest. For seventeen murders."

"Eighteen, now, *Agent Xidas,* but I think you're forgetting that it only takes one, and you're the one who clicked off the cuffs for me to do the deed. The blood on my hands looks an awful lot like the blood on yours. Not to mention the blood on your jacket, and in your hair, and seeping through your jeans and staining that pretty little FBI laminate they issued you." I didn't like being curt with her, but I needed the balance of power to start balancing out.

She put her glasses back on and looked away, out the passenger window. I heard her breathing hard over the quiet hum of the engine. She sniffed and rubbed her eye behind the reflective frames. Nothing easy about waking up a cop and being a fugitive before sundown. She pulled a loose strand of hair behind her ear and turned to face forward again, cracking her neck to the side.

"By the way, I didn't think you had it in you to do that."

She looked at her jacket and ran a finger along the blotched streaks of caked on blood, mindlessly scratching at it as though it were a nail file. "What? You didn't think I'd trust you?"

"Hell no, I still don't think you trust me. You probably trust me less than ever."

"Then you didn't think that a woman had the guts to go through with it?"

"Says the woman who was pistol whipping me twenty minutes ago. The same cruel woman who insisted I wear jeans with a goddamn button fly." This time the laugh softened. Nothing easier than letting your lips switch from shaking to smirking. "No, Iggy, it wasn't that. I just didn't think you had it in you to give up control. To be a spectator instead of acting on your own, that's all."

We endured a silent stretch, Agent Xidas picking blood off her jacket, me blinking at the lane dividers.

"Frogg," she said, staring straight ahead, "I'm sorry for kicking your ass."

"It happens." I exhaled. "Sometimes frogs get their asses kicked. You know, in Greek mythology, there's a story about some frogs that wanted a king. They asked Zeus to provide one and Mr. Lightning told them that a log was their king. What did he care about some tiny frogs? He had goddesses to impregnate. But the frogs complained that the log wasn't good enough, it just sat there like a log. They wanted a real king. So they pestered the big man again. Zeus shrugged and assigned them a stork to be their king. The frogs loved him for it, until the stork king started eating his subjects."

I looked across the dash at Agent Xidas and smiled. She didn't. Only twenty more minutes to Chilton.

"Are you crying?" Agent Xidas asked.

"Incredulousness doesn't suit you, Agent," I said, rubbing my eyes on my left sleeve. "You must have punctured my tear duct with the butt of your firearm."

In truth, I was crying. Nothing easy about waking up a fugitive and working with the Feds before sundown. But the twist of fate didn't cause the waterworks. The homecoming did. Men of principle, with or without principles, understand the complex set of rules regarding adult males shedding tears. In this circumstance I couldn't locate a principle to justify the emasculating effect of a slow crawling salty discharge plowing its way down my gravel and blood stained cheek. A single tear clearing out debris like a facial Zamboni. It seemed, in my daily trek towards sentimental old age and the big 4-0, that I had developed a disproportionate attachment to my soup can.

The trailer conformed to one of my most consistent principles: Don't take up space. All my life I took up space, and I despised it. What right did I have? I filled parking spots, job openings, places in line at movie theaters, seats on public transportation. I explained to Ed once over a drink, just before scotchlogic had set in, but not so early that I couldn't apply scotchlogic if need be, my feelings on the travesty of cemetery burial. Think about it. Massive fields of dead bodies taking up space. Square miles of subterranean filing cabinets for decaying flesh. And for what? So loved ones can come stand over a rock with someone's name on it once or twice a year? If these people really cared, they'd bury grandma in the back yard and pay their respects every time the dog had to piss. Ed agreed, saying, "We're all eaten by worms anyway; may as well toss me to the wolves. I'd much rather be eaten by wolves than worms." I promised him that, in the event I had some say over the disposal of his corpse, I would find some hungry wolves.

That's why I loved the trailer. I thought I'd never see it again and, after only a few hours, I missed it. It took up minimal space. Truly an ideal home for a man of principle such as myself.

I pulled up in front of my trailer and killed the engine (this didn't count as kill number nineteen, though) just as Agent Xidas had earlier that morning and waited for her to step out of the vehicle. She didn't.

"You really think I'm going to let you drop me off so you can run off with my car?" Her eyebrows rose above the frame of her sunglasses and I imagined just how wide her disbelief could stretch those sky eyes.

"Iggy," I dropped my head to the side to showcase my mangled ear. "You really think I would if I haven't yet. Like it or not, we're in this together." With this I reached across her, careful not to graze any, let alone the most appealing parts of her body, and popped open the passenger door. "Do what you got to do. I'll pick you up after I poke around at Ed's place."

"Not, Frogg. I like it not." She shut the door. "Drop yourself off at Ed's, I'll take the car and pick you up. Then we can get out of here."

"Get out of here *together*," I winked and started up the engine. She crossed her arms over some of the more appealing parts of her body.

Minutes later I dropped myself at Ed's and Agent Xidas shimmied over the center cup holders to take the car back to the Solutionist. Like my mother, she insisted upon punctuality in regard to the prearranged pick up time. "Yes, dear," I said. She rolled her pretty eyes, rolled her window up, and rolled off to the end of the block.

Ed lived in a single story house with yellow aluminum siding and a robin's egg blue door that hadn't been locked since he moved in. He kept the windows glistening and made sure I kept the gutters clean by issuing semiannual invitations for what would turn out to be a fake Italian holiday celebration. I'd show up all smiles and hand him the booze, he'd be all smiles and hand me the rubber gloves, graciously pointing out where I could find the ladder.

Ed belonged to that exclusive, neurotic community of people whose homes never acquired dust. To check up on his membership,

I ran my finger along the top of a picture frame as I entered the house, upon inspection finding my finger somehow cleaner than it was prior. I didn't often spend time at Ed's house, the general cleanliness acted like garlic to my inner vampire slovenliness, but I had been over enough to know my way around. Agent Xidas mentioned documents with my name on them, but the place looked undisturbed. *How much of what she says is the truth?* I shook my head. There had to be something in this house, something concrete, that I could use to piece this whole thing together.

I told her I wouldn't run and she believed me. Hell, I believed me too. But that was before I stood in Ed's house by myself, looking out the window towards a future free of prophesized murder and missing men. A man of principle without principles can change his mind, right? Agent Xidas trusted me, but not enough to give me the keys. Right about then she'd be talking to a faceless spirit in a red hut looking for answers to questions she refused to clue me in on. Yet I still felt the need to stick with her. Something in the way those sky eyes fixed on me, like she were studying my face, searching my eyes to make sure I was real. She hadn't been here before; I realized that as soon as I walked in. Those documents she mentioned didn't exist. Yet she still showed up at my trailer knowing about Eddie and my friendship. She didn't add up. I knew I couldn't trust her. But where else could I go? I considered surprising Mother. "Hey Ma! Sorry you haven't heard from me in the last several years; I've been busy murdering people for a living." It'd kill her. Anne's doorstep represented an equally unappealing option. Men of principle don't crawl back with hat in hand. Especially this one. It's not often the path of least resistance is the one paved with pistol whippings, but Agent Xidas came out the big winner.

Entering Ed's house felt like walking into an improvised, low budget Italian Embassy. Paintings of Venetian canals hung from the walls, framed photographs of the old country sat on the mantle, and a prevailing odor of olive oil lent the home an unsettling, transitory feeling. I crossed the border to Ed's Little Italy without a passport, though I did have the oral backing of a recently crowned fugitive FBI agent who left me to my own devices while she attempted to find answers from a silent mystic. It had been a strange day, the type that warranted a drink. I went to find one.

By standing directly in the center of Ed's kitchenette I could access every cabinet, drawer, and shelf of the fridge without taking a step. That's where I stood when I realized that the half-cup of coffee I shared with Agent Xidas (a memory I had begun to think of as a first date) wouldn't suffice as the only fuel I had in the tank. The cabinets turned up mostly red wine, though the one directly above the toaster oven housed a pyramid of canned cat food. I may have forgotten about Ed's cat in all this mess, but I had no intention of forgetting him again. I decided on a principle: No pet left behind. Rolo, short for Barolo, represented Ed's only New World possession. An American Shorthair that, like its owner, had attained an advanced enough age to let itself go. Hopefully, its blubber supply kept it alive since Ed disappeared. Rotating in my centralized point, I surveyed the drawers and quickly located the can opener and left a tin of Rolo's dinner at my feet. Yet another example of how my mother's cooking days instilled in me a progressive, nearly preternatural understanding of culinary storage. When Mother needed a measuring cup, she needed it *now.* Put me in a kitchen anywhere in America and I'll tell you with confidence where to find the casserole dish, coriander, colander, and coffee grinder.

Deciding to skip the drink, I instead grabbed a loaf of not-too-stale bread and explored the house, ripping off chunks in the style of a wolf with a rabbit between its jaws. Or maybe more like a stork with a frog in its bill. I left a trail of crust flakes on the pristine floors leading to Ed's bedroom. The bathroom door stood ajar and I finished the bread on the toilet before facing myself in the mirror. More sore eyed than a sight for sore eyes, my face was so badly mangled I had to convince myself that Ed hadn't replaced his mirror with one from a funhouse. Agent Xidas's pistol had turned me into an expression of cubist extremism. Turning side to side I found my nose looked the same in profile as it did head on. *Good God,* I thought, *The Woman pummeled me into the 2nd dimension.* Still, despite being closer to death than ever before, I never looked or felt more alive.

Ed used to credit his grandmother for his glorious head of hair, attributing it to her apothecary-like use of olive oil as a medicinal ointment. During his formative boyhood years she'd sit him down and lather his locks with her homemade supply, and thus, he spent his adult life with a comb in his pocket leaving flocks of old hens giddily giggling in his wake. Despite knowing this unique aspect of his personal history (one of the few personal details I did know of his upbringing), I still performed a double take when I noticed a bottle of extra virgin beside his "sensicare" toothpaste.

As I splashed water on my open cuts and sores, I heard the entitled meowing of a fat, disgruntled cat. Rolo perched himself expectantly atop a chest at the base of Ed's bed. Attached to the front of the chest a sizable lock dangled, staring me in the eye. I remembered Ed mentioning, amid the haze of scotchlogic, that if anything should ever happen to him, there was information in his house that could be of use to me. Could anyone really blame me for neglecting Ed's chest once Agent Xidas's perked up on the scene?

I rushed from the mirror, knocking aside the olive oil and causing poor, fat, Rolo to exercise his springing muscles for the first time in a decade as I slid to my knees in front of the chest. Once situated my heart rate kicked up, making it impossible for me to focus on cracking the password protected padlock. It had five knobs, each with letters printed around the outside. I tried to think of what Ed would have made his password. Being a man of principle, I decided to try smashing the damn thing first, finding the heaviest hard-bound tome on the bookshelf and bringing its spine down against the lock with all the force of a man of principle. Hard enough to stub my thumb something awful, but not enough to force even a crack in that sucker. I'd have to solve it. Staring at Rolo, an indignant and mocking look in his eyes as though to say, *Not my problem, asshole,* he sprawled on the bedspread and it hit me. Ed had been telling me for years: Remember the Alamo.

A-L-A-M-O. *Click.*

I lifted the lid and discovered massive piles of documents. Far more than I could look through in the handful of minutes I had before Iggy's scheduled return. If she even planned on coming back.

With or without her, I couldn't afford to delay with Officer Taupe Suit's DNA still clinging to my person and the inevitable posse out for justice. I rifled through the first manila folder, scanning two-dozen documents before I realized they were written in Italian. I guess I wasn't thinking straight, which is known to happen to people who just had their skulls busted up and have to deal with the constant stress of wearing button fly jeans.

I tossed folders and newspaper clippings around the room like wayward fireworks, hoping whatever it was Ed wanted me to find would explode on the scene. My antics failed to amuse Rolo, who rose and strutted across the queen bed with the air of a third generation old money aristocrat, haughtily bemused by my frantic peasant movements. The obese feline ambled over with his chin held high, regal and proud. He came towards me and leapt over the top of the chest, landing heavily atop the remaining packets and folders. As he landed, the base of the chest released a long, cricket-like *Creeeeak*.

My world switched to slow motion. The mind worked separately from the body, reacting to sensory stimuli but unable to tell the body what moves to make, like when you see a spider on your arm and know to knock it away, but it seems like minutes pass before your hand flails in. The chest squealed, but I remained caught in that moment of paralysis. Ten black widows walking on my arm couldn't break my transfixed gaping.

Rolo's pudgy cat butt conceded to gravity and as it frumped down atop the papers the baseboard fell in, revealing a hidden compartment. I don't believe any other cat in the universe had the necessary combination of leaping ability and excess body weight to accomplish this feat. "Thanks, tubby," I said to Rolo as I lifted (with great effort) the fat cat out of the way and removed the decoy files to gain access to the compartment. Kneeling over the chest I reached underneath the false bottom and discovered a single black folder. I opened it as Agent Xidas honked from the front of the house. I had only an instant to examine the contents, but long enough to notice the FBI logo and take in the header:

Debrief: Agent Eduardo Mondo

Case #: 8350723
Suspect: Bogdan Woland AKA The Solutionist

I stuffed the folder in the back of my jeans beneath my shirt. Difficult as it was picking up the cat, I had a tougher time picking up my jaw. Outside, Agent Xidas leaned against the hood of the car holding a pair of zippered jeans and wearing a too big smile. "I think I know where to find Ed Mondo," she said. I nodded without listening and caught the sun peeking out from behind the horizon, as though it too had something to hide.

I didn't speak much in the car, didn't argue when Iggy insisted on driving, didn't ask about Ed's whereabouts, didn't ask where she planned to whisk me off to, didn't even change pants. I would have changed pants, but I wanted to keep my discovery of the folder to myself. At least for now. It felt good to be the one keeping a secret for a change. I didn't ask about the Solutionist, either. She tossed a few concerned looks my way as we rolled through the dimmer and dimmer Land of Lincoln. Like the background of a cheap cartoon, the sights of the Illinois intrastate route system repeated again and again, but not so often as to distract you from the action of the characters in the foreground. I wanted to focus on Agent Xidas's action, but something told me to keep quiet. I ignored the Mystery Machine and kept my eyes glued to the barn, field, crops, mile marker, barn, field crops, mile marker, barn, field, crops, mile marker that were never meant to be noticed on US-IL 67.

At first we continued west. She may have wanted to drown me in the Pacific. Maybe she thought Eddie went to Wyoming to find refuge in the cowboy culture, turn the final act of his personal opera into a live action spaghetti western. We weren't far from the Missouri border, so I didn't rule out an old fashioned Huck Finn adventure on the Mighty Mississippi. Frogs are better for fairytales than The Great American Novel. Whatever she had planned, Agent Xidas didn't seem suspicious of my lack of interest in whatever she had planned until we reached the motel and I failed to fight her on the separate rooms issue. "Perfect. Get some rest, Iggy." Did I detect a hint of disappointment that *I* didn't have something planned for her?

The bald headed toad across the counter pulled back the keys he'd held outstretched and squinted at me. He held my gaze long enough for me to wonder whether he suffered from cataracts, was coming on to me, or thought he could use Jedi mind tricks. A southerner's lifestyle, an Asian's face. China meets Chattanooga. Dark, greasy hair, thick glasses, stout faced and drowsy, he moved like an ensemble cast member from a kindergarten stage production, lurching from scripted position A to B and so on. I didn't want to find out what twisted accent his thin-lipped, mandatory line of dialogue would sputter out in. I didn't want to find out whether I'd be eating a multi-continental breakfast or if it'd require chopsticks. I just wanted to read the debrief of a certain "Agent Mondo." I opened my mouth to ask what the problem was when he twirled on his feet and opened a drawer. He removed another set of keys that he held out on an upturned palm without a word. Eager to get some reading done, I ignored the odd behavior, snatched the keys, and forced Iggy to take Barolo. "See you bright and early." I took off for the privacy of my motel room and left a dumbfounded Agent Ignatz Xidas wondering which one of us had lost their mind. She may not have wanted the Frogg, but she definitely didn't want the motel toad. Just then, neither Big nor Little Carl could be bothered.

The motel's neon vacancy signed burned red against the royal blue sky. Stars in the prairie, a hundred miles from anything that could be considered half a skyscraper, double in number and triple in candlepower. Maybe Iggy took the time to appreciate the view, but I didn't.

I raced to my room, locked the door, and shut off the lights. After tossing the folder on the bed I grasped the front of my waistband with both hands and yanked the fly apart, launching the buttons across the room and scattering them on the damp, stained motel carpet. I pulled down on the jeans too fast and fell sideways onto the bed, careful not to crush the folder, finally freeing myself from that denim prison forever. I picked up the folder, made a beeline to the bathroom, flipped on the lights and sat down to read.

73

As I opened the folder, my body tingled and a surge of heat rushed through me. In the dingy motel mirror my reflection fell forward off the toilet, but my body stayed seated as I watched it. The strange fever blurred my vision. I tried to stand up as the world went blank.

The Yes and No of Eduardo Mondo in Germany
Friday, June 2nd, 1967

"Omnipotence is not a constant. Not even for a solutionist. Knowing comes in waves. The range of my advanced consciousness fluctuates like a night sky, often clear and illuminated by candescent starlight, yet sometimes muted behind a layer of cloud. It is important to remember, of course, that clouds are only temporary masks, transient partitions of air and water that do not block, rather, merely obnubilate the depths of my awareness."

Eddie Mondo removed his egg-shell panama hat with its black ribbon and wiped the sweat from his brow with the back of his hand. "How about that?" he said, moving to the foot of the gauze wrapped patient's bed in room 319 of the Orlando Regional Medical Center. *Egg-shell?* He thought, recalling the enthusiasm of the airport haberdashery salesman. *Looks more like dark white to me.*

"But you are not interested in all this, Agent Mondo. My lunatic ramblings, you are thinking. You've come to find out about the fire. How did it start?...Who is responsible?...How did I survive?...Yes? I'm afraid the origins of that story stretch well beyond the blaze at the carnival. My behavior in regard to the incident in question, like the actions of my benefactor throughout history, represents the force that forever wills evil and forever works good. For you see, Agent Mondo, it was the Devil himself who bestowed my powers unto me."

"That's really something, pal." Agent Mondo lifted the patient's chart at the end of the bed.

Name: Bogdan Woland
DOB: NA
Country of Origin: Poland

"A Polack, huh?" Agent Mondo dropped the chart onto the crisp white bed sheets, the papers chirping as they fluttered and crashed into the clipboard. The middle aged FBI field agent plodded his stumpy body to the knuckly, skeletal chair to the patient's right side and sat down. He stared at the light blue wallpaper and measured the repeating pattern of the floral print along the trim that circled the room. The immobilized patient faced Ed's chair, but when Ed glanced through the apertures in the bandages around Woland's eyes, he found them closed. "Long way from home, aren't you?"

"Poland?" The patient spoke with mock indifference. "If I had a home at all, it would assuredly not be Poland. My home is no longer in this plane of existence. Here I reside only in body."

Agent Mondo exhaled a deep, drawn out breath, resigning himself to yet another long day. He stretched his arms backwards over his head and knocked into an electronic display monitor resting on a wheeled cart. Turning, he saw the black screen reflected an empty room. The dark box didn't frame the hospital bed nor contain the image of Bogdan Woland, but what worried Eddie Mondo most of all was the absence of his own face. Eddie shook his head, but the screen remained a void. His heart rate revved into second gear, and he found himself closing his eyes and giving himself a "you'll get through this" pep talk.

The trip to Orlando provided ample time to acquaint himself with the case. He read the briefing on the Herzig Bros. Carnival, had looked over the relevant documents and testimonies as closely as he could during the turbulent flight. Big fire. No causalities. Fifteen hospitalized including suspect. Witness accounts suggest suspect incited riot outside his carnival booth with proclamations of apocalypse, judgment day, and displays of magical illusions. Among the remains of the damaged area one remnant had survived peculiarly intact, a wooden placard that, in the heart of the fire, should have burned to ash but instead remained unmarred. Affixed to the placard rested a ball chain security pen and on it large red painted letters read: Solutionist. *And here is that Solutionist,* Agent Mondo thought. *A real nutcase.*

Ed Mondo said, "You may not be at home here, pal, but I certainly am. And seeing as you don't look like you'll be going anywhere for a while, why not tell me why you started that fire?"

"No, Agent Mondo. I am of sound mind. These bandages may give me the appearance of a madman, but I assure you my thinking is clear. The firmament is twinkling with starlight. My body, this vessel, it suffers. But I exist separately. You wish to know the origin of the fire, but that story takes time. In fact, it is a story that begins in Poland."

The air in room 319 stalled between the patient's breaths. Through the window on the opposite side of the bed, Agent Mondo saw the indecision of an evening sky settle in. A blending of unnamed hues hung over the distant horizon, waiting for the inevitable violet night to take shape. Ed wanted to check his watch but didn't. Instead he looked over the patient; the facts of time were no longer a pressing matter inside his mind, inside room 319. Beyond the door the hospital buzzed with activity. Doctors, surgeons, orderlies, interns, all whirring and whirling through the corridors, fighting the endless rush of endangered lives, working against the will of nature in its role to work both for and against the survival of our species. Agent Mondo stared at the door and felt disconnected from the world beyond the baby blue wallpaper.

The fluorescent light hummed with the slow, steady confidence of an ocean's tide. Ed slouched in his chair, resting his round face in his hand. A psychological specialist sent to endure the nonsensical ramblings of a halfway-demented arsonist only to check a few boxes on the paperwork and return home. Another day, another dollar for the Federal Agent. There was talk at the Bureau of a promotion, very hush-hush operation, and his name had been floated around. *Just keep it together, play it by the book, get out of here, put in your time.* He scratched a lump behind his ear, where his thick locks had eagerly skipped gray and begun to shine in white streaks like lighting. "The devil, huh?" Ed thought he saw the bandaged head nod. "When did the devil appear to you, Mr. Woland?"

"No, Agent Mondo. I found him."

"And he told you to burn down the carnival?"

"Agent Mondo, your sarcasm is unbecoming. I will show you."

"And how ar-"

The dismissive rebuttal caught in Ed's throat as his mouth clamped shut, pursing, like a child refusing his Brussels sprouts. Ed's body locked in living rigor mortis, confined to the bony armchair. He fought to move his limbs, straining, sweat from his chest dampening the front of his undershirt, the muscles of his stocky legs (already sore from flying coach) tightened and ached.

"Breathe," the voice from the bed floated into the air, mingling with the hum of the lights and dissolving into the otherworldly current of room 319 until permeating Ed's senses. Ed's body loosened, though still he couldn't move it, but the tension had lifted. A warmth sputtered into life beneath his feet and spread over his toes. It filled his penny loafers and crept up his ankles like a carnivorous vine. A dense comfort followed the heat, unlike any tranquility he'd known. The warmth reached his waist and curled around his barrel-chested torso like tentacles suckling against him. It advanced towards his head, its tendrils sidling up his neck. His skull felt heavy and tired, but he couldn't droop, still paralyzed by the unknown force acting upon him. His vision darkened and blurred, as though the fluids surrounding his brain had thickened into molasses. If he could've moved at all, he'd have smiled. Instead, he fell asleep.

"Agent Mondo." The voice rang loud and clear, rousing the Federal Agent into an upright position in his chair. Ed Mondo searched the room, looking over both shoulders and reaching for a gun that he'd purposefully left at his hotel room. The memory of the warmth stretching over his body flickered, unreal, but still he wondered how long he'd been out. "Are you hungry, Agent Mondo?"

"Yeah..." Ed surveyed the room to regain his wherewithal. He blinked to stop the walls from spinning, saw the empty monitor behind him and bounced his knees to test the command of his body. He looked out the window behind Woland's head and noted the lack of movement from the sun. The sky beyond room 319 radiated with strange light, a hazy combination of yellows and greens as though seen in the reflection of the nearby water of the Everglades. Ed scratched at his stomach. "Yeah, actually. I am pretty hungry."

"They are always hungry after experiencing the soluse. Go then, and find food. You will need strength. If you do not wish to hear my story, very well. Fill out your forms, recommend me for asylum, prison, the death penalty, whatever you see fit. However, Agent Mondo, if you wish to return and hear me out, please come back and I will show you all I can of how I became the Solutionist. Perhaps, in turn, you shall find solutions of your own."

Ed got up from his chair with hesitation, testing the strength and control of his legs. He walked to the door. With one hand on the knob he asked, "And what exactly is a Solutionist, anyway?"

"One who provides solutions, Agent Mondo. That's all." Ed rolled his eyes, though with less conviction than he had before the strange occurrence of his unexpected nap. "For example," the patient offered, "D5."

Ed left room 319 and lingered with his back against the door. The pace of the hallway stunned him, shocking him back to a world of responsibility and order. Here he felt no warmth. Out in the hall, the world of time and order didn't only exist, but accelerated. Faceless staff members hustled by with fierce focus as Agent Mondo remained planted against the door. He counted to three and jumped into the jet stream of the outside world. In making his way through the corridor to the waiting area Ed collided with a nurse who ignored his apology. He saw an orderly pushing a patient in a wheelchair towards him, but couldn't react fast enough to get out of the way. Again his apologies and polite smile garnered no reaction. Ed peered into the faces around the hallway, all blurred and suspicious in their unwillingness to meet his gaze. He rubbed his eyes with the base of both palms and headed for the vending machines by the elevator.

Facing the machine, he looked into the reflection. Among the chips, cookies, and candies, the cartoon trade characters and granola bars, Ed saw an opaque image of himself. A funhouse mirror, a carnival illusion, an amusement park version of national authority staring back from the glass pane. His short-sleeved white button down shirt, his pressed ecru khakis, and his stern professional demeanor all had been reduced to a wavy, tie-dyed, adulterated contortion of the truth.

Before deciding on whether to return to Bogdan Woland and the heavy air of room 319, he'd have to decide on his snack. *Haribo Gold Bears? No. Chuckles? No. Curly Wurly? That's the one.* Ed Mondo reached for the keypad and checked the corresponding code. D5. Grinning, he realized his decisions had been made. He pressed the keys and watched as the chocolate-coated caramel leaned over the cliff's edge, unleashed from his reflection at the center of his chest, and dropped into the unknown abyss, utterly unaware that it would soon be wholly consumed.

"I've never been one for caramel," the patient said as Agent Ed Mondo emerged from the whirlwind of the hospital corridor. "Doesn't it get stuck in your teeth?"

Agent Mondo, candy bar in hand, returned to his post beside Woland's bed. "From what I've read, teeth are the only part of your body that shouldn't be a pile of ashes right now. Care to explain that?"

"That is," the patient said, "if a solutionist even has teeth."

Ed leaned forward once more to look through the bandages into Woland's eyes, wondering what the man beneath the wrapping actually looked like. He swore that for a moment he saw a xanthic green shade shimmering from within, but it extinguished in an instant. *Must have been the lights*, Ed thought, chomping a hunk off the end of the chocolate bar. "Well I've got teeth, pal," Ed smacked his lips as he chewed. "So while I eat, why don't you give me something to chew on?"

"So it appears," Woland began, "that my parlor games have filled you with sufficient amusement? Abundant curiosity? Willing to pay twenty-five cents more for another round at the Solutionist's booth? The soluse settled your anxiety, did it not?" The patient chuckled beneath his integument of soft-edged cotton bandages.

Not quite believing, yet not the cynic of twenty minutes prior, Agent Eddie Mondo leaned back in his chair and crossed his legs, resting one ankle atop his opposite knee. "Hell, why not? I don't fly out until the morning." He interlocked his fingers on his lap, Curly Wurly pressed between his palms. "Tell me, Bogdan Woland: What brought us here today?"

Agent Eduardo Mondo, as a rule, did not humor his suspects. Rarely in his tenure with the Bureau had he casually conversed with a potential perpetrator. Small talk happens, but he'd always taken mental notes on the suspects' psychological tics. The suspect in room 319, the mysterious cocooned figure, disarmed Ed Mondo. The interrogation transitioned into a biography, and Ed did the reading, not the writing. The patient sprawled inside his casts, motionless, head listing to the right side against the pristine cleanliness of the hospital linens. To his left, a window to the blended greens and yellows of an ethereal sky. To his right, Agent Ed Mondo, pupils expanding in eager reverence as a focused, specialized gravity drew him to the patient's story. Ed's conscious mind resisted the pull, but deep down, as he turned an ear towards the soft voice of the bandaged man, he knew he'd listen through the story's end. Though whether he'd believe what he heard remained to be seen.

"I was born in Poland, yes. So I suppose I am a 'Polack' as you say. Only, I did not stay there long. This was before the war. I can tell you of my time there, not from stories told to me by relatives, but from the yet-to-be formed memories I have since reconstructed. Waves, remember. Today my sky is clear and shimmering, my vision extends beyond the bounds of memory. After my ascension, the concept of time, of past and future ceased to exist. Only waves determine my awareness."

Agent Mondo ripped a chunk of Curly Wurly, meditatively chewing as he struggled to keep up with the supposed supernatural powers of his arson suspect.

"It was 1937, a dangerous time for Polish Jews. I lived with my parents in a mixed neighborhood; there were some Jews, but not enough that we could escape daily persecution. People worried, the clouds of war formed all around us, and even in our home the atmosphere bubbled with the undercurrent of fear, like living in a teapot about to boil. Our neighbor, Abram Pupa, came to us and urged my father to move to Russia. They'd argued late into the night, and eventually, with the support of my mother, father relented and agreed that we should leave before it was too late.

"One night, Abram announced he was leaving. We could stay with him in Russia, at his cousin's home until we found permanent housing. I was only an infant, but now I can see clear as day my parents packing what possessions they could in coarse paper bundles. We left the following day."

As the patient related his personal history, Ed Mondo saw shaded images appear in his mind, memories not his own, opaque and fragmented. The warm sensation from earlier, like a golden bulb lying in wait in the cavities of his body and mind, filled him with pale, pleasant heat.

"Poland's weakened economy burdened the rail system. Trains ran less frequently, were understaffed and often oversold. When we boarded, which we were lucky to do at all, we found ourselves standing against a wall, where my mother held me snug against her breast beside a small barred window. A miserable cold rattled through the compartment, and my mother held me tight beneath her scarf."

Ed Mondo squinted in focus, trying to make out the faded faces of Woland's parents. He felt the pressure of his mother's embrace and the chill of the wind against his skin. He asked the patient, "What were their names?"

"My parents...I prefer not to recall..." Agent Mondo opened his mouth to speak but held back, unsure if he had offended the patient. Instead he waited, concentrating on the warmth coursing lightly through his legs.

"Do not worry, Agent Mondo." Woland said, heaving a heavy breath from beneath his mask of bandages. "Russian soldiers stopped the train at the border for inspection. My mother, through the window, made out the uniformed men boarding the front car. Soon, she saw men forced to line up beside the tracks. Women wailed in protest. The soldiers pressed on to the second car. Any woman who lashed out too strongly received harsh treatment from the Russians. They taunted the offending women with threats of work camps and escorted them from the train. The soldiers poured into our compartment and removed any man fit enough to fight and forced them to enlist in the Russian infantry. In running from the war we had arrived in it."

Ed witnessed the scene through a dense fog. The red star on the soldier's cap, the reflection of pale sunlight gleaming from the caramel-colored belt buckle above a soldier's hips. A hand grasping the arm of a faceless man Ed sensed was Woland's father.

"Yes, my father was taken. My mother tucked me beneath her scarf on the floor and swung her feeble fists helplessly against the soldier's back. She, too, was taken from the train. I would never see them again."

Ed shifted his weight, releasing soft gasps of trapped air from his seat cushion. He waited for Woland to continue but the patient said nothing. Outside, the tinged green sky grew pallid and milky. Ed cleared his throat. "With your, uh, ascension and all...couldn't you have found out what happened to them?"

"Waves, Agent Mondo." the patient whispered, his voice sounding harsh and weak, "Waves. In some circumstances, I have found it better to build dams than to allow oneself to drown. Tell me, in my position, would you rather know the details of their fate or allow yourself to hope? Not knowing, too, is a great power."

Another weighty pause hung between the bed and the chair. Ed leaned backward, rolled his neck back and looked at the ceiling. He brought the Curly Wurly to his lips but didn't bite into it.

"The train entered Russia and, miraculously, I went undiscovered and unharmed. Barely beyond infancy, a small child wrapped in a dark floral scarf, it amazes me still that nobody found me. That is, until a Russian porter performing a routine spot check at a depot in Smolensk picked me up. He glanced over his shoulders, crouching over my body. Assured that nobody remained besides the two of us, the porter held me in front of his face, examining me to ensure that I was, in fact, really there. Convinced, he hugged me against his face and scratched my skin with his beard. My cries caromed from train car to train car like a bullet through the barrel of a gun.

"Despite the gravity of my childhood misfortunes, certain memories can only be recalled as lucky. The porter, Viktor

Petronovich Avilov and his wife, Sofia, could not conceive, and thus Viktor smuggled me to his wife, still wrapped in my mother's scarf, as a gift. There, in the home of the porter outside Smolensk, I would survive the war in open hiding."

Ed Mondo tore at the Curly Wurly with the unmistakable fervor of a carnivorous mammal. He nodded and spoke as he chewed. "That is a stroke of luck if I ever heard one." Ed stood, taking advantage of the break in the story to unbutton his shirt, folded it, and hung it neatly over the back of his chair. Giving in to the heat of the Florida climate as well as that of the story, he settled back down in his undershirt for more. He picked up the remaining hunk of the candy bar, crossed his arms, and nodded to Woland. "So you knew you were adopted?"

"Adopted!" The volume of the retort produced by the mound of bandages made Ed jump in his seat. "I do not think so, Agent Mondo. Sofia cared for me, yes, but was always quick to remind me, as well as her neighbors and relatives, that I was not her son. I was her onus. Her charge. Her contribution to the war against the Nazis. She'd raise me, but would never be my mother. Nor would Viktor fully embrace me as a father. She resented her husband for bringing me home and resented me for reminding her of her infertility.

"I cannot say she loved me, but I can say that she came to accept me as her responsibility. She took pride in my accomplishments, imbued me with her spirit, and shared what she could of her food and her knowledge of life. She kept me in good health and away from trouble. But I was never her son. If I erred in any way, stumbled when walking, spilled my milk, misbehaved or acted indignant, as all children do, she was quick to point out, 'No son of mine!' When the war ended and the death camps of Germany were liberated she seemed sad, though not reluctant, to send me back to Poland and out of her life."

Woland returned to his heavy breathing. In the restful pause, Ed thought about the miracle that the patient could speak at all. His eyes scanned the length of his interlocutor's body, every inch of which burned and encased in a structured pool of gauze. *And still, he speaks.* No morphine, no analgesic. *What am I dealing with?* Ed thought.

"This time in Russia, it too pains me to recount. In my omnipotence, I can assure you my troubles paled in comparison to those suffered by others of my birth and blood. Yet still, it is difficult."

Agent Mondo reached out to console the patient, but stopped short at the return of the warm feeling in his limbs. He leaned back again in the chair. "We don't have to talk about it," Ed said. He did want to talk about it, but he also wanted the patient to keep talking. As entrenched as he found himself in the story, his professional interest in the patient as a suspect remained the priority. "Take your time, Bogdan."

Another heavy breath escaped the bandaged face. "Thank you," Woland coughed in response. Agent Mondo got up and pointed to the door, offering to return to the chaotic tempo of the world beyond room 319 for assistance. "No. Please sit." Ed shrugged and returned to the chair and nibbled on his Curly Wurly. The hum of the fluorescents droned above them.

"When the war ended," Woland's voice trembled, but had regained some its early strength, "Viktor brought me with him to the train depot and arranged to ride with me to the border. By now, I was nearly ten years old and had wits enough to survive on the train, but beyond that I didn't know what I'd do. This was very frightening, you understand, to travel with no destination, to a home country I had never been to, where I would be alone, with only a few sparse words of the native language.

"We didn't speak on the train." Ed closed his eyes, could see the outline of Viktor's profile beside him in the train car. A silhouette against a deep background. "This time, I created my own luck. I saw at the station a group of children supervised by an American soldier. Distraught, I sidled away from Viktor's hip and hid amongst the throng of children, each dressed in rags, thin as rails, and all of them Jewish. The Americans herded us onto a train. Turning as we left the platform, I saw Viktor twisting frantically in search of me, waving my mother's scarf over his head."

"Do you know what happened to the scarf?" Ed asked.

"Sofia used it as a kitchen rag."

"Oh. I'm sorry, I didn't-"

"It would only have drawn attention to me. It was better I not have it. With it, I may never have made it out of Russia and into Germany."

"Germany?" Ed lifted his hand, still holding the candy bar, to quiet the patient. He scratched at the black and white hairs behind his ear. "I thought you were headed to Poland?"

"Viktor intended to send me to Poland, yes. But there were thousands of children like me, who had lost their families and left their homes. It wasn't so simple as heading back to one's hometown. Many of us didn't know where home was, and for some who did, home had been destroyed. The American soldiers escorted us to Germany. There I would live out the most formative time of my life. And there, in Germany, I would find Satan. In Germany. Among the displaced Jews of Neu Freimann, I would make my first true home."

Agent Ed Mondo's body remained rooted by the inexplicable warm sensation. Beside him, the bandaged frame of Bogdan Woland released a steady ebb and flow of oxygen. Ed's empty stare concentrated on the wallpaper and its ring of violets along the trim as he tried to maintain a grasp on reality. *Can't forget the fire.* Ed's head drooped, his vision blurring as his brown penny loafers faded in and out of focus. *You have a job to do.* The warmth crawled up through his torso. "What is this?" Ed asked.

"The soluse, Agent Mondo, is a physical embodiment of solutionism implanted in another form. It is the fuel without which solutionism could not operate. The life force. The blood. The connective tissue that binds me to this world. Through it, I can see into your past and your future, if I so choose, can enter your present and allow you into the minds of others. Of course, it is not always so simple. There are costs. Severe costs. For me, and especially for others. Not every person can contain its heat, for weaker minds it proves fatal. You, however, have extraordinary tolerance. Extraordinary..."

The warmth, the soluse, throbbed lightly in Ed's ankles, releasing his fear and stress with each pulse. "But, how?"

"Two ways. I can force it upon you. Introduce it to your being as a means of connectivity. The soluse allows for our meld. For you to see into my memory. Also, in rare cases, the human form has been known to reproduce it on its own. But this is rare, very rare. The soluse, like many aspects of solutionism, is finite even in its endlessness. It too comes in waves. It can be broken. Now, let us return."

Ed blinked and opened his eyes to the sights of Woland's memory.

"I was shocked by the hollow cheeks of their faces, could see the structure of their bones through their emaciated frames. At the time I could not even imagine what horrors they went through. I stared at the floor as the train rolled west, never meeting the eyes of another child. At intervals the soldiers would distribute small hunks of dark, heavy bread. It was old, stale and dry, but we needed it. It got us through the train ride until they herded us into trucks. Some of the others struggled, trying to stay off the trucks. The automobiles a reminder of their families, lost to them perhaps forever. Like me, transportation had separated them from loved ones. The sight of a truck sent one girl into hysterics. Later, I would discover her father had thrown her from a truck headed to a death camp. She was not eager to trust the foreign soldier smiling as he gestured towards the rear door."

In Agent Mondo's mind, children pleaded with empty eyes. Collage-like images of defeated compliance and tear-filled faces flitted by one after another. These he saw with greater clarity than those of Viktor and Sofia. Bogdan, while suffering in body, communicated clearer through his mind. Ed could now see the freckles of the girl who ran from the truck, the unrestricted fear and the resignation to her fate as they pulled her aboard. Ed squeezed his candy wrapper and felt a pang of guilt.

"You see her, Agent Mondo. She ran. As did a few others, but the soldiers captured them without much strain and piled us on board. We rode in silence. I know now that only one of that group

87

would reunite with a relative. Two had lice. One suffered from the early stages of typhus. One would become the Solutionist, as well. The girl who ran, Ella was her name, poked me with her elbow and directed my eyes to a small boy. He smelled his fingers and placed one in his mouth. He did not bite it, though.

"When the door opened, the light of a Neu Freimann afternoon flooded the carriage like sunbeams through the gates of heaven. Before exhaling our first breaths of free air, they marched us to the orphanage for processing.

"This is one hell of a trip, Woland." Ed Mondo said, tossing his crumpled Curly Wurly wrapper towards the trash bin beside the door, only for it to unravel in mid flight and crash lightly onto the tile floor. "Must have taken a toll on you."

"Yes, it did. The Americans distributed a few bites of chocolate from their Red Cross rations during the drive, which endeared them to us a great deal. But these were meant mainly to lessen our fears than appease our hunger. Of course, not everyone shared their treasured treat. For the small boy there would only be the smell of his fingers. For him, like all of the children, hunger was a part of life. They had no memory of living any other way."

Ed rose to his feet, still experiencing the warmth in his lower extremities. He walked without feeling his feet on the tile, picked up the candy wrapper, tossed it the remaining distance to the trash, and glided back to his seat with a grace he hadn't felt since childhood.

As Ed sat back down Woland coughed violently, shaking the bed and his gauze wrapped limbs. Before Ed reacted, the fit ceased and a surge ran through Ed's body, sending the strange sensation of heaviness up his spine and into his head. It stayed for a moment, then receded steadily back down to his gut, pulsing like an alternate heartbeat.

"Do not be alarmed." The voice didn't originate from the patient, but rather from an internal source, an untapped region of Ed Mondo's mind functioning under another's control.

"What is this? What's going on?" Frantic, Ed shot glances over his shoulders, even bent forward to look between his legs underneath the chair. He found nothing but deactivated medical equipment, baby blue wallpaper, and the reflected fluorescent light bouncing off the tile.

"Do not be frightened, Agent Mondo. This body I inhabit...it's...weak. It is easier for me to speak to you this way."

The voice rose once more inside Ed's head, and the heat intensified over his ankles and up to his knees. He released a sigh and slouched, sedated by the soluse but still in command of his mental faculties. *Ok*, Ed thought, *This is Ok.*

"Post war Germany was a land in transition." Woland's voice softened with a newfound strength inside Ed's mind. "Nothing functioned as it had. Everything, everyone, was repurposed. Neu Freimann, once a work camp, became a site of recovery. Its two-story single-family homes now housed multiple families. Only the idea of a family had been repurposed as well. Fragments of families filled these units, redefining what it meant to be a neighbor. Privacy was out of the question. You asked about the orphanage, Agent Mondo. Well, during the war it was an army barracks, but it too took on a new role as a temporary home for us, the lost children. Even the administrative building where the Camp Director had his office had been an etiquette school for German girls before the war. A place to learn to cook and sew."

Ed grinned in his visitor's chair beside the patient's bed. He watched the scene unfold in front of him as Woland described it. The distant mountains beyond the rows of houses, the hand painted sign reading "Orphanage" in English letters above the door of the former barracks, the possibilities of new lives brimming within the faces of people on the street.

"The director worked in the building adjacent to the orphanage, both of which faced a public square with a large fountain. When I first alit the truck I saw him, the Director, speaking to another man who gestured wildly towards the water in the fountain. Director Cohen stood with his spindly arms crossed in front of his chest. He had boyish features and a long neck, atop which his military cap nearly engulfed his undersized head. Some thought him too young for his position of authority at only thirty-two. However, I believe his inexperience with bureaucracy stood as his greatest trait."

Ed saw the young director, gangly and silly in his baggy uniform beside the fountain. He felt a mysterious admiration for the man, one that wasn't his own. "This guy meant something to you, huh?"

"Oh yes," Woland said. "Director Cohen would be the great inspiration, a key object of my attention during my time in the camp. He captivated me from the first moment I saw him. You see, Agent Mondo, he did not argue with the man by the fountain. It was merely a negotiation of logistics. The man, David Adler, practically ran the black market inside the camp. He had bartered with local Germans and procured a substantial quantity of carp to sell for Shabbat dinners. The fish delivery came early, and he had no place to store them until the Shabbos. Cohen not only allowed Adler to use the fountain, but turned a blind eye to the handful of violations Adler committed in bringing the fish into Neu Freimann. Cohen recognized the value of people's joy following the horrors of war. Much like my benefactor, Cohen used evil means to good ends. A provider of solutions, I used to think of him."

"So did he fill the fountain with fish?" Ed asked.

"Yes, Agent Mondo. Look." Ed closed his eyes and discovered himself at the base of the fountain, staring into a shallow pool crowded with panicked carp. "Within the hour, we had an aquarium. Like I said, repurposed. Everybody traded with the Germans, not just men like Adler. Many did so by necessity. Even housewives engaged in a daily give and take of illicit trade. People like Adler, however, suffered damaged reputations. Trading with a local farmer for fresh food was one thing, but manipulating the black market for profits was another. He wasn't a crook, more an opportunist. Still, there existed a saying in Neu Freimann: If you shake Adler's hand, be sure to count your fingers."

"Ha!" Agent Mondo perked up, nearly amused enough to break free of the hold that weighed down his lower body. "I'll have to remember that one."

"Do not worry, Agent Mondo. When the time comes, you will remember everything. I assure you." Woland whispered in Ed's mind. He had taken residence there and Ed accepted his presence,

90

trusted his voice, and saw his memories as clear as his own. He lived the story of Woland's childhood as much as he listened to it, feeling his hunger, his fear, inhaling the musty odor of the truck and breathing the fresh air of the public square. He yearned for more, his mouth watered, his craving for the rest of the tale dominated his senses. All he could do was sit, wait, and listen.

"At the orphanage, they brought us into a large room where we joined another group of children. More truckloads would arrive before nightfall. In all, we numbered one hundred thirteen. Nearly all of the orphans wound up illegally shipped to Palestine. After two or three months, a fresh batch would arrive."

"But you couldn't have gone to Palestine, right?" Ed spoke his question aloud and blushed, realizing the man who penetrated his mind and body didn't require verbal communication. *What do those bandages cover?* Ed thought. *A man? An illusionist? A conjurer of dark magic?* Ed lifted his head as high as his sedated body allowed and stretched his neck forwards to peer through the eyeholes of the patient's mask of bandages. The voice returned with a reassuring tone.

"No, Agent Mondo. Not an illusionist..." Ed saw the closed lids twitching. The skin of Woland's eyelids glistened with a raw, pink sheen. His lashes badly singed. "...And certainly no conjurer..." Woland lifted his eyelids. "A Solutionist," he said, exposing Ed Mondo to two eyes matching the tinged chartreuse flare of the sky beyond the window. Woland's irises shifted with a fluidity of greens and yellows that mimicked the dynamic, otherworldly firmament outside room 319. They did not blink. Ed trembled, his teeth rumbled like a snare drum as he tried to force himself to look away. Transfixed by the patient's glare, he felt sweat beading behind his ears and over his lips. "A Solutionist," Woland repeated, closing his eyes and releasing the Federal Agent from his grip. "The Solutionist has no need for the fallacies of men."

Ed panted and dabbed his forehead with the shirt he had laid out behind him on the chair's backrest. *I'm sorry, I...*

"No. I am sorry. I should have warned you. I did not wish to scare you, only to prepare you for what is coming. Let us continue."

Ed allowed the voice and the supernatural warmth of the soluse to enfold him, breathing slowly through his nose with heavy huffs. Woland's past opened to him again. Not in fabrications of his imagination, but with the actual sights and sounds of Neu Freimann. "No, never to Palestine," Woland continued. "By another stroke of luck, my experience differed greatly from that of the typical displaced orphan. I owe my ascension, my gift, as much to the assignment of my bed as any other act of fate.

"Overcrowding forced the American soldiers to set up cots along the halls of the barracks. Children scattered all about, filling the rooms on both the first and second floors. Upon arrival they behaved as docile, frightened children, but once they grew comfortable in the camp they became an unruly tribe of imps. They knew no rules, had no basis of polite behavior. On arrival they took us to a room functioning as a cafeteria. We sat shoulder to shoulder at long tables with low wooden benches, where they issued us each another slice of dark, heavy bread and a dented tin bowl containing a thin stew."

Ed could taste the stew. Through the melding of his mind and Woland's, he felt the cold wooden bench beneath him. With each passing moment spent in Woland's memories Ed gained greater fluency with his senses, grew more accustomed to the ways of the soluse and the rules guiding this internal world of Solutionism. He gained an element of control, an agency in choosing what stimuli to explore. Using this limited control, Ed focused on the girl from the train, Ella, and watched as she slid her bread beneath her shirt. He felt the hand of a female soldier fall on Woland's shoulder, saw the uniform lean over Woland's body and explain to Ella that storing her food would no longer be necessary. The girl smiled. Ed wanted to reach out and hug her, but it wasn't his body to control, not his limbs to manipulate, not his memories to recreate.

"The boy with the fingers," Woland's voice returned, "you remember him. See how he looked at his spoon with confusion. He had never learned to use one. Look, Agent Mondo, look how he drank from the bowl. With both hands he lifts it to his lips, wary eyes scanning over the rim." Ed watched the boy as the memory faded out.

"What were you saying about your cot, Bogdan? What made it so special?"

"Yes, my bed. A single cot, not part of a bunk. I slept on the second floor on the south facing side of the barracks hallway. I had a unique location because my cot blocked off a door to a storage closet. The knob would not turn, but being a child I imagined amazing things must lie in wait on the other side. It didn't take long for curiosity to get the best of me.

"The first night I fell asleep amidst the soft cries of my fellow orphans and woke to the voices of the Jewish socialist group which operated the facility during our group's stay."

Agent Mondo cut in. "I thought the Americans ran things?"

"The Americans handled the administrative work in the camp, that's true, but for the most part the internal operations of Neu Freimann were left to elected officials among the displaced persons. The orphanage was no different. Americans registered us, took our information and sent inquiries to see if our families had survived. But the responsibility for day-to-day care of the children fell to certain citizen groups. Jewish orphans like us were a special circumstance. Nobody knew what to do with us. The young boy from the truck with the smelly fingers, he was labeled as 'Politically Undesirable' on his identification card. Only five years old, he didn't know how to use a spoon and yet he threatened to destroy an entire continent's way of life through his politics. Ha!

"Zionist factions lived within the camp, and they knew most of us would be sent to Palestine. They each wished to indoctrinate us with their ideals, so they rotated. For my group, the socialists, *the Mapai*. The next batch may have the workers' union, *the Mapam*. A crooked shoe for a crooked foot, the people said. We were orphans, what choice did we have?"

"So you were a socialist?" Agent Mondo asked.

"I was a child. We all were. They called us down the next morning to introduce our new way of thinking, to convince us that Palestine was our rightful home, the unofficial state of Israel our final destination."

Ed returned to the world of displaced orphans. He smelled the dusty air of the hallway, heard the garbled languages of Europe growing distant, and the empty hallway materialized around him. He felt in his hand, in Woland's child's hand, a cool, thin pin.

"I found the needle in the room on the other side of the building where local women volunteered to teach sewing to the girls," the voice explained. The young Woland sat up on his knees atop his Red Cross issued blanket and jimmied the lock to the utility closet. Despite Ed's determination for the memory to accelerate, to see what treasures, or even what horrors Woland found beyond the door, he had to endure the inefficiency of Woland's effort and the incessant nervous glances over his shoulder. Ed felt the syncopated beats of his heart and the one he shared with the boy, and together they skipped a full uneven beat as the lock clicked open. Woland's hand reached out and turned the knob. "I slipped inside," the voice rang out with joy as the memory of the room came into focus. Ed Mondo looked at the empty space, no bigger than a broom closet. Not wide enough for a grown man to walk through, not deep enough to fit a mattress. *Not even enough room to iron a shirt,* he thought.

"That's right, Agent Mondo, but I didn't have any dress shirts at the time. The size may not impress, but the privacy should. It was my own space. All my own. I'd pass hours in the small closet, staring out the window." Ed looked up through dusty pane and spied the fountain in the square to one side. To the other, the administrative offices for the entire camp. "Look, Agent Mondo, through the window of that building. That is the office of Director Cohen." Ed saw the man, seated at his desk with his back to the orphanage. He recognized the unmistakable look of the Director's hat drooping over the edges of his ears. The sight of Adler's face across the desk only confirmed Woland's claim. Ed took stock of the closet once more, wondering what use it had in the barracks to begin with.

"Rifles, Agent Mondo. The Germans stored rifles against the walls." Woland's voice softened. He paused beneath the weight of his memory. "I have since looked into the matter. It was an error. The room wasn't meant to exist. A careless architect misprinted the dimensions of the rooms and in the haste of wartime construction, the walls went up with excess space. The foreman on site decided the remaining expanse was too large for a crawlspace and could perhaps be utilized by the inhabitants." Woland brought Agent Mondo back to the scene in his mind, back to the hallway. "Look at the door. See it is thinner than the others, built of a different wood? The extra room required a smaller door, and one was found in city with the proper measurements." Ed watched Woland's nail pick at a small chip in the door's exterior. It was once a gorgeous blue, but the German's painted it brown to match the others."

The image floated out of Ed's mind, and once more he discovered himself staring blankly over the bandaged Bogdan Woland in room 319. "The room wasn't meant to be there, Agent Mondo." Woland's voice played on inside him. "It was a void, an overlooked stretch of air, a pocket of what never should have been."

"Something tells me you didn't find the Devil in the closet." Ed said.

"No, but I would not have found him without the closet. Watching Cohen take meetings through the window, I witnessed the inner workings of the *Komitet*, the camp's committee of elected officials. Sometimes, I would sneak away from the orphanage and follow him through the city."

"Let me get something straight here, Bogdan." Agent Mondo tried to stand but his legs remained rooted under the influence of Woland's spell. He shifted his upper body, causing the chair to creak and moan. "You just came and went as you pleased?"

"Yes."

"You must have been seen. People had to be suspicious of a kid on his own. What would you say to talk your way out of trouble?"

"I wouldn't talk my way out of trouble. I wouldn't talk at all. I spoke no Hebrew and no English. Russian, yes, and I understood some Yiddish. I was bright enough, even before the bestowal of my omnipotence, to keep my mouth shut."

"Still," Agent Mondo said, taking the side of the law, "some authority figure must have nabbed you, right?"

"Agent Mondo, in a place where the authority's responsibility lies in helping break regulation, where people are living in a space

95

designated as anything but their home, is it so unbelievable that a quiet child could walk the streets undisturbed?"

Ed reclined with a sigh. He looked at his watch but didn't register the time. Outside the sun disappeared beyond the icy green clouds of a Solutionist's sky. *Is he sticking to the facts?* Ed thought, scratching behind his ear at the slick streak of white hairs, *If there are any facts to stick to in the first place...*

"Facts, Agent Mondo, were hard to come by in Neu Freimann. It is a fact that I stood by the window of the closet for hours each day. It is a fact that the Devil resided in the camp. And it is a fact that I was led to him by the foul stench of a goat." Agent Mondo blinked, hard, and rubbed the inside of his ear with his index finger. Before he could speak the soluse returned to his core, and he slipped back to the consciousness of Bogdan's remembrance.

"General Eisenhower came to visit Neu Freimann. I watched crowds massing in the public square, some going as far as to climb into the fountain to gain better vantage, as the future leader of the free world's arrival neared. I stood in the closet, but I didn't watch the square. As always, I looked in on Cohen's window, which framed an irate director reprimanding two shabbily clothed men who, in the hectic circumstances of Eisenhower's arrival, had managed to bring a goat past the receptionist and up into the office.

"Of course, Cohen couldn't have the General walk in on such an imbroglio. After all, Eisenhower's report would eventually wind up in the Oval Office. Cohen forced the two men out the back door and rushed to open the window as the General's caravan pulled up to the square. The Director raced to meet the envoy of rumbling military Jeep convertibles, straightening his cap as it wobbled out of place with each gangly stride. He prayed his office would not retain the smell of a farm. The mob roared with gratitude and waved to the American military brass while behind the building the two men argued over the goat, gesticulating wildly in the universal body language of disagreement."

Ed strained to see through the peripherals of the young Woland. He had always admired Eisenhower's career.

"I could tell you about Eisenhower's tour of Europe, could recite the relevant passages of his official reports, thus satisfying your boyhood fascination, Agent Mondo. I could tell you how his wind-beaten face stretched in awkward approval as the Neu Freimann school children performed their entirely phonetic English rendition of the Star Spangled Banner. I could tell you about his confused smile, unable to understand a word of it, and also how he had the tact to compliment the children on the beauty of the performance nonetheless. I could tell you, but not from my own memories, only those borrowed from others in the camp. Instead of the General with the uniform, I chose to follow the men with the goat. The bleating of the poor, poor creature would prove to be the siren's call that thrust me into a life of omnipotence."

"Hold on, Bogdan." Ed Mondo stood, the soluse shifting within him, buoyant, wavelike in its movements through his limbs. His body accustomed to it now, accepted it as an organic component of its interior, a bodily humor acting as an analgesic, coating his organs and bones. Ed raised a finger in disbelief as he paced at the end of the hospital bed, pointing to the ceiling beside his pumpkin shaped skull. "You aren't trying to tell me that the Devil appeared to you as a goat?"

"Don't be rash, Agent Mondo. Patience is, as they say, a virtue." The G-Man continued pacing as Neu Freimann returned to him. "I followed the men down Ohio Street, dodging a pack of wild turkeys that scurried through the alleys in the camp." Ed Mondo took in the city as Woland moved through it, reading the temporary street signs, hearing the voices of the displaced persons mispronouncing the American states. Oheeo, Kentootsky, Meshugeen. He followed the patient's memory past rows of Bavarian houses with empty or half-filled flower boxes in the windows and orange shingled roofs until he saw the men with the mangy goat, yanking the stubborn beast into their home.

"I waited in solitude for the men to leave. Eisenhower's visit lured people to the main square. The only man I saw came by picking up trash. The *Komitet* paid people, in rations, to do these types of jobs. The sun receded halfway behind the mountains by the time the men left." Ed watched them leave, bouncing through the door with yellow smiles. Next, he saw Woland's reflected face, blurred in the fading light of the window as he slid it open and climbed inside the house. Bedsheets hung as partitions between repurposed bedrooms, lending a false privacy to the broken families sharing the house. To Ed, the kitchen looked ransacked, with open cabinets and barren cupboards. Between the dried milk and eggs the families subsisted on a diet designed not to live on, but to avoid dying on. *But where's the goat?*

"I'll show you," whispered the voice.

Back in the house Ed Mondo stood, in the body of Bogdan Woland, in front of a dark sheet. The sound of the bleating animal emanated through the air, rippling its way through the curtain. Woland pushed the curtain aside and Ed gazed down a flight of wooden steps. He felt the dank stone walls on either side of him, inhaled the goat's musk and shivered at the sound of the chains binding the goat in cramped captivity. Ed felt the trepidation of the young Woland in his own quickening pulse. He sensed, as even the young Woland did, that the cellar was built by the inhabitants and not as a part of the original blueprint.

Agent Mondo succumbed to the pull of an unknown force. Woland lifted the curtain and stepped past it, releasing it and shutting the light of Neu Freimann away. Standing in the darkness, he listened to his breathing against the hawing of the goat. He took on the first step, lightly, but still produced an echo in the void beneath the stairs. One hand dragged against the cool stone wall, guiding him in the darkness as the other reached tentatively in front of his face, unseen, to protect against invisible enemies. Then everything vanished.

Agent Mondo coughed upon his abrupt return to room 319. He leaned over the silent patient and peered through the eyeholes at serenely closed lids. Standing over the patient's sedentary form he felt the warmth disappear from his limbs, evaporate from the trunk of his torso. He held his hands over Woland's body, afraid to touch the bandaged patient. He looked at the door, then back at the patient. "Bogdan? Bogdan, what is it? What's wrong?" Ed tried to put himself back on the stairs, but the memory felt obscured and inaccessible. He twisted at Woland's bedside, glaring at the medical instruments and examining his shirt resting on his chair with a perplexed anxiety. *How long have I been here?* Ed's stumpy legs started him to the door and the bustling reality of the hospital, but as he reached for the knob, he paused. He turned back to face Woland, straightened his posture and took a deep, long breath. *Focus...Don't give up on this yet. Woland, you can hear me. The top stair. Take me back...*

Agent Mondo clung to the hazy memory of the cellar steps. He listened for the goat, and from the corner of his eye he caught a strip of muted light from beneath the curtain. The skin of his arms tightened to the cold, the creaking of the steps whimpered in his ear. *We're there, Woland. I'm there.*

"Yes, Agent Mondo. Prepare to look upon the eyes of Satan."

Soft braying wafted from the goat at the base of the stairs, no more than twenty feet from where the young Woland shook on the first step. Reaching with his toe, he ventured one further, the screech of the wobbly step heightening the panic in the goat's guttural bleating. Woland had crept halfway down, with Ed experiencing each quiet movement, when his foot didn't meet with a step, but instead the vacuous air of empty space. Unable to see the missing step, Woland's bony leg sank beneath the stairs and acted as an anchor to keep him from becoming a human avalanche. Ed Mondo felt the sting of the wood against his face as Woland collided with the steps. Sitting in the hospital room he cringed at the spark of pain, clenched his eyes and covered the left half of his face. Woland's knee crashed into another step and sang out in a reverberating chorus of pain.

Woland landed, facing away from the goat, towards the dust-caked blackness beneath the steps. Through Woland, Ed felt his head lying flat on the step, the muscles of his leg pulled awkwardly like bare tree limbs in winter storms, dangling through the stairs. His vision blurred the surroundings, but a glowing golden light glinted near the floor beneath him. He tried to focus on it but it moved, always further down out of sight. Woland closed his eyes and took two breaths. He opened them to an upright world, dark still, but clear.

The light remained, shimmering inches above the floor beneath his twisted body. The stinging pains dissipated, but he failed to notice. He only stared at the light, subtly bouncing in place. Transfixed, he watched it move slowly away towards the wall beneath the door. First came the feet, bare and upward pointing, then a mound of tattered cloth. It was a man, Woland recognized, a very sick man. The form struggled to breathe, hardly able to lift the decrepit blanket over its chest with the power of his lungs. The light moved over the emaciated torso and revealed a pale face striped with lengths of sweat-drenched black hair. The glowing amber rested in front of his face for a moment, and began pulsating. From the step, Woland watched the ethereal light source flow into the body of the defeated form, and as the light disappeared from the room its power remained, providing a soft glow. In the light Woland saw the man's ashen, slumbering face. Ed sensed what Woland had sensed, that this sleep delved beyond the subconscious dreams of mortal men. There was a flash of light, like that of lightning in a heat storm, and Woland recoiled with eyes sealed from the glare. Once the flash subsided, Woland opened his eyes to meet those of the man. In them he saw a subterranean concentration of darkness that penetrated straight into his heart. Ed felt it too. Both he and Woland knew in that instant that the man needed help, knew he was sick in ways no human could fathom, knew they had looked upon the eyes of the Devil.

"Sir?" Agent Mondo felt a hand shaking his shoulder. "Sir, visiting hours are over for the day. You'll need to exit this ward."

Ed popped up and reached for the holster that he'd left in the safe of his hotel room. He surveyed the scene with shifting eyes and licked his lips. Outside the window, the sky returned to its routine beauty of faint reds and oranges against a spectrum of blues. He smiled at the nurse.

"If it's not a problem, Miss," he held the gaze of the plain vanilla face while removing his badge, "I'd like to stay and ask a few more questions of the patient."

The nurse gawked at him and hiccupped a nervous laugh. She noticed Ed's demeanor wasn't deadpan comedy, but sincere gravitas.

She erected her posture straightened her uniform with her palms and looked back and forth between the patient and the squat, tired man beside the bed. "Sure," she mumbled, "Just don't tell anyone I said so. And if he does wake up, be sure to find the on-call resident. Word is this coma could last months, even years."

Picking up on physical tics for a living helped Ed Mondo develop an incredible ability to mask his own. He masked his surprise behind a solemn nod. "Of course, sweetheart. Anyone asks, we never met. I'll just be a few minutes with paperwork, boring stuff." She offered a closed mouth grin of minute duration and left the agent alone with his suspect and his new set of doubts.

"Paperwork...Not a bad solution, Agent Mondo." Woland's voice returned, this time in Ed's ears and not in his mind. Ed breathed a sigh of relief in his chair, leaned forward with his elbows on his knees and his forehead on the base of his palms.

"Jesus, Woland..."

"No, Agent Mondo, quite the opposite, in fact."

"How can I know if any of this is real?"

"Agent Mondo. Ask yourself: Have you ever known what is real?" Ed slid his hands over his face and rubbed his eyes. Through his fingers he made out the misty green waves of the sky outside the window. "You know what you see. What you feel. What more reality can there be? The reality of the Devil in Neu Freimann." Ed wiggled his toes, The soluse wriggling its way back into his feet. He had followed Woland's tale deep into the forest, too deep to find his way back. The only way out was through to the other side.

"I hurried out of the stairwell and out into the street. The sight of his demonic gaze remained with me, branded into my eyelids." Ed saw them still. They occupied his focus, eliminating thoughts of the goat, the nurse, the sky. But he felt no fear, only a desire to aid the suffering entity. "You feel it too, yes?" Woland asked. "The compassion. It drew me back to him and I returned that night." The melding of minds resumed as Ed heard the muffled breathing of sleeping orphans.

The young Woland sat up in bed and cradled his blanket under his arm. He slipped out the orphanage and, thanks to his months of tailing Cohen, followed a direct route through the brisk night air back to the house with the goat. He lifted the window and listened for movement from within as he cowered beneath the pane. The scent of the goat gushed out of the house, like steam erupting from a pot once the lid has been lifted. The heavy darkness and the grating snores of the yellow toothed men covered the sound of Woland's entrance. He tiptoed to the curtain and heard the goat cry out in its sleep, an unnatural, arrhythmic arpeggio of huffs and squeals that set Woland's hair on edge. Ed rubbed his forearms in his bedside chair. He remembered the high-pitched yelp of the stairs beneath Woland's weight and tensed in his chair, willing the boy not to continue. To his surprise, Woland stopped at the top step, bent down, and dropped the coarse blanket through the gap. He stole away before hearing it land.

"That, Agent Mondo, was the first act of kindness that would lead to my reward."

"Kindness to an ailing Satan?"

"Exactly. He was weak. Tired. The war was brutal, even for him to endure. Like others in Neu Freimann, he needed to rest and recover his strength. But unlike others, that was all he could do. The rest of us needed a distraction, a mission, and for me caring for the Devil would fill that void.

"Sounds like a big job for a kid, Bogdan."

"Yes, but we all needed jobs. Some refused to work. Surviving Hitler's genocide, they believed, entitled them not to. That entitlement ruined them, I think, for it left them with nothing but thoughts of their tragic past. I can't say definitively that they were wrong, but keeping busy with work allowed the displaced lives to find meaning again."

The warmth returned to Ed, enveloping him from inside out, and the sight of the public square appeared before him. The bright German sun shone high above and the young Woland wheeled about in pursuit of a short, slouching man. "The man we are chasing," Woland's voice returned, "is a tailor. I knew this because I had seen him present a suit coat to Director Cohen as a gift. Cohen had agreed to sign off on a forged medical form that ignored the slight case of

Pott disease he suffered. Notice the hunchback in his right shoulder." Ed watched as the man waddled with uneven steps through an alley, one shoulder dipped well below the other. They passed small stalls selling overripe fruit purchased from Germans on the black market, operated by grisly housewives. "This way, he could immigrate to Canada, where they were always looking for skilled workers. Tailors, woodsman, *holtshakers* and the like."

"Cohen would do that?" Ed asked, keeping an eye on the memory of the tailor's jilted movements.

"Of course. He was, as I said, a great provider of solutions. Hundreds of would-be immigrants came to him in need of assistance with medical records. A misdiagnosed spot on a lung from five years past could still prohibit a man from entering America, or Australia, or Romania. Cohen always strove to help."

Ed watched as the memory played on and the tailor returned home. He entered the door and came out minutes later, beaming, brandishing a slip of paper and holding his wife in a single armed embrace. The change of his medical status warranted a celebration with friends, and in the excitement he failed to even shut his door. Woland approached the house, recognizing it as an exact replica of the Devil's abode, only without the makeshift basement. As he climbed the stairs, Ed noticed yet another missing step in the flight. Powerless to warn the young Woland of the potential booby trap, he braced for another shared experience of pain. This time, however, Woland gracefully skipped the step without hesitation. "Stairs disappeared for the same reason the door was left open." The patient's voice sounded in Ed's mind. "These weren't the homes of their inhabitants. They borrowed them. A wooden stair could keep a fire alive, why not burn a step that once supported the enemy? It was a simple solution."

Once upstairs Woland located the tailor's fitting room, a space hardly larger than the orphanage closet, insulated on all sides by stacks of fabric. Rifling through the mounds, Woland snatched up all his arms could carry. Hugging the new wardrobe against his chest, he blindly staggered back down the stairs, deftly skipped over the diminutive divide, and stored the loot behind the house beneath an overturned wheelbarrow.

"I skipped meals that day, waiting for night to fall so I could return to him. Soon after his presence became a part of my life I felt isolated, as though I existed apart from others living in the camp. I lost weight, but was never hungry. I slept less and less, but was never tired. My transformation began before I was aware of what I would become.

"That night, I returned to the tailor's house," Ed's perception once more inhabited the surrogate body of Woland's youth. Sitting in his chair he felt the untamed grass tickling his ankles as Woland skirted across an empty field beneath a violet sky. "This field was used by Zionist groups to train young boys destined for Palestine in basic soldiering. War hardened many men, and some would never soften. Violence became their constant companion. Cohen didn't like it. He even went as far as shutting down parts of the operation. When he discovered the horrifying nature of live stabbing simulations, which involved burlap sacks of live cats, he cracked down on the whole procedure. That was the difference between people's experiences of war. For Cohen, it was disgusting, repulsive cruelty. But for the men who had seen so much worse, it did not faze them in the slightest."

Ed looked at the barren field as Woland's twig-like legs carried him through it. He pictured the cats shoved into the sacks and thought of his own Siamese back home. "I had been to see him many times by this point," the patient continued, "and I began to realize that something cloaked my presence. I was careful still, but I no longer feared being seen. I worked with a borrowed confidence. Weeks had passed and I'd brought stolen fruit and bread, dropped them through the stairs without venturing below myself. I did the same with the clothes that night."

Back in room 319, Ed Mondo blinked in quick succession and shook his head as though drying his hair. Breaking free of the sedative effect of the soluse, he raised an open palm and slapped his cheek three times before looking at his watch. The hands blurred and swayed. He slid the gold band over his wrist and dangled the timepiece in front of his face from two fingers. Somehow, it felt both lighter and heavier, dulled yet more vibrant. Woland's voice whispered, hardly audible but clear as day in the back of Ed's mind. "You may forget, but one day you will stay close to me and listen to me." Ed nodded with hypnotic assent. He slid the watch back over his hand and laid his arms flat on the armrests.

"It went on this way until I had become fully accustomed to the odors of the captive goat. The operation ran smoothly up to the day I attempted to bring him a pair of shoes. Citizens in the camp took classes in basic skills. The more skilled a person was, the better off they'd be finding work in the future. Besides, Cohen encouraged people to enroll by rewarding them with extra rations. A man like Adler would, at least on paper, learn to lay brick, repair timepieces, and make shoes. And he'd do all this at the same time.

"I ascertained where a former cobbler taught shoemaking classes and, with a pack of cigarettes I pilfered from an orphanage administrator's jacket, made my way through camp. Timing is everything. I'm sure you've heard the expression, Agent Mondo, and mine was abysmal that day. I hoped to open the door to an abandoned room and instead encountered an ensemble of men huddled over a worktable, each speaking over his neighbor."

Ed listened to the chorus of voices as Woland sidled up to the side table loaded with mismatched footwear. A pudgy man with a face like a sponge presided over the debate by banging a steel shank against the table like a gavel. Once the mob settled, he cleared his throat with a shake of his jowls. The mob quieted down just as Woland pulled the two closest shoes from the table. Ed gritted his teeth in tandem with the young Woland as the boy turned on his heels to find eleven sets of eyes fixed on him. *Run, Kid, Run.* Ed thought.

"Relax, Agent Mondo," the patient's soft voice said. "It was a different world than the one you've lived in. Some men were to be avoided, surely. But many looked out for one another."

Ed endured the standoff a moment longer, still willing his shared body to flee. The boy took a deep breath and exhaled through trembling lips. Back in room 319, The Federal Agent mimicked Woland's mouth movements. In all this time, he realized he had not heard the boy speak a word. Woland bit his bottom lip and Ed felt the force of his young voice building in his diaphragm, but another voice cut in. "How's this for a deal, son," an older man, the cobbler, with a salty corona of thinning hair, elbowed his way through the crowd as though paddling a canoe. "You give me the rest of those Lucky Strikes sticking out of your pocket there, and I'll let you trade in one of those left feet you got for an honest pair. Deal?"

The shoemaker's room faded out, replaced in Ed's vision by the rectangular fluorescent light humming down at him. He picked the back of his head up from his neck, struggling to establish the realm of reality from the common ground of the patient's history. "I will not show you what happened that night, for I do not like to relive the horror of it. I brought him the shoes, and as I dropped them through the stairs I heard voices, the men with the butter yellow teeth had returned. I ducked below just in time, for they came directly to the cellar. In the moment they crossed the curtain, I spied a gleaming blade. You see, Agent Mondo, they had procured the goat in the hopes of using its milk. Through Adler, they had obtained a form of saccharine and aimed to produce ice cream to sell. It would have been quite a treat for the children in camp, but the goat, due to malnutrition, yielded sour milk, and little of it at that. The men had decided to cut their losses. I watched from beneath the stairs with a hand over my mouth. It was horrible. The blood pooled and flowed towards me. The sound of the animal's heft crashing down haunts me still. I shivered as its last breath reverberated through the dark air of the cellar. Worst of all, the men dragged the felled beast up the steps, scraping its clotted fur against each step with loud thuds. The blood dripped from above, covering me in warm, thick, crimson streaks.

"When the men had left, I opened my eyes and he was awake." The soluse had steadily returned to Ed's body, clinging to his mind like tentacles engulfing their prey. He returned to Woland's consciousness and looked upon the ocular abyss, dark rivulets of blood coursing over his eyes and cheeks. Neither Ed nor Woland attempted to move. Nor breathe. The amber sphere of light formed between the Devil and the orphan. *The soluse*, Ed thought. Once more it pulsated with energy, bobbing slightly up and down. The light shone dim at first, but as it moved towards Woland's young body it intensified, growing brighter, sharper, and hotter. The Devil lowered his head and the ball stopped inches from Woland's chest.

A voice, distant and unfamiliar, speaking an unknown language, murmured a brief message, an incantation, a warning, and in it a hint of gratitude. The ball exploded in a blaze of white light, but only for an instant. When Woland recovered from the blast the figure had vanished, and he recognized he was lying on the floor of the orphanage closet.

Agent Mondo came to in the hospital room with a start. He jumped from his chair and again reached for his phantom pistol. The vise grip of Woland's memories released its suction hold and Ed staggered back and caught his balance by throwing a hand behind him onto the chair. The room spun, he heaved for oxygen. The idiosyncrasies of his middle-aged body replaced the lithe durability he had enjoyed in Woland's form. He rubbed at his eyelids and coughed, slapping his thick chest with a tight fist. "Bogdan," he coughed out, "What happened?"

"It was my reward. I had been the Devil's solution, and in exchange he gave me the power to offer the same service to others."

"The soluse..." Ed went to the foot of the bed and sat down on the hospital sheets, staring at the floor. "Damn," the Agent smiled and shook his head. "I don't know what to tell y-"
Eddie Mondo turned to face the bandaged man but found only an open window to a clear blue morning sky.

Fore for Four
Saturday, May 18th, 1985

The third kill was, as I stated earlier, easy as pie. Number four, however, required a touch more effort and two touches more pain in the ass.

Established in 1895 on the Atlantic coast of Virginia, Harbor Hills Country Club originally served as a gentlemen's hunting outfit. By the time this old Frogg hopped to the cast iron gates it had transformed into one of Old Diminion's most upscale social clubs. For Mark IV, Harbor Hills represented a home away from home. Unlike his cursed precursors, it didn't take long to understand why this Mark had it coming. I killed him for the same reason someone wanted him killed: Large sums of money. My latest Mark owned one of the largest beef distributors in the nation. He saw the product from the feeding of the mother cow to the birth of the calf, kept tabs on growth and development at the farms, monitored activities in the slaughterhouse, and even managed the supply chain that shipped the end product to his consumers. Based on his unusual girth, I assume he sampled more than his share of the product for quality control purposes. Money Mark, as my memory saw fit to classify the jowly dignified southerner, had acquired in his career the type of wealth that necessitates top of the line home security and, as is so often the case, a level of paranoia that leads a man to bug his own office.

Couldn't hunt him at home.

Couldn't whack him at work.

No choice but to pop him at play.

I had followed him this far and felt eager to put Money Mark on the books. Something about the South, and not just the hillbilly South of Mississippi, but even the hoity-toity colonial South of Virginia, just didn't sit well with me. Before I could get out, though, I'd have to get in. My black t-shirt lacked the mandatory collar. My denim jeans lacked the mandatory lack of denim jeans. Security officer Larry Funk asked a fair question: What exactly was I doing there dressed that way? A man of principle on a murder mission doesn't fail to size up a rent-a-cop named Funk. Part of me said *I gotta have that Funk*, but I opted to give up the Funk and go with a fib.

"I'm with the band."

"Where's your instrument?" Couldn't argue with the man's logic. He stood with his arms crossed at an absurd angle, forcibly pressing his palms up into his armpits. He didn't intimidate so much as bewilder, but not enough to throw me off my game.

"Piano." I wiggled my fingers without missing a beat.

"Keep your tux in the server room, huh? Risky." And just like that, Officer Funk opened the gate and pointed me to my disguise. I offered to shake the man's hand but he backed off, citing that he didn't want to damage my moneymakers. Instead, he returned my friendly finger frolic with a wiggle of his own. I ambled up the tree-lined driveway whistling Dixie with ample enthusiasm to ensure my sarcastic bent, all the while maintaining a veracity of tune and tempo such that any Confederate in earshot would have offered a solemn nod of rebellious camaraderie. Approaching the main clubhouse, I came upon two teenage valets slouched forward beneath their polyester white vests (as well as the additional weight of their adolescent blonde mustaches and shaggy haircuts). They gaped as I danced on by as though they'd never seen a Unioner in their lives.

Flecks of black dotted the chalk-white stone steps, so walking up to the colonial mansion felt like climbing a giant scoop of manicured chocolate chip ice cream. I stood in the center of the front atrium, basking in the opulence of Harbor Hills. Underdressed, out of place, and en route to engage Money Mark in the most hostile of hostile takeovers his career would ever know. But first I'd have to practice my scales.

I love music! Anne's letter said. I'd written to her about my childhood at the piano bench taking lessons on scales from the two-headed dragon of Mother and Mr. Sootsky. Even as a child, I could see through his lascivious intentions with my mother as easily as I could see through his comb over. With me, his lips scrunched inwards and trembled with hatred, but with Mother his smile pushed the corners of his mouth wider than the outside of his eyeballs. He doubled as a teacher and a tuner, and I always suspected he intentionally mistuned the thing so I'd sound worse, thus requiring more visits from him to Mother's home, the home my father once lived in, to correct either me or the instrument I so thoroughly detested. They went on one date. I broke two lamps that night.

Did your mom ever date anyone besides that Sootsky weirdo? Maybe she was just desperate for a night out! She'd have to be to go out with that guy. Speaking of dating, a boy from school invited me to a concert. Not just any concert, either. We're going to see MADONNA! He's picking me up Saturday morning and we're driving all the way up to Chicago to see her on the 18th. I. Am. So. Excited. Like a virgin...maybe not for long! We're spending the night in the city at a hotel. I can't believe it. I may never come back!

Needless to say, I was not a fan of this mysterious Montague making moves and playing Casanova with my Capulet girl. Just what I needed: another Sootsky to worry about stealing the woman in my life. I put it out of mind though. Focus. Focus on the job at hand.

A few Harbor Hills members eyed me for a fleeting moment, but a man of principle doesn't warrant more than a passing glance from an entitled trophy wife on her second vodka of the early afternoon. I located the club restaurant and followed the lone waitress into a back room where I gave her a line about surprising a member on his birthday (me being his old college buddy or some other forgettable bullshit). She showed me the communal backup tux hanging beside the restaurant's two-week shift schedule and I pulled it off the hanger. I flashed the young lady a not-so-innocent wink and suited up for an impromptu concert.

As a general rule, a disguise should decrease one's conspicuousness. General rules, I've found, are generally meant to be broken. Not unlike the seams that strained to maintain the structural integrity of some other, much shorter man's tuxedo. Walking across the restaurant towards the piano, I caught a glimpse of Money Mark with his moneyed cohorts, cigars ablaze and scotchlogic not too far off. Continued visual reconnaissance would have to take a backseat to maintaining cover. I Frankenstein waddled my way to the piano. The tuxedo pants stymied my mobility something awful, seeing as I

110

never learned an alternate method of walking that didn't involve bending my knees.

The help was so far below the members at Harbor Hills that the pianist wasn't worthy of watching the superior social class imbibe. I sat at the piano bench—hiking up the cuffs of my borrowed pants and exposing two mismatched socks and a pale stretch of my ankles of principle—only to look above the sheet music through the floor to ceiling windows that lined the room out onto the Harbor Hills golf course. Behind me, Money Mark whistled for the waitress. He and his cronies sat directly in the center of the restaurant at a round double-clothed table, each finishing a mess of pulled pork and a neat Glenmorangie.

The bartender glared and approached, tossing a polishing rag over his shoulder. Every inch as big as me and about a foot more intimidating, and that measure includes the additional fear I inspired by practically flexing through my tuxedo. "You're not Jerry." I'm not sure whether he meant to ask where Jerry was or who I was, but he appeared pleased with having formed a sentence and uttered it aloud clearly enough to be understood. I said Jerry couldn't make it, that I knew him back at the conservatory and he called in a favor. The lunkhead scratched his lunk of shaved head, leaned over the bar and whispered, "You like Ratt?" He lifted his sleeve and showed off a fresh Ratt tattoo. I mumbled something about classical being more my style and the bartender went back to polishing burgundy glasses and crystal decanters, nodding his head to an internal guitar riff. Clearly, the clown in the too small tux wasn't worth his precious time. Not quite easy as pie, but so far still a piece of cake.

Harbor Hills may have lacked intelligent employees, but it made up for it in Swanky amenities. Even the well drinks came from the top shelf. Everywhere I looked I saw extravagance in style and spending. The club didn't skimp on the latest luxuries. Hell, it was 1985; even the Coke was new. The club architect ruffled a few feathers when he imported Brazilian Rosewood for the bar. Members of Harbor Hills prefer to buy American. They didn't seem to mind so much when they saw the sheen coming off the end product. More impressive than the wood was the plastic. You should have seen the bells on these southern belles. It didn't matter how old they were, what color hair they grew, how they felt or what time of day it was; without fail each of the female members had D-cups pressing against her knit sweater vest, blonde waves cut to shoulder length, a permanent smile held together by staples beneath her skin and a martini glass of clear liquid in one hand. Hi Carl! Welcome to Stepford!

These women kissed each other hello on both cheeks without making contact with one another's faces. As for the hetero hellos, it looked to me like the men went after their friends' wives' lips with the casual impunity of practiced swingers. Almost every piece of artwork and furniture came from generations past, possibly because this generation of members inherited their fortunes from the folks who actually paid for the place. It was the kind of joint I'd hesitate to fart in. But only for a second or two, of course.

I didn't lie to Officer Funk about my instrument. I'm no Mozart but I've got some art. My mother's insistence on my childhood mastery of scales provided the muscle memory to throw an arpeggio into the oxygen of the stuffy dining room without suffering an anxiety attack. Unfortunately, her insistence of total mastery of scales prevented me from learning anything beyond them. For example, how to play songs on the piano. Perhaps my hatred for a certain Mr. Sootsky contributed to my poor progress at the piano keys, too. Either way, two decades of nothing but warm-up exercises and there I sat, ready for the recital.

With my back to the room, I diddled a quick series of C Majors, starting low and raising the octave. Only three missed notes. The bartender shot a glare my way, but Money Mark couldn't be bothered to listen to me. I, however, had nothing but open ears for his flavorful twang.

"What can we do?" One of Mark's cronies put up his hands in surrender. "If Adler changes his product line, that's his business. We either adjust, or we lose him."

"Well," Money Mark wiped barbeque sauce from the corners of his mouth. "I didn't get where I am by smiling as my biggest accounts broke their contracts. If he thinks he can hang me out to

112

dry..." Money Mark coughed and patted his chest. "We can't alter our production to fit his needs. Impossible. If we can't keep him, I don't want him going someplace else. We'll freeze the bastard out. Monday morning we call everyone in food services, distribution, equipment, everyone. Conway, Banks, Goldberg, everyone. I don't want Adler to so much as rent a refrigerated truck in this country. Simple message, gentlemen: If you do business with Adler, you won't do business with me." Money Mark's face reddened and sweat pulled at the wisps of hair striping his receding hairline. The room fell silent after his tirade.

The cronies exchanged glances until one cleared his throat and spoke up for the group. "Adler's no pushover, boss. You've heard the rumors about his son's death. A lot of people don't think it was a coincidence. And that PR stunt he pulled afterwards...it seemed a little too neat."

"Let him try it," The fat man whispered into his chins.

Nobody cared that the unruly pianist hadn't played a note in minutes.

"Anyhow, we're still on for the afternoon, right boys?" Mark asked, pulling at his collar to cool down. His smile steadied the nerves of the sycophantic circle.

A dancing D minor.

"1st tee at 1:15?"

A flirt of F sharp.

"$100 a man on the front, back, and full 18 sound good?"

A babbling B flat major.

"You sound confident for a man who can't keep it in the fairway." A brave crony chimed in.

Fanning himself with his barbeque sauced-stained napkin, Mark answered, "I swear to God, my slice will be the death of me."

You don't know how right you are, I thought, closing the key guard and rising from the bench. Between Officer Funk, the valets, the waitress and the bartender, I'd been overexposed. I'd meet Mark and he'd meet his maker out on the links. The bartender owl-eyed me as I wobbled by with a shrug. I told him I forgot something in the car and skulked out through the kitchen looking like a giraffe stuffed into a monkey suit. Before leaving, I heard the crony toss out an all too appropriate bit of golf gambling trash talk. "You made the bet, Sir. It's your funeral."

I let myself out by the dumpsters, but not before snagging a paring knife from a small drawer. If only the Agency paid me to locate kitchen goods instead of killing people.

"Harbor Hills' private golf course, known to players worldwide as "The Bull," challenges players of all skill levels. Hitting straight off the tee is imperative to scoring well here at "The Bull," as dense stretches of woodlands and thick cut rough lie in wait for those who fail to hit the fairways. An elevated tee box at the 18th offers beautiful views of the Virginia coastline and the majesty of the Atlantic Ocean."

I dropped the scorecard back in the trashcan on the tee box of the 7th hole. As a man of principle I enjoy a beautiful view of anything, be it a majestic ocean or even a lesser, perhaps fog covered ocean. But work is work, and the 18th hole would have to wait for another time. I chose the 7th because it had a dogleg left, meaning the best way to play it is a shot that moves from right to left. Thanks to Crony's trash talk, I knew Mark had trouble keeping the ball from moving left to right. It doesn't take a man of principle to recognize that two wrongs don't make a right. In fact, in the game of golf, two wrongs make a shot go doubly right. Mark would undoubtedly aim further left to compensate for what weekend warriors refer to as his "banana slice," and that would result in a ball bending even more drastically the opposite way, where I would be waiting in the woods to kill the fat, drunken aristocratic linksman.

He thought he was taking on The Bull, but instead he'd get the Frogg. Leaves and twigs crunched below my feet as I estimated the likely landing spot of Money Mark's misfired drive. I checked my watch to calculate what hole the unfortunate foursome might be playing and reasoned that prior to killing Mark, I'd have to kill some time. My knee pressed against the polyester pant leg as I calmly coaxed the taut fibers into bending. I managed to contort my limbs into a sitting position with my back against a tree trunk and my legs splayed out like aboveground roots. Looking up through the canopy of budding leaves and branches, I made out thin traces of the sky.

What am I doing here? Is this what I am? I thought about my sleepless nights. About Mark Hilson reaching towards third base. About the look of Professor Mark lying in the snow and the sour taste of the stale pie from Mark #3's fridge. I picked up a green leaf the size of my hand and peeled its flesh along its slender veins, mindlessly rolling the surgically removed foliage in my hand. *I could give it up. I could learn to play songs and get a job at Harbor Hills playing piano for the rich folks. Can't beat the free booze and the eye candy.* I thought about my mother. It'd kill her if she knew. A caterpillar crawled up onto my ankle. Normally, I'd have flicked that sucker into early cocoon retirement, but I didn't have it in me. When it comes to deadly sins, once you go mammal, you never go back.

I thought about Anne. In a few hours I'd lay Money Mark down to rest and she'd just be laid. Funny how clearly I could see her and the little piss-ant boyfriend in my mind despite not knowing what either of them looked like. The caterpillar slipped off my pant leg and back onto terra firma. *Focus. Focus on the job at hand.*

That's when it hit me. The rush. I couldn't give it up because I didn't want to. The surge of life that accompanies death. That's what made it worthwhile. Not the money. If my reasons filled the air then money would be the oxygen, taking top billing but only comprising a fifth of the substance. The rush was like nitrogen to my lungs. Working with interesting people was as fleeting as carbon dioxide, and the opportunity for advancement held as much weight as water vapor. I took a deep breath.

While I pondered the breakdown of my work atmosphere, Money Mark's voice rang from the clearing.

"FORE!"

Sure enough, he'd sliced into the woods. I heard a rustle in the branches followed by what any amateur golfer would recognize as the unmistakable knock of a golf ball on wood. I followed the noise and located the dirt-smeared orb in front of me, only not quite far enough from the tree line to provide ample cover. A man of principle keeps an honest score on the golf course, but he also doesn't get arrested for murder. With the latter in mind, I scooped up the Titleist 2 and moved it into deeper cover, placing it atop a mound of green grass in plain sight to lure Mark the Bull into Carl the Frogg's clutches. Crouching behind a nearby tree I waited for the grunting, out of breath gastropod to scratch and claw his way into the depths of the greenery. How did I know he'd come in search of the ball? Golf balls cost money, and you don't stay rich by buying more golf balls. Relying on my ears to keep tabs on the man, I listened as his elephantine tramping grew louder, and louder, and stopped. Mark released a moan as he leaned forward to pick up the ball and then turned to drop it somewhere closer to the fairway. A no-no in both etiquette and integrity. Emerging from my hiding place I announced, "Now Sir, with $100 on the front, back, and full 18, I don't think your playing partners would appreciate your club choice of the hand-wedge."

"What the fuck? Who are you?" The blimp exhaled. "Why are you dressed like that?"

I sprang on him, subdued him by the neck and pulled out the paring knife. "You folks really like asking about my clothes in these parts." I yanked back the floundering walrus's head. "Remember what you said about your slice?" *Fwipp.* I dropped the massive man like a beached manatee. *FORE! For four,* I thought as I raced deeper into the woods.

Escaping back through the club would lead to anything but escape, so I'd have to take my chances searching for civilization on the other side of the woods. The cronies would come help Mark find his lost ball in a minute so I couldn't risk heading back towards the course. I glided through the trees with all the grace one should expect from an adrenaline fueled size 38 squeezed into a pair of slim fit 32s. My legs moved like tree trunks, plodding me forward like a man on stilts. A subdued scream from a crony assured me I had made it out to a safe enough distance. Minutes later, I happened to cross a narrow clearing and an abandoned train track, overgrown with rust and weeds. I stood between the rails, took off my tuxedo jacket and flung it over my shoulder. Nothing down the track one way, nothing

116

down the track the other. I started walking, whistling a C Major scale as I went.

Bless This Mess
Tuesday, May 9th, 1989

    I woke up with a fat cat sprawled across my chest. A steady beat thumped in the back of my head and sunlight worked upon my eyes like a natural blindfold, which forced me to squint at my surroundings. I realized then that I must have slept walked into the back of a car, but how did I get in? My head weighed me down and I couldn't lift it, or my arms and legs. Peering to the front seat, I made out the hazy outline of a driver and couldn't believe my eyes. "Mom?"

    "Jesus Christ, Frogg," Mother wouldn't take the lord's name with such aggressive inflection. "You really need to see a shrink."

    "Iggy?" From behind the groggy veil of stupefied semi-wakefulness I observed the driver sitting upright with her hair down, wearing a bleach-white baseball shirt with green three quarter length sleeves and an all too familiar pair of Aviator shades. "Iggy," *Did I drink a gallon of single malt last night?* "Where are we?"

    "Just lay down, try to relax." I felt my strength coming back and started to shift my weight around, but still my brain cried out in agony with each fresh pump of oxygenated blood. Rolo leapt up to the front seat and I peeled my upper body off the leather interior and rested on my elbows. "Hey!" Iggy snapped at me in the rearview mirror while never taking her sky eyes off the road. "I said lay down. Don't make me stop this car." My head sank back to the seat and I wiggled my toes. Fitting horizontally in the back of a sedan left me with one knee cocked upwards and another splayed out like a chicken wing. My legs looked like a denim rollercoaster track winding its way through the backseat. What a ride I'd been on. I knew we went to the motel. I remembered ripping apart those jeans (at which point it occurred to me that I had my new, zippered pair, in place, signaling the second platonic encounter between Iggy and Big Carl). After the denim demolition, I went to the bathroom to read the debrief-*SHIT.*

    "Iggy we gotta go back to the motel. I left my, uh...something behind."

"Listen Carl, right now all I need you to do is lay down and rest. Whatever you were on or into last night doesn't matter. Just sleep it off."

"No, it's not drugs, it was a folder, with a-"

"The screenplay?" Iggy unleashed another of her flying monkey cackles as she eased the sedan down the yellow brick road of the Great Plains.

"What screenplay?"

"The motel manager had to let me into your room. He wouldn't do it at first, but I told him my pet frog escaped and got in there somehow. We found you in the bathroom passed out with all these papers spread on the floor. The guy threatened to call the cops and accused you of breaking into his office and stealing his screenplay. You must have gotten drunk and taken it in the middle of the night. 'The Devil Under the Stairs,' he called it. Said it's going to be a horror flick, his ticket out of that dump. Did you at least read it?"

"I guess not..." This felt like as good a moment as any to adopt a principle regarding my ability to either throw punches or roll with them. I figured finding out my best friend and my neighborhood mystic have a complicated secret history, confusing the Federal Agent I'm trying to knock boots with as my mother, and waking up in the back of a car unable to move might be God's way of telling me to holster the haymakers and ride this one out.

"Get some rest. I'll wake you when we get close."

"Close to where?"

"Just sleep it off, Frogg."

"I like your shirt." I said, succumbing to heavy eyelids.

"It's my only change of clothes and I'd hate to get it blood splattered." Agent Xidas pushed her shades down her nose and turned to the back seat to look me over. "But if you don't quiet down back there, I'll give you another taste of the great American interstate."

"I hear you," I yawned. "Just brings out your eyes, is all." She returned to the road and left me to my backseat bedroom.

The forest blocks all sound and light. Only the distant keen of a whistling train penetrates the trees' sensory obstruction. I put one foot down in front of me. The soft ground accepts it, willing me forward. I stop. I listen for the next whistle. It comes from ahead of me. Turning, I run blindly in the night, trusting I'll come to no harm. I sense I'm not alone. *Whoever you are, get out.* No answer. I feel winded and heavy, weighed down at my feet and up to my knees, but lighter than air above them. I slow and come to a stop. The Solutionist's hut looms above me, higher and darker than ever before. Its window sits in the canopy of still branches. I cannot see the sky beyond it. Suddenly, I fall to my knees and retch, clawing at the damp night grasses around me. The blades coat my fingers in a slick film of dew, a silver oil. When the spasms pass, my eyes trace their way from the base of the structure, back to its original size, up to the window. *How did you get here? You don't belong here. This place is mine. Not yours.* The hut makes no answer. *Creeeeak.* The window opens and I shuffle onto my knees and raise my hands together as though in prayer. Through the mesh wiring a glimmer of amber shines through. *I'm so tired. I want to go back. Take it, please. Take it from me.*

The amber glow erupts through the wire partition and illuminates the forest around me. Deep purple shadows strafe in streams between the tree trunks against the bottomless night of the forest. The force of the light knocks me backward and disappears into the forest in all directions. Still on my back, I look to the hut. A circular clearing unfolds in the trees, revealing the violet night sky above it. The leaves of the trees croak and in them the faces of a thousand bullfrogs watch me. A hand emerges from the window and takes hold of a cord. *No. Not that. Anything but that.* Next, the top of his head. *It can't be.* White as cotton in the purple light, a solemn Eddie Mondo materializes from the hut, his eyes closed and lips pulled tight in a content grin. *Don't do it, Eddie. Please.* He pulls the cord and opens his eyes. Sky eyes glowing like twin suns. The sound of a hundred train whistles whirls down from the starless purple firmament. The frog leaves open their mouths and project the horrid noise from all sides. The whistling manifests in currents of air, spiraling down from above. It grows louder and faster and bears down on me. And all the while Ed Mondo hovers above in the hut, watching with someone else's eyes.

I woke up with a fat cat sprawled across my chest. If Iggy thought I'd willingly submit to another game of Mad Mom Minivan she had another thing coming. I rolled Rolo off of me and sat up in the middle of the backseat. "How long was I ou-," I didn't see a need to finish the sentence with nobody else occupying the automobile. *If a Frogg croaks in a Sedan and no Federal Agent is there to hear it, does it make a sound?* We must have been on the road a good while and I'd slept through all of it. The sky took on an afternoon coloring, deciding which shade of eveningwear to outfit itself with that night. The face in the rearview looked pretty natty, all things considered. Agent Xidas must have cleaned me up before hauling my ass out of the motel. Don't get me wrong: my face still represented Exhibit A in my police brutality lawsuit, but I knew I'd like her in my corner as a cut-man if I had to go a few rounds on the canvas. A few moments of vanity passed before it occurred to me to take stock of my situation.

Question 1: Where was I?

Question 2: Where was Agent Xidas?

Question 3: What did I make of that dream?

Question 4: Was that Anne?

Question 3 would have to wait. I had answered question 4 (yes), and in the process felt a serious desire to answer question 2 (so I could kill her). Then, I made the gradual realization of the answer to question 1: I was in Hell. Or at the very least, Hell's driveway.

Little had changed. Out the right window, the garden burst with floral fecundity to the delight of the local bee population. Alstroemeria, gladiola, aster, chrysanthemum. I knew them all by sight and scent by the age of seven, otherwise no TV. The hose coiled without a single knot, like a lime green Slinky still in its original packaging. The yard to my left mowed, not a blade out of place. Behind me the Johansons' schnauzer would be shitting on the sidewalk, if it was still alive. Below me, my feet. Above me, the roof.

Nowhere to go but straight ahead, to the regrettable answer to Question 1: Mother's house.

I'm a man of principle. I can handle an occasional dose of unsolicited time with less than beloved loved ones. As such, waking up in my mother's driveway after more than half a decade of absence, while difficult, fell under the umbrella of hardships that could be handled through the up-sucking of it. I prepared to suck it up. Then, I saw once more the round pink profile of Anne peering sideways out of the kitchen window at the conspicuously parked sedan. I don't think an industrial strength wet/dry vacuum had what it takes to suck it up and face those ferocious foes simultaneously.

She disappeared from the window. *Good, that should buy me some time.*

She appeared at the front door. *Shit Shit Shit.*

Rolo shot out of the car before I released the door handle. He broke for the porch steps and caterpillar shifted up into the waiting embrace of Anne's arms. "Rolo! Eddie will be so happy to hear you're ok!"

Mom once received, as a gift, one of those kitschy "Bless This Mess" placards. She tossed it out the next day on the grounds that nobody would accept that Eileen Frogg's home had ever been a mess, needless to say that God would run the risk of leaving Eileen Frogg's home unblessed. That afternoon, two exceptions broke the rule of cleanliness: Rolo and myself. Like Eddie, Mother belonged to the dustless homeowner community. Unlike Eddie, I never witnessed her do any physical cleaning. Dust knew better than to settle on her turf. I sat at the kitchen table admiring the sameness of everything. It felt like entering a home design magazine, the air charged with a glossy, pristine quality and the scent of lemon squares. Streak-free windows looking out to calm weather, pastel hand towels that matched the drapes and dangled serenely in front of the oven, well-stocked jars of sugar, flour, and baking powder lined up in descending height order along the smooth, shimmering countertop. And then a sweaty Carl Frogg rocking back and forth, twitching at every bird chirp and passing automobile, equal parts museum curator and paranoid psych ward inhabitant.

"Relax, Frogg," Anne stood by the sink, leaning backwards and facing me where I sat in the center of the room. Distant voices seeped from the countertop radio, hissing about Burger King's policy on breaking the rules, reminding us that Donnie's Discount Autos is having a spring blowout, and punctuating any silence that hung between Anne and myself. "She won't come home until dinner. Hardly left the church at all the last few days." Rolo slinked between my ankles, which I noticed trembled behind their denim covering. I had spent most of my childhood in that chair, could take inventory of every chopping apparatus, countertop gadget, and baking spice in the room without opening a single cabinet or drawer. And still, I had never felt more lost. "Whatever you and Eddie were up to it really shook her up. She did a total 180."

"So Ed's here?" I steadied my breathing. "Right now?"

"No. Are you alright? You look like you got hit by a train." Anne trudged towards the fridge and removed a mason jar of Mother's home brewed sun tea, uncapping her half filled bottle and swigging with ecstasy. "Have you had this stuff? It's incredible." She recognized my expression and jumped into a rebuttal. "I don't know why you say such horrible things about her. She's a saint."

"That's exactly why." I didn't like Anne taking Mother's side, even if I didn't want her on mine. "Doesn't it bother you how perfect she is? Every mistake I've ever made has felt exponentially worse when looked at by her. Perfection is nothing but another form of evil. A passive aggressive evil, the type that makes you hate yourself no matter what happens, feeling awful for not being as wonderful as she is. Think about my life, Anne. You've seen her. You know how she is. Anything that went wrong, any error in judgment or behavior traced back to me. Never her. She doesn't make mistakes. So when they're made, who else is there to blame? Tell me I'm wrong."

She rolled her eyes over the sun tea. "I'll tell you you're insane. I'd never been around anyone so genuinely kind and generous. For your sake, I didn't tell her about your lost years. I knew she still loved you. Until..."

She grimaced at the thought of Mother's deflated spirit, dropping her head and scrunching her chin into her neck, producing parallel ribbons of fleshy mounds like rolling desert dunes. Her ellipses opened the floor for news radio to take center stage.

Authorities are still scrambling to uncover the motive behind the murder of Officer Daniel J. McManus. Police say the veteran officer's neck had been snapped clean. Listeners are encouraged to contact their local police station with any information that may aid the investigation.

"Isn't it just awful? That poor man." She switched it off.

"Until what?" I asked, eager to avoid the airwaves, more eager to get answers out of her. She looked sideways and shook her head with the involuntary spasm of a horse's leg muscle shooing off flies. "Anne. Look at me. Until what?"

"It was Eddie." She spoke the words in a pleading tone, as though begging for forgiveness. "He was here, but he hardly spoke to me. He seemed dazed, was mumbling a lot. Something about the Solutionist's plan."

"What plan? Slow down, babe." I hadn't meant to use the endearment, but it cheered her up so I let it hang in the air. Tepid sunlight pushed through the kitchen window.

"Well," she sniffed and wiped her nose with the top of her index finger, the way a connoisseur smells a cigar. "I didn't get much from him before he took off, but he did mention 'the farm.' Eileen didn't offer much more, only telling me that he needed to come clean about what you and he have done. Since then, she's been a wreck. Like the life was sucked out of her. She's always at the church praying and when she's home, she just sits quietly in the living room. She hardly eats a thing."

The realization that Ed had somehow known about my work with the Agency didn't come as such a shock. Especially after reading his debrief on the Solutionist case and hearing about his early FBI affiliation. He must have worked to shut me down. Maybe that was why he came to Chilton in the first place. Later, after thinking it all through, it seemed so obvious I was embarrassed not to have caught on before. Then it hit me.

"She knows," I whispered, mostly to myself, staring at my hands resting palms up on the kitchen table. I watched them sway in slow elliptical orbits as the world around them blurred into a misty gray. The fresh lemon scent faded, my muscles tensed and skin tightened. Cold sweat beaded across my entire surface area. A low train whistle blared in my ears. Just as I thought I would lose consciousness, Anne moved towards me and took my quivering palms into her own.

"Carl, I don't care what you did." I looked at her without registering her words. Her mouth moved, a tear rolled down her cheek. My mouth was open but I don't know if I spoke. *She knows.* My stomach contracted and my tongue tasted of vomit. I grasped my belly and ran my opposite hand over my face from the forehead down to the chin like a squeegee. "Carl? Are you listening?" Anne was still going and I perked up just in time for her grand finale. "That's why I'm here. I was worried about you. I missed you. I thought maybe she'd help me back into your life."

"I wouldn't count on it, honey." We turned and there she was, baseball shirt tied up behind her back to show off a stomach flatter than any acre in the Land of Lincoln, resting a raised elbow against the doorjamb, sky eyes glistening. Agent Ignatz Xidas: The girl next door. Anne let go of my hands and shimmied to her feet.

"Who in God's name is this?" She asked me. I made no answer, still open mouthed in shock for reasons I could no longer keep track of. A man of principle, facing down the inevitable 40th birthday, worried sick over his Mother's shame, a twenty-three year old girl trying to win back his heart, and a Federal Agent winking a supernatural sky eye his way. Somewhere a fat cat purred.

"What? He didn't tell you?" Iggy sashayed to my side with a full allotment of va-va-voom. She yanked me up effortlessly by my armpit and slid her hand around my torso and into the back pocket of my jeans. I liked that, especially because I knew Anne couldn't even see it, and that Iggy knew it too but did it anyway. Pressing against me she popped onto her toes and, smiling, nibbled my ear. Anne released a 'this ain't a cold symptom' cough. "Oh, sorry." The Federal Agent smiled, "I'm the girlfriend."

I'm a man of principal. In my former line of work I had seen people at their most vulnerable, lives flashing before their eyes, desperation emanating from every inch of their person. None had ever looked half as defeated as Anne in that moment. Who can blame her? She stood there, the piggish sidekick catcher who just discovered the long-legged face of the franchise star pitcher had secretly been screwing the new team manager she'd just professed her love to. To make matters worse, Big Carl—as usual, utterly unaware of the context of the moment—had perked up in the excitement and, despite the confining qualities of denim, began to make his presence known as little Carl stood gaping like a post-op lobotomy recipient.

"G-girlfriend?" Anne stuttered.

Iggy beamed up at me. "Engaged to be engaged, as they say." The force of her words drove Anne backwards a half step and caused her to bring a hand over her gasping mouth. She shot me a 'say it ain't so' look that would have broke my heart if my heart weren't half way up my throat trying to ask my brain for instructions on what to feel.

I didn't want to wait around. Not for Anne to explode, not for Mother to return, and certainly not for the two thousand pound, double rigged C4 bombtiger Iggy had let loose in the room to go off.

"Listen, hon," speaking to her this way without the threat of potential pistol whippings gave me a chill. "I think we should probably take off." I raised my eyebrows. "If we're going to get to your folks place tonight we should really get going then, don't you think?"

"But baby," she said through smiling teeth, "I thought there was someone who might be here that you'd like me to meet." She pinched my arm. "Remember? An *old friend.*"

"No." I squeezed her tight enough to force the air out of her lungs with a wheeze that almost made her break character and cuff me. A man of principle doesn't subject the piggy ex-girlfriend to schmaltzy pet names any longer than he has to. "Mother can wait. And besides, Mr. Mondo has already left for a new destination." And with that, she had heard all she needed, dropping the act entirely, turning on her heel and marching out towards the sedan. To my great surprise, I didn't focus on her ass as she stormed away, but instead on the number six and the discoloration from where an ironed on

126

nameplate on the back of her baseball shirt had fallen off. I looked at Anne's stunned silence. "Sorry about that," I stammered, wondering if emotional murder would count towards the Solutionist's prophesied trinity of death. Rolo strutted between us to break the tension. "Uh..." I nodded to the fat cat, "you keep it." And much like my faux beau, I turned and fled the scene.

Agent Xidas sat behind the wheel, upright, shades on, looking straight ahead as I jumped into the passenger seat. "Where is he?"

The car rolled out of the driveway and I watched the house drift backwards with my forehead pressed to the window. *She knows.* I could see her at the church, sitting in the front pew with her eyes glued to the floor, clouded by a steady weeping. In my mind, she trembled with the same expression she wore on the first Sunday I refused to go with her to morning mass. Heartbroken, she still didn't argue. Everything she did in life, she did for me. And this is how I repaid her. The world's most benevolent saint left to her own devices to raise a son and manages not only to bear the onus, but executes her role flawlessly. Only to find out in the end that she's mothered the embodiment of sin.

She knows.

"She knows." I said to the window.

"Carl, where is Ed Mondo?"

"I never thought she'd find out."

"Carl," she flailed a hand into my arm. "Snap out of it. Where did that woman say Ed went to?"

"Huh?"

"Where. Is. Ed. Mondo." My hometown. Mom lived about twenty minutes from Monmouth, an hour or two (depending on whether Iggy or I pressed the gas) from the Illinois/Iowa/Missouri border. Three times the population of Chilton, but all of them could have lived in a city block in downtown Chicago. Having Iggy drive me aimlessly through the residential streets gave me the same sensation as rereading a favorite book (think *Siddhartha,* not *Victoria's Secret April Preview*). Certain details came to light that I'd never noticed, but mainly the most memorable parts retained top billing. We passed the gas station where I'd once tried to buy cigarettes as a minor with a fake ID from a clerk who had twice babysat for me (including the Sootsky date night, in which I was guilty of multiple lampocide). He didn't sell me the pack of cigs. Next, we passed the baseball diamond where I'd famously failed my teammates on countless summer days. I thought of Mark Hilson. Poor guy.

"Hey! I can't just drive in circles all day, tell me where we're heading." The affectionate inflection of my kitchen fiancé transformed back to the hard-nosed bark of my police escort.

"He went farming.'"

Her eyebrows peeked over the Aviators and she took three quick breaths. "You'll have to do better than that?"

"I can't."

"Well, then. Maybe I'll just drop you off at the church for a reunion?"

"Jesus. Don't do that. I've had enough misery for one day. Why'd you bring me here in the first place?" I shot a glare her way and held my eyes on the side of her face, realizing the validity of the question, as up until that point I'd taken for granted that somehow she'd been correct in catching up to Eddie's whereabouts.

"It wasn't my idea. It was the Solutionist. I asked where to find Eddie Mondo and he said to take *you* where you'd least like to be. Figured this would be a good place to start."

I let loose a blue whale exhale. "You can see why."

"He also said to remind you what you asked him for. And to trust him."

"Trust him?" I scoffed. "Shit. Who else am I supposed to trust?"

She didn't answer. Or maybe she did by not saying a word.

The sun dove towards the cornhusk horizon as we rolled onto southbound Route 67, no destination in mind but still rushing to get somewhere, anywhere. Out of dodge. Fields full of ears on either side of us and not a single decibel from our quiet commute. Until I broke the silence.

"So what, The Bureau plays The Company in company softball?"

She smiled, but didn't say anything. I shrugged and looked back toward the crops. As we drove by each farm, I watched the array of stalks glide by. If I looked straight through, I could see all the way to the dusky light beyond the field for the briefest of instants until the next row of stalks took its place, like watching the earth rotate through a flipbook.

"It's from high school," she said after I'd long forgotten what I'd started her on.

"What is?"

"I played fast-pitch. Was pretty good. Almost threw a no hitter one time in the playoffs. Played a little in college out east."

"Wicked," Not exactly an accent of principle but it was close enough. "So if school was out east, where's home?"

She stopped as suddenly as she'd began, cracked her neck by rolling it to both sides, then cleared her throat and focused on the road.

"Pitcher, huh? That explains the uppercut," I smiled. She didn't.

We took on a western heading at Route 34, silently succumbing to the gravitational lure of the American frontier that pulled patriots across the Great Plains for generations. Now and then I'd offer to drive but Iggy wouldn't falter from her seat, or her posture, so I slouched for the both of us. I spent the ride in and out of consciousness, semi-awake and fully disoriented. With heavy breaths I counted off my kill list in my head, Mark after Mark after Mark. Everything reminded me of death. I saw Mother when I closed my eyes.

The ancient Egyptians prayed to a deity with a woman's body and the head of a frog. Heqet was a goddess who brought fertility to otherwise arid fields. Inundation of the Nile dispersed an otherwise stagnant frog population well beyond the borders of the river, and with the flood of frogs came fecundity in the fields. Growing up, I imagined Heqet and my mother as one and the same. Wherever she went a flood of happiness followed. What was Heqet doing now?

Praying for her son's soul. She'd been responsible for the lives of thousands of frogs. Could she save mine?

I watched the road and thought of Officer Taupe Suit. Smelled the fresh starch on his collar, heard his body crumpling to the asphalt like an unmanned marionette, saw his limp shoe bouncing at the end of his breathless bulk as I dragged him off the road. Why did he have to be patrolling that stretch of highway? Why couldn't I have kept my mouth shut in the car? I just *had* to provoke her...

Iggy. Agent Ignatz Xidas. Looking at her, I only saw two more blank slots on my deadly dance card. *Trust the Solutionist.* He may as well have told me to dig my way out of a hole. An even twenty. For what? More guilt? More pain? Eighteen felt pretty damn even as it was. *Trust the Solutionist.* Where was he now? On my lawn. Next to my beloved soup can. What sort of principle could I ever hold to justify murder on behalf of a small town clairvoyant? A secular yogi trapped in a picnic basket of a hut? None. No principle for the man of principle without principles.

Iggy pulled off the road without my noticing and rolled up to a fast food drive through window. We were somewhere near Iowa, but I'd spent so much time lost in my own head I couldn't be bothered to keep from getting lost outside it, too. She ordered a handful of hamburgers and a chicken sandwich combo meal, no tomato. The speaker could have been broadcasting from a bunker in 1944 Stalingrad with a lethal case of laryngitis and the amount of static and interference wouldn't have been any scratchier. "Anything else, Ma'am?" The cracking teenaged voice didn't help the communicative effort.

"Yeah, my son here has had a rough day. Let me have an ice cream cone." I didn't care for her tone, and would have preferred a cocktail, but beyond the mocking sarcasm Agent Xidas had at least acknowledged that she'd put me through an emotional wringer. Besides, a man of principle can appreciate soft serve as much as hard liquor. She pulled up to the next window, traded a handful of cash for a stomach-full of empty calories and parked in the lot so we could eat.

Fast food always fascinated me. In the long run, we all know it will kill us. In the short term, it makes our bodies sluggish and miserable while constraining our ability to travel outside fifty feet of the nearest toilet. At rock bottom prices we'll happily allow the grade of beef to slip from A down to C, even D in certain specialty franchises. But that wasn't enough. Still, rumors circulate about the descent of beef grades that kindergarteners can't comprehend without further study of our standard English alphabet, and certain specialty franchises consult with linguistics professors on ancient Cyrillic characters to accurately designate just how bad things have gotten. These poison hawkers, they should be in jail. Somehow, they've convinced us that we're valued customers while simultaneously labeling each individual as one of the "Billions Served." We, the human cattle, line up at the counter in tighter proximity than any living creature besides the cows and chickens we're lining up to consume. And yet, damn did those grease-ball burgers smell good.

Agent Xidas adjusted her seat back several inches to give herself room to operate, both in the sense of moving her arms as well as performing surgery on her chicken sandwich, much in need of a tomato-ectomy despite her modest request.

"Not a tomato fan, huh?" The small talk got smaller as it tried to force its way through my crunching molars.

"You really didn't know Ed Mondo was onto you? All this time?" She snapped at me, sky eyes exploding with reflected light from the illuminated drive through menu. I shook my head, feeling childish for having spoken with a mouthful of meat, and swallowed a too-large hunk to clear some space.

"Not a clue." Whatever I had learned, or thought I'd learned from the file I found in Ed's bedroom, I decided would be best kept to myself. "He never let on in the slightest."

"Hmm," she leaned her head back, her slender neck exposed, smooth, elegant, and glowing in the half-light of the parking lot. Crumpling the tissue paper from burger number one, I started into the ice cream before it melted. Chocolate and vanilla swirled beside one another in a safety cone. Like God and Satan trapped at sea in a big yellow raft, dripping sweat under the relentless heat of the

Pacific sun. "Frogg," she said, taking a long breath. She hadn't taken a bite of her sandwich. "Can I ask you something?"

"Shprout." I mumbled over a mouthful of safety cone. "Sorry," I swallowed. "Shoot."

"Why'd you do it?"

I'm a man of principle. When a man of principle sees a set of eyes like Iggy's looking for an honest answer, he doesn't bother to bullshit.

"Honestly, I was addicted to the rush."

"Then why'd you stop?"

As a man of principle, what choice did I have but to tell her?

Small Frogg in a Big Pond
Tuesday, November 18th, 1986

  The sixteenth kill should have been easy. I flew to New York, keeping my sunglasses on the entire flight, checked into a hotel under the pseudonym Mark Markson, took the elevator up to my room and slipped the file out of the crisp, unmarked Agency envelope for the Nth review of latest target. Mark XVI: Late forties by the picture, a home address, work address, and the going retail price for his head on a stake listed somewhere in the middle of the six digit range. Studio apartments and club sandwiches weren't the only things that cost more in New York City.

  I slept on my back. Rather, I lay on my back like Chicken Little, staring at the ceiling as the electricity of Manhattan's highrises twinkled in the periphery as though the sky had fallen. The Sandman must have had trouble catching a cab. I opened the mini fridge and gulped a mini water bottle, executed fifty elbow-to-knee abdominal crunches, one hundred diamond pushups, and hopped in the shower. I took hot showers back then. As hot as I could get them. Steam seeped out from beneath the door, and inside the hotel bathroom the excess towels sweated in the impromptu sauna conditions.

  Sometimes, the night before a kill, I'd stand in front of the mirror with the shower running at a scalding temperature, engaging myself in an endless staring contest. When the mirror fogged around the edges, I'd settle in and control my breathing. With each minute the air grew denser and the steam closed in towards the center, inching towards my reflection, blocking out the rest of the world. Eventually, the cloud cover overtook me, and then I'd step behind the curtain and let the water pound into my chest as I meditated on the power of mind over matter. By the time I toweled off, my body would glow, red with sensitivity, the harsh fabric of the linens stinging my skin. If I was lucky, I could sleep after that.

  The morning of the kill, I rolled out of bed and dressed in black jeans and a white undershirt. No, that's not the way to say it; makes me seem much too human. The morning of the kill I rose at

5:30 a.m. without need of an alarm clock. I didn't dress, as dressing implies some level of subjective decision making and style. I outfitted myself in an unofficial uniform, unfurled my toiletries bag and squeezed (from the back of the tube) three quarters of an inch of styling gel onto my left index finger to slick back my hair. I slid into my camel-colored fall jacket (custom fit, but otherwise modest and forgettable) and went to the lobby to purchase a decaffeinated tea and a selection of fresh fruit, which I ate on a bench across from Mark's office building in the Financial District. In the ensuing twelve hours, I left my bench twice to use the bathroom and once to purchase a granola bar. Otherwise, I passed the time honing the skills of my mind against the illusions of reality (which was actually something I did back then). This involved keeping an eye trained on the door for Mark's coming and going while shutting down all other sensory perception. Blocking out the grumbling buses and honking taxis, ignoring the heavy scents of roasted peanut and hotdog vendors, and feeling as little of the surrounding world as possible. Now and then, to take a break I'd try my hand at cloud bursting, with little to show for it.

This also involved severing the emotional connectivity between Anne and myself. She had written me about her plans to drop out of community college and return to Chilton. Her parents had passed and left her the house as well as a little money to live on. I didn't respond. A rock feels no pain. An island never cries. A Frogg doesn't console. A killer can't afford to grieve.

With my feet flat on the ground, heels directly beneath my knees, I kept my spine erect and my hands resting upwards in my lap without interlocking the fingers. I had read interlocking the fingers while meditating lead to aggression and violence in one's inner self, and seeing as I already had my share of sleepless nights with my fingers serenely uncrossed, I always paid special attention to that particular aspect of meditative practice.

In my intentionally inattentive state, a young girl approached and sat beside me, pondering the mystery of the meditative mister, the absent-minded amateur ascetic. "Are you ok?" She asked. Focused on not hearing her, I didn't hear her. It's not that I wasn't a man of principle, only that at the time the ever changing river of my

134

principles had been flowing upstream, clouding my mind with ideals of physical and mental perfection, achieving an emptiness of what I'd convinced myself were the material world's many illusions, in search of spiritual oneness with some greater force I hadn't yet decided on, or maybe hadn't quite committed to believing in.

Not feeling meant not feeling bad.

"Mister!" The girl tugged at my jacket sleeve, perhaps unsure if I were asleep, alive, or a wax statue placed by some bohemian guerilla artist. By this time, the lunch hour had long since passed and the time for Mark to leave the office neared. The tug at my arm broke my mindless spell and brought me back to the whirlwind of stimuli unique to Manhattan. Waves of pinstripes and briefcases, an undercurrent of streaking yellow from the passing taxicabs and the stark shift between the masses unable and unwilling to notice a man on a bench and the unsolicited concern and acknowledgement of a child checking on a stranger's wellbeing.

I shot her a sideways look, hardly turning to face her. She had on a pink backpack featuring a series of female farm animals standing with their arms, hooves, paws and talons around one another. A clique of anti-amphibian exclusionists smiled away the day without any female frog friends to muck things up with their webbed feet. The girl's hair hung in deep red, verging on chestnut brown pigtails, with one braid falling in front of her shoulder and the other behind. She smiled with her mouth closed as I turned, and when she spoke again, I noticed she had lost her left incisor and the right, if it subscribed to a realist school of thought, would have finished writing its last will and testament by then, as it dangled so tenuously the wind from a passing horse and buggy could have snapped its remaining roots clean through.

"What's wrong?" She asked, but before I could say anything a young woman trotted over and took her by the arm.

"Sweetpea! There you are." The woman said, somewhat concerned but not at all surprised the girl had run off. She kneeled to meet the girl's eyeline and scolded the child. Turning to me, she added, "Sorry, she just loves talking to people. Her mom would fire me if she knew how often I let her scamper off." I watched them go but the girl didn't turn around. They disappeared around the corner.

Mark left the office through the revolving glass doors and made his way on foot in the opposite direction of his apartment. A bachelor according to his file, he lived close to Wall Street. One of those 'Married To My Job' types. I could relate. Outside of the little girl on the bench, I hadn't spoken to someone in a non-professional capacity since arriving in the city. I got my first good look at the guy and didn't like him from the start. As a man of principle I never trusted people in the Northeast with yearlong tans. Short, but not short enough to qualify for a Napoleon complex, he took quick steps. Always in a hurry. I remember thinking he wore such a wide tie knot to trick people into thinking his head and neck extended a little higher than they did. The strategy didn't work on me. I sensed he maintained his look with frequent (and expensive) haircuts, and due to his close-set weasel eyes I had no trouble classifying him as evil and eliminating any emotional attachment to his imminent demise at my hands.

I followed him at twenty paces through the rush hour pedestrian traffic, disguised by the mob even though my brown jacket stood out in the sea of navy blue and black suits like a log floating in a pond. To help fit in, I carried my briefcase. I wasn't taking my work home to stay a leg ahead of my colleagues and not wind up fired. I was taking my firearm to Mark's home to stay on my rigid schedule so my bosses (if the Agency even had bosses) wouldn't send a colleague (if I even had colleagues) with an envelope with my picture in it and I wind up cremated. With my principles aligned as they were at the time, I viewed stress as a material worry, an illusion. So I tried to ignore the threat of death and the pressures of work. Tried.

Mark ducked into a garden level door, noteworthy only for its need of a new paint job. An elderly black man sat on a stool just inside the door and patted Mark on the shoulder with a smile before the darkness swallowed them back behind the door. Curiosity served as an Achilles heel for me in my professional life. Nearly cost me a kill with Professor Mark. Still, even in the prime of my career, I couldn't shake the urge to expose myself now and then to find out just a little more about the lives of those unfortunate souls who didn't yet know they'd eaten breakfast for the last time. I let fifteen minutes pass and opened the door to a murky, poorly lit bar filled with poor, lit customers. Cigarette smoke wafted up and crashed in silent explosions against the dim ceiling. Though crowded, the customers hardly made a noise. They left that to the band.

Jazz: the antithesis of my musical upbringing. Listening to the standing bass and scaled down drum set unraveled every lesson I'd learned sitting at my mother's side on the piano bench. Mr. Sootsky never told me that the ordered, structured, predetermined foundation of scales could lead to such chaos and improvisation. I didn't look for Mark. I didn't look at anything. I only sat at a small round table in the back corner, alone in the dark, blocking all stimuli besides the music and occasionally practicing cloud bursting with the wisps of cigarette cirrus, nimbuses infused with nicotine, and clouds of tobacco tinged cumulus hanging all about me.

Time melted into the illusory realm, which means I had ignored it. When the band called it a night, I came out of my trance and discovered the room still well populated, but without any sign of Mark. I stood and peered through the smoke over the heads of the jazz cats (not nearly as intimidating as bombtigers) and asked the man behind the bar if he knew him. He tilted his head back and looked down his nose at me, as though scanning me with a laser implanted in the base of his chin. He asked why I wanted to know, and I made up a story about how I thought I saw him drop his wallet in the corner. The bartender took a few steps towards where I'd indicated the incident and I got the hell out of there. Seedy bars have proven to be less than ideal places to ask questions. My plan for Mark's murder went awry. The sheet music shredded, the scales tossed aside, I regressed to my old self. Returning to an old principle I decided to improvise. I walked to Mark's building without a plan, whistling what I remembered of the bassist's solo.

On my way to Mark's, I caught a glimpse of myself in the tinted window of a minivan. Tall, sleek, and strong in a less exaggerated style of a comic book superhero whose waist measured about a third of his chest, my torso the shape of a funnel. Staring at the window, I thought about the scrawny sniper on the youth center rooftop. How much he'd grown up since then. The Agency's trust in me developed from small town contracts to big city moneymakers. I once received an envelope with the photo of a prominent government official and the special instruction of "Standby for approval. Make necessary preparations for deadline." I'd have done it, too, had they ever sent approval. Some Senator with a stance on childhood obesity that didn't end up dead (at least not by way of Frogg). I became a rising star within the organization. That is, if the Agency had rising stars, or any sort of organization to begin with.

The Agency profile on Mark included his apartment number, thankfully, as the high-rise loomed over thirty stories. I loitered outside, swinging my briefcase back and forth, leaning against the wall of the neighboring building and tapping my fingers on my leg to the irregular beat of my internal jazz combo. Typically, I made my big city jobs last no longer than they had to, never caring for the bustle of urban life. This time felt different. I had decided after Money Mark's killer slice and my multiple mile traipse down the abandoned tracks that the time had come to grow up. More by the book and less by the seat of my pants. Being a man of principle, I stuck to the new regime. I dressed the part. I was careful. I was cool, calculated, controlled, and concise. A few kills later, I started meditating. I'd lose myself for hours, entire days sometimes, inside the quiet recesses of my mind. But still I couldn't sleep, couldn't rid myself of whatever curse kept me from feeling at peace. My inner Om never shed its resemblance to the distant train of my subconscious.

While my personal life developed in more free spirited directions, my professionalism had other plans. The Agency's envelopes may have been light on information, but that didn't mean I had to be. Sure, I was the type of idiot who'd scratch his chin with a loaded pistol, but I was also a man of principle, and I was no dummy. My performance reviews, if the Agency even had performance reviews, would've shown top marks with the amount of research I did on my Marks. I knew Wall St. Mark's business history better than he did, and certainly better than the SEC. A few years earlier, Mark saw an opportunity to diversify his portfolio by investing heavily in the initial public offering of a national restaurant chain that specialized in pescatarian fare. Gone Fishin', a not quite fast food not quite sit down establishment with locations across America featured fish sandwiches, fried cod filets, fish'n'chips, and other under the sea delicacies. I'm guessing Mark caught a news program detailing early cases of Mad Cow Disease in England and jumped to a few conclusions regarding Americans' panic responses and willingness to give up on McDonald's. Not the most prudent decision, but I admired the guy's ability to stick to his guns. Too bad I was in New York to kill him with mine.

Another household name in the national restaurant scene had made headlines at the time for reasons that brought about the tried and true cliché, "Any publicity is good publicity." Once known as Burger Corner, a standardized, reliable chain of franchised storefronts that always occupied primo real estate on a street corner, the family friendly sellers of hamburgers and shakes had seen better days. Their CEO's son was found dead on the campus quad at the university where he taught philosophy and later the company changed directions and abandoned their McMockery of a copycat McDonald's product line and developed into a seafood purveyor. In doing so, their national contract with a certain Virginia beef provider got shredded. And there I sat, wondering what exactly Wall St. Mark had planned to protect his investment against the new competition. It had to be something. Otherwise, he wouldn't be a Mark.

Yet another chapter in the unwritten secret history of murder that drives the fast food industry of America, as performed by Carl Frogg.

The sun yawned its way below the skyline and I took a seat at a bus stop on a hard wooden bench that advertised one of those lawyers who already knows he'll win your case and won't bother charging you until he does. I closed my eyes and took two deep breaths, sitting up like a flagpole with my briefcase between my feet. *No,* I thought, the jazz combo striking up again. *Not this time.* I opened my eyes, slouched with my elbows atop the backrest, and decided to take it in. Half an hour passed in total absorption. The autumn sky melting from orange to navy, the soft crackle of a leaf pile blown into the air by a bus landing en masse on the sidewalk, the air cooling my fingers. I stretched my arms above me, pointed my toes out into the street, and inhaled to full lung capacity, holding the oxygen as long as I could.

A Chinese kid glided by me on a bicycle, long straight hair whipping beneath his helmet, carrying three oversized brown paper bags. He locked his bike to a 'No Parking' sign in front of Mark's building, deftly shifted the bags around in the air to see the stapled-on receipts, and flipped one to his opposite hand before speed walking towards the entrance. *Time to improvise.*

"Hey, kid," I said, indicating he come my way with a nod. He stalled, his body caught in a game of freeze tag, still facing the door as to limit the precious seconds lost as the food cooled down. He moved his head but didn't take the bait. "You got a delivery for this building? I'll give you $200 for it." He turned, looked left and right to make sure the cops weren't planning some sort of Szechuan sting, and tiptoed a few half steps my way. "$200," I held out the bills, "No questions asked."

He started to hold the bag out and then pulled back. "Two fifty," he smiled. "Unless you aren't really that hungry?"

"You're a smart kid," I said, reaching back for my wallet and handing him the surcharge. "Go buy yourself a haircut."
I took the bag with me around the nearest alley entrance and deposited my Fabrique Nationale (which I shipped to myself at the hotel) into the fragrant void of beef and broccoli, hot and sour soup, and newly wanton wontons. I flung the briefcase into the dumpster, took a deep breath to compose myself, covered my giddiness with an irritated scowl and walked into the lobby.

"Got one here for..." I hefted the brown sack onto the doorman's countertop and inspected the delivery receipt. The bag began to darken, blushing with the deep tones of leaking grease. "Littman? 5B?"

"Sign in..." The doorman didn't indicate the register, but eyed me from atop the perch of his high stool like a juvenile court judge about to question a teen vandal. "You aren't the usual kid." He floated in the indeterminate waters of middle-aged bachelorhood. Anywhere from forty to sixty, had always lived in the city, knew at least three guys named Mahoney and probably participated in a dart league at a bowling alley with one of them. Eyes wide set like a halibut. Stubbled salt and pepper chin. He refused to wear his uniform cap but had worked in the building long enough that nobody said anything. A man of principle, perhaps, but seeing as the family-sized bag of Funyuns hadn't left his hand since I entered, I assumed one of those potential principles involved never hoisting his ass off its perch.

"Where is he?"

"Went home sick, the little prick." This guy wouldn't know a bombtiger if he pulled one out of his Funyuns. My leg shook behind the counter, the familiar lilt of the imminent rush. "Which means the Assistant General Manager," I pointed to my face without lifting it from the sign in sheet (where I pedantically scribbled "Ernest Bunbury"), "has to handle the fucking deliveries."

He leaned back as though my anger may cause me to spit fire, or perhaps some other, equally hot Chinese herbal condiment. Whether it was the year of the dragon or not, I can't say, but I'd done enough to convince him to buzz me up and lose interest in me. I pressed the elevator button for the 33rd floor. *Sorry, Mr. Littman 5B. You'll have to cook tonight.*

The elevator door reflected a cubist rendering of myself, splintered and cracked, the colors smeared and wavy like the face of a weeping, overly made-up call girl. I bit my lip to stop from beaming with an overtly murderous smirk, making sure to keep my head turned just far enough to the left to stay out of the security camera's sight. My recent foray into professionalism faded with each story of the elevator's ascent. *13...14...15...*I let my shoulders slouch, lifted the bag to my nose to inhale the aromas of the Far East...*22...23...24...*I pictured Mark's apartment, a metallic, modern, not so modest box in the sky. He probably had a private tanning bed. He probably had a projection screen and a camcorder. He probably clapped to turn his lights on and off. *31...32...33...DING.*

I stood facing Mark's door and craned my neck to both sides. Bending my knees, I set the bag down and dipped a hand in to locate my silenced tool of the trade. The Fabrique fluttered out from the forest of plastic containers like a butterfly released from its cocoon, like grasping a wisp of smoke, a handful of oxygen concentrated with airborne poison. My palm cooled at its touch, not a bead of sweat, not a glimmer of hesitation. Only the deep gratification of the rush. I walked two inches above the ground, riding the high of my adrenaline, breathing without breathing, acting without thought, but with the confidence of a crusader who trusted in God to protect him. With my finger pressed against the peephole in the style of a dorm building RA, I knocked twice and mumbled "House of Jade." A chair squeaked across a hardwood floor beyond the door, followed by the soft echo of Mark's final footsteps.

"Finally!" His voice less harsh, less evil than I'd imagined, with a distinct warmth to it. "We. Are. Starving!" *We? The file didn't mention a We. Too late.* The doorknob turned to the side as the Fabrique turned up towards his chest from beside my hip. He swung the door back and I shot, but not before what seemed a thousand tanning sessions passed between us. His eyes first landed on the bag at my feet as mine fixed on his pink slippers and blue striped pajama pants. My jaw dropped and his followed suit after his gaze locked onto the thick chrome cylinder covering the business end of my firearm. The bullet penetrated his chest just as our eyes met, equally shocked expressions mirroring each other for reasons that couldn't have been more different or more the same. He stumbled backwards and fell to the ground, eyes open and unmoving. Sliding the bag through the door I shut it behind me and stepped quietly over Mark's carcass.

She appeared halfway down the hall from another room and collapsed to her knees, keening unintelligible strings of vowels with the occasional N tossed in for flavor. Looking up from the corpse she met my gaze, and that of the one-eyed Belgian I aimed at her forehead. She cried with passion, a human elegance that meant she was a wife, not a girlfriend. The Agency botched the file and I'd have

142

to clean up the pieces, and seeing as she was seeing me, I couldn't leave a witness behind. She wept with a girlish quality, too. I could tell that when it came to Boys and Girls, she had always been deeply entrenched in girlhood. The type who, at thirteen, read *Seventeen* magazine, and at thirty still acted on the relationship advice of yesteryear's high school gurus. Actively waiting two extra rings to answer when a new boyfriend called. Wearing a headband when her stylist took a little too much off. Always leaving him wanting more. I wondered if *Seventeen* ran obituaries.

I fired again, catching her in the neck and silencing the unexpected mourning session. Two bodies meant I needed to get out of the building twice as fast and four times as undetected. I turned back to the door but stopped when I heard someone else coming from the end of the hall. I twisted and ducked as I turned to take aim, firing without looking. *Click.* Empty chamber. *Thank the lord.*

It was her. Still with one braid in front and the other behind. Mark's daughter. She stood, shaking in place with her arms crossed and her knees slightly bent and pressed together like an underdressed fan shivering on the sidelines of a December football game. She tried to speak but the words got snagged somewhere between her diaphragm and her lips, only the tattered remains pushing through in hardly audible gasps of carbon dioxide. The heft of the gun returned, forcing my hand to fall to the ground as though gravity had arrived late to the party, already a few drinks deep. I stared at the ground, my head pounding, my principles eroding around me and drowning in the puddle of sweat that leaked from my temples and dripped down from the tip of my nose. Raising my head, I found her expectant eyes boring into me over the threshold of her parents' bodies. Shining spheres in the darkness of the hall. I said nothing. I couldn't say anything. *I'm sorry, Sweetpea.* I tried to say it but couldn't.

I crashed down 33 flights of stairs, banged through a garage exit, and promised myself never to work for the Agency again.

The next morning I left for Chilton and a clean slate with my Pen Pal.

Bang! Pow! Resco to the Rescue
Tuesday, May 9th, 1989

To be honest, Agent Xidas was a terrible kisser. She opened her mouth as wide as possible and lazily swirled her tongue with all the imagination and inventiveness of a ceiling fan on its lowest setting. Not to mention a total lack of regard for tooth on tooth clattering. Believe me, there's a difference between reaching first base and reaching the first molar. Still, it *happened.* As Iggy drove us from the burger shack to a pay-per-night campground and RV site, I told her my sad tale of death, shame, and early retirement. When I finished, she took my cheek in her hand and planted her thin, forbidden lips onto mine. As much as she liked the story, I promise you, as a man of principle, that Big Carl liked her reaction twice as much, offering a standing ovation in his own right.

Parked in our private campsite, a small wooded area somewhere in the middle of the United States, we united the middle of our states. Iggy sailed over the center console and straddled me in the passenger seat, a colonizing force with a perverted manifest destiny on her side that gave her control of my lips and everything west of them on my body until she met the Pacific. At first I kept my hands up in surrender, unsure what to make of the conflicting behavior of the sky eyed woman with a history of inflicting pain now bringing a heavy dose of pleasure to the table. She pressed her face firmly against mine in a nose-melding meeting of mouth meat, hair cascading over my eyes and elbows interlocking behind my neck. Somewhere in the rush of blood and frenzy of limbs, my right hand reached for the seat back adjuster and, yanking the handle, sent our bodies tumbling into a nearly horizontal, dentist's chair type recline. A maniac's grin spread over her face as she pillaged deeper into my peaceful native land. She placed her palms on my chest and dug her fingertips into my collarbone like a tigress preparing to go in for the deadly jungle hickey. "He was right," she whispered between quick, heavy inhalations, "He's always right."

Still mentally a few moments behind the pace of reality, I stared dumbly up at her, though my fingers, living very much in the

144

moment, had taken a firm hold on her hips. That body. Muscled in the places it served to be muscled and soft where softness better fit the bill.

"The Solutionist told me we'd come together after a few days, if we could last that long without killing each other." *What didn't the Solutionist say to her?* I thought briefly, for she leaned down and started working my neck with all the sensuality of an English bulldog slobbering at the bottom its food dish. I laughed at her, but luckily she interpreted it as a reaction of disbelieving gratitude. Rising up to meet me face to face, she asked, "You're a sweet guy, really? Aren't you?"

If there's a man in the world who'd have been dumb enough to say "no" it might have been me, but I was so too metaphorically tongue tied to talk my way out of the ensuing literal tongue tying. I cupped her head in both hands and planted a kiss of principle.

Iggy accepted my answer, leaning back and pulling her baseball shirt over her head, the neckline getting caught around her chin like a four year old trying to get out of their complicated church clothes, thus trapping her face inside an inverted cotton screen. I'd have thought a woman so physically attractive would have behaved in a less amateurish manner and displayed a more impressive, or even intimidating, command of her own sexual competency. This felt more like a college dorm room scenario. Cramped, chaotic, and capable, if not likely, of ending badly. Iggy tried to squirm free of her shirt, but I didn't pay much attention to the activities above her shoulders. Before she could wriggle her head free, I reached around her back with one hand, took the hooks of her bra in my supple, dexterous fingertips and carefully, expertly, ripped the undergarment to shreds in one clean pull. A man of principle, especially one as out of practice as I was back then, doesn't waste time or take chances when it comes to clothing removal in non-traditional sexual arenas.

Finally unencumbered from her upper body wardrobe, Agent Xidas raised her eyebrows and ran her tongue across her upper lip. I felt the zipper of my jeans slowly coming open. "Looks like you were right, too." She leaned forward so her breasts hung lightly above my panting mouth and whispered wetly into my ear. "The button fly would have been a disaster."

Fucking is too crude a term. Lovemaking, too passionate. Somewhere on the spectrum between the two, Iggy and I had tender, awkward sex in the sedan. Fucking and Lovemaking can happen anywhere, a king size or a car seat, so I don't consider location the deciding factor. If one were to take into account the fact that my pants never made it lower than my ankles, or inspect the imprints in our skin where seat belt holsters jabbed into our legs, one may then classify the haste as an indication of Fucking. However, if one factors in the sensual contact between our foreheads and the abundance of, and welcome attitudes towards heavy, passionate panting, one would draw more intimate conclusions that point towards Lovemaking. Semantics aside, for one wonderful moment she put aside her badge and her Aviators, I emptied my mind of the Solutionist's prophecy, and neither one of us felt alone.

Since pulling into my driveway less than forty-eight hours earlier, the sedan acted as a backdrop for our entire relationship. Whether I had the wheel outrunning bombtigers or Iggy secretly chauffeured my unconscious body into the eye of Hurricane Mom, the sedan saw us through all our highs and lows. And after that night, it saw us through our ups and downs, side to sides, back and forths, and ins and outs. We needed a break from the sedan as bad as it needed a break from us, so we cracked the windows to air it out and sat on pre-cut stumps of tree trunks on either side of the campsite fire pit. Using the twigs and pine needles left behind in a pile by the previous campers and the cigarette lighter from the sedan's dashboard, I managed to get a small fire going. I rooted my rear to a stump and sat across the flame. She didn't look at me one time in the silence. I can attest to the veracity of that statement because I didn't take my eyes off her, not even to blink, which proved a tear-inducing challenge with the smoke filing through my pupils and deep into the cavernous space that used to house my brain prior to what, for me, was an evening of mind melting meat mingling.

Iggy sat with one leg crossed tight above her opposite knee and her arms dangling limp at her sides. Safely back in her softball uniform, she looked like she had just given up the first single in her legendary playoff "almost no hitter." Through the quiet hum of the flame, I fixated on her eyes as they absorbed the orange of the fire and mixed it into a mélange of chartreuse emerald tinged light, the same fiery irises that first signaled to me that destiny, if in fact the Solutionist dealt in the medium of destiny, would tie me to this woman. "Doing ok over there?" Nothing. "Not too bad for an old man, huh?" My crisis of virility could have done with at least a smirk. But again, I got nothing. The Iggy I'd grown so attached to in the passenger seat drifted into a smoke blurred phantom, replaced by the zipped up windbreaker and Aviator shade inhumanity of Agent Xidas. "You know," I said, walking around the burning logs and moving a nearby stump beside her to sit down. "You never really answered any of my questions."

"Questions." She exhaled without looking up from the base of the fire.

"Yeah," I put my arm around her and she shook, a vibrating pressure-sensitive security alarm shooting through the dendrites and axons of her spinal column, an involuntary spasm of initial rejection followed by an uncharacteristic slackening of acceptance. "When you first showed up at my trailer. Remember? I asked about your name."

"And?"

"And," I squeezed her shoulder and pressed her against me. For someone so recently eager to lie atop me, she'd become intriguingly standoffish. "I still want to know."

"I changed it on my eighteenth birthday."

The firelight ebbed, the embers pulsating with a crimson blush. A breeze rattled the leaves and I rubbed her arm with my palm to keep her warm. And to keep her talking. With each minute she dipped further into her sedated state, and unfortunately I don't think her stupor came about as a result of my performance so much as the fact that the show had gone on in the first place. "I knew it. *Ignatz*. Impossible. Nobody in this day and age likes *Krazy Kat* enough to find a namesake in it. You planning to tell me what your parents wanted me to call you?"

I kept smiling, trying to lift her spirits. Her body nestled into mine like two pieces of a jigsaw puzzle that you find in the box pre-connected, unwilling to let go but unable to look at one another. Adjacent bricks in a wall, locked in place by the mortar of circumstance and Solutionism.

"Crazy as it sounds," she turned her head up to me for a moment, but broke away as our eyes met. "Part of me actually wants to say 'fuck it' and tell you."

She picked my hand from her shoulder and inspected it in the dwindling firelight, rolling it between her fingers. She held my index finger up in front of her face and curled it in along each of its joints. She kissed the inside of my fingertip, covered the outside of my hand in her palm and held it out towards the dying embers. She pushed the index finger one more time and whispered.

"Bang."

Who is this woman? I could still see the glow of the fire pit through the trees but had made it far enough into the woods that I couldn't make out Iggy's silhouette. A man of principle makes certain to remove himself a safe distance from a lady when shitting in a non-traditional bathroom arena. *I don't know her name.* I dropped my pants. *I* still *don't know what she wants from Eddie.* I scooted backward on an uprooted tree. *I don't know what she wants from me.* I mimicked Rodin's The Thinker and did my thinking (and my business). *Hell, I don't know what to use for toilet paper.* I looked up into the unmoving branches and nearly spoke to God, or at least nearly tried to speak to God, when the call of my family name croaked up at me.

"Ribbit," the bullfrog said. "Ribbit, Ribbit." He stared up at me with eyes like toy marbles, poised on the edge of a fallen branch. Growing up I obsessed over frogs. How could I not? I memorized folklore and proverbs by flashlight ("When the snake gets old, the frog gets him by the balls," or so the Iranians say). I completed annual science projects on amphibians and wetlands and spent countless

Halloweens explaining to neighbors that I wasn't supposed to be Frankenstein or The Hideous Sun Demon or whatever green monster Hollywood had released on America the past summer (Yoda was still a few years out, thank God, because I was a spitting image). This one, an American Bullfrog (*Rana Catesbeiana*) measured about 6 inches, right about average, but had impressive hind legs with beautifully symmetrical mahogany stripes. I tried to read his mind. As it turned out, he did sound an awful lot like Yoda.

"It's past midnight, a little late for you to be up, huh?"

"Ribbit. Ribbit Ribbit."

"Maybe you're right." I said.

"Ribbit?"

"Yeah, I have come this far."

"Rib-"

"No. That's not fair. Don't try to talk me out of it. I trust her."

"Ribbit."

"Exactly. It *is* my life."

My thinking complete, my business conducted, I picked up the branch with my miniature rannochio and started back to the campsite. I'd give the little mound of mucus to Eddie, if we ever found him, as a replacement for Rolo. I wasn't counting on Anne to bring the fat cat back anytime soon. "How do you like the name Barbaresco? Maybe Resco for short?"

"Ribbit."

"That settles it then."

Nearing the clearing I heard Agent Xidas speaking, not to me and not to herself. Peering through the remaining forestry I spied a second form. I couldn't hear either of them but the lack of movement gave the scene a Showdown at the OK Corral vibe. I moved closer, on tiptoe, still carrying Resco on the end of his stick, either oblivious to or unconcerned with the potential stranger danger. Crouching into a catcher's stance, I leaned from behind a trunk to listen in, catching pods of words from either of them and squinting at the new arrival.

"No. I know what I saw." Her voice rasped out like a fairy tale hag.

Iggy stood in the I-beam posture of Agent Xidas, her back to me and her words muffled by the surrounding trees.

"You tell me where he is or I'll cut you and bait him out with blood." The knife reflected the dying flame of the fire between the two women. The predator's body undulated in the thin stream of smoke, which billowed behind her towards the open windows of the sedan. She had long, greasy, dirty-blonde hair that should have just been blonde but needed a wash. Red-eyed. Strung out. White tank top covering the rail thin body of a teenage boy yet to fill out in the shoulders. Olive green Capri pants tattered at the cuffs. Track marks. Facial twitches. The embodiment of harmful unpredictability. Knife in hand. It didn't matter whether or not she knew how to use it.

"Pretty girls like you don't come around here. Fancy cars don't come around here. I want money. I want the keys. I like them shoes you're wearing too."

Well, Resco, I looked at my new friend, *I might need your help on this one.*

"Ribbit."

I stood up, careful not to snap a twig or crunch a leaf, and strafed through the trees with my back bent low and Resco's stick in my hand. I paused as I reached a nice access point in line with the fire pit between predator and prey. Iggy looked resolute, prepared if not confident to take the junkie on in hand-to-hand combat. As a man, I'd have loved to see a cat fight between these two bombtigers, but as a man of principle, I had no choice but to throw my frog into the fire, or so the saying goes.

Grip it and ribbit. I scooped Resco from the branch and offered him a firm nod in salute of his sacrifice, then sent him up up and away. He came down in the heart of the smoldering embers, creating a tiny flash in the fire pit and rustling the remains of charred twigs into a scale model of Hiroshima. He leapt out like Godzilla over Tokyo. The women looked down as Resco put his powerful hind legs to work, leaping from the fire onto the dirt, dancing wildly in search of water to cool his webbed feet. In the brief chaos that ensued, Agent Xidas exploded with energy. She never struck me as the bible reading type, so I figured the raining frog wouldn't fill her with thoughts of

Exodus but rather give her some confidence that I was nearby. She took the hint, leaping the fire and taking the woman's wrists in her hands, grappling to loose the knife from her grasp. The woman kicked the inside of Iggy's leg and brought her to a kneel, but still the Agent held to the pale, eerily vascular forearms. She dropped the knife but managed to raise her right knee into Iggy's face, sending the Fed sprawling to the ground. In all the noise and flutter of feminine ferocity I sidled towards center stage with Resco's branch clasped tight, the bark digging into my palms. The woman bent for her blade as Iggy, clutching at her eye with one hand, attempted to crawl towards the sedan. The woman came up panting, standing over the defeated Ignatz Xidas with wild-eyed determination. As far as she knew, within seconds she'd finish the job and drive off with the spoils of war. Unfortunately for her, she knew only as far as she could see, and the waning firelight didn't offer much of a view.

"Excuse me, miss," I said, causing her to wheel around in horror at the sight of me wielding a branch of principle over my head. "Have you seen my pet frog? I could swear he came this way a moment ago." I brought the wood down just above the eye.

Pow!

Her journey involved a 270-degree twirl and a 90-degree rotation that ended with her skull landing in the heart of the burning embers.

Agent Xidas, now leaning up against the front tire of the sedan, kept her hand over her eye as she struggled to catch her breath. I trudged over and sat beside her, both of us watching the back of the burning skull with blank expressions until the smell of singed flesh brought us back to life.

"Remember how the frog jumped out of the fire?" I asked as she lifelessly slouched against the sedan. "It's funny, if a frog sits in a pot of room temperature water on a stove and somebody comes by and turns on the flame, it won't jump out. It'll just sit there as it gets warmer and warmer until it boils and dies. But if a frog falls into a pot of already boiling water, it'll jump out right away." Agent Xidas didn't say anything. She wiped a tear from her eye on the back of her hand. "I guess the Honeymoon's over," I added.

"Thank you." She took my hand.

"Two down. One to go."

She leaned her head onto my shoulder, careful not to put pressure on her swollen eye.

"That's really what he told you? To kill for me?"

"To kill for you to find our missing man."

"And you believe him?"

"Iggy, I'd take out a hundred strung out forest freaks if you needed me to, and I wouldn't need a man in a box to prophesize it either." She gave my palm a squeeze. "What do you say we get out of here?" I sniffed and shivered, nodding to number nineteen. "Leave our new friend behind and look for my old one?"

I helped her up and opened the passenger door for her. "No, I'll drive." She rubbed her eye, blinked like a camera on shutter mode, and took the keys from her pocket. "You've done enough for today. You should rest. Lay down in the back." She grabbed my wrist and turned me to face her. Standing on her toes, she kissed me half on the lips and half on the cheek, slyly adding, "Big Carl must be tired."

Laying in the back seat on my side, facing the trunk in the fetal position, I closed my eyes. "Hey," I said without looking up. "What's the female equivalent of the name Mark?"

The engine grumbled out of its slumber as Iggy whispered, "Mark...Mark...Mark..."

I stand knee deep in a swamp, reeds and cattails rising up around me. My fingers hang at my sides in the warm murky waters. My feet lock into the mud at the base of the wetland, entrenched and unmovable. I lift a finger to my eye and, although the fluid coating my fingertips drips slow as honey and takes on the swirling lemon lime chromatic pattern of the sky, my instinct assures me it is blood that I'm wading in.

My attempts to move prove futile, even as I pull at my thighs with both hands. A frog croaks. Then another. Their voices rising up in a rumbling chorus from all sides. The resonating tones permeate my skin, reverberate through my limbs and cause me to take short breaths. I look down at my clothing, pants and shirt stained with the shimmering chrome blood of the swamp. The frogs' groans grow louder, louder than should be possible, but still the lyrical amphibians refuse to emerge from the reeds. Wiping at my shirt and jeans with wild swipes of my hands I fail to remove and instead disperse the blood further along my body.

Louder and louder and still nowhere to be seen.

Floating. I look down on the corporeal form struggling in the swamp. Like quicksand he sinks deeper into the sage-green streaks of metallic fluid, encased by it. He tastes it but I am free of him. The Solutionist's hut appears for a moment, glowing with pulsating amber hues. I feel my heartbeat synchronize with the rhythmic aura. I try to locate my body in the swamp but it has drifted too far behind me. *What have you done?* I try to speak but have no mouth, no tongue. *Why have you brought me here?* My disembodied form receives no answer, and I grow aware that the Solutionist's hut never glowed beside the swamp, only an illusion, and a mirage. A small shed takes its place.

The shed's windows blackened by wooden planks, hastily nailed in. In the back of my mind a muffled voice urges me to turn, but the shed pulls me closer. I coast on air, a ghost, lucid and unafraid. In the shed I see him. Eduardo Mondo.

He sits in a dust-drenched recliner with padding bursting through its seams. His leg extends atop a stack of crates, one shoeless foot resting there. A homemade brace of duct tape and padding from the recliner sets his ankle straight. It has swollen to the size of a grapefruit and taken on a similar color and consistency beneath its amateur cast. He wears only a sleeveless undershirt, stained with another man's blood, his own sweat, and splotches of briny juices. Above the shirt rests a double-breasted holster. Strapped on both sides with long barreled single-six magnum pistols. On his right side an enormous burlap sack of crawfish leans against the armrest. To his left a pile of discarded shells, twisted carcasses and sucked-out exoskeletons. He stares forward, a silent sentinel, chewing through the side of his mouth, prepared for a war of attrition. His eyes possess a strength his body long since bid farewell. A glare free of sleep, free

153

of the need for sleep. A transcendent inhumanity. A depth known only to those who have achieved peace or the appropriate lunacy required to believe they have achieved peace. The eyes of Bogdan Woland. The eyes of a man I'd never laid eyes on before.

I know where to find Ed Mondo.

Long Ride to a Little City
Wednesday, May 10th, 1989

I woke up without a fat cat sprawled on my chest, but in the now familiar circumstance of coasting at the speed limit, limbs contorted by the constraining dimensions of Agent Xidas's backseat. The adventure took its toll on me, but the only time I felt like I was "too old for this shit" came when waking up in that car. The cobalt blue of a predawn highway surrounded the sedan. I rolled over from stern to bow and smiled at the reliable posture and outfit of my Aviator shaded chauffeur. Clinging to the memory of my dream I bolted into an upright position and leaned forward between the two front seats.

"Iggy! I know where Ed is."

"Oh yeah?" She looked into the rearview, I think, hard to tell with those shades on.

"Well, sort of." I rubbed the back of my neck and wriggled my body to loosen my muscles. After a few hours of the sardine lifestyle an old man's body gets awful tight. "I had this dream..."

"Oh really?" She pursed her lips and nodded. "You were dreaming? Let me guess. About frogs?"

"Yeah!" I made an abrupt but imperceptible transition from rubbing my eyes to wake up to rubbing my eyes in disbelief. "How'd you know?"

"You were sleep croaking for hours." I saw my face redden in the rearview and gave a sheepish grin. *Hours? Really?* I hadn't slept so much in a decade. "So where do you think we're headed, Frogg?"

I opened my mouth to answer but realized I had no idea. I knew an ailing Ed Mondo waited in a shed somewhere, surrounded by a swamp of frogs. I knew it. The dream felt so real. A dream of principle. Undeniable in its earnestness, its lucidity. Not one moment of it had faded from my mind, I could relive the entire experience of the dream to Agent Xidas without missing the slightest detail. But I wouldn't. Not yet. "Farming, Ed said. It's got to have something to do with what he told Anne."

Agent Xidas released another of those uniquely feminine, earthquake-inducing sighs. Only this time it contained a hint of jealousy instead of repugnance. Or so I thought, having mentioned Anne's name. Impatience, it turned out, brought about the change in the air currents. She reached into the center console and produced a tri-fold pamphlet. "As helpful as your fantasy world has been, I think this may be a little more informative." I looked at the pamphlet, a tourist sightseeing promotional booklet with an enormous smiling cartoon bullfrog on the cover. "I saw it at the campsite offices when I was paying our way out of there."

Uncle Haywood's Fantastic Frog Farm! The cover read. Flipping to the inside pages, I saw an image of a swamp infested with gigantic bullfrogs, easily twice the standard size. *Marvel at the incredible beauty of God's happy hoppers.* The same swamp from the dream, no doubt about it. *Listen to the riveting ribbiting of these amazing amphibians!* This was it. We'd found Eddie Mondo. *Uncle Haywood's: A Missouri landmark unlike any other!* And we'd be there soon.

Fun for the whole family!

With hours to go until we'd reach the farm I climbed into the front seat, sidling in feet first, and settled in for another painstaking session of blinking at the lane dividers and staring through crop fields along Route 94. We moved on in our usual silence. I thought about my dream. About the viscous swamp blood and the image of Eddie Mondo using heavy pistols like antiperspirants, packing heat under both arms and trying to keep his busted shin elevated to reduce swelling. *Why crawfish?* I tried to remember what it was like, dreaming, back before my insomnia set in. It couldn't have been this wild. Growing up, I'd dream about what my dad might have been like had he lived long enough for me to get to know him. Or sometimes, I'd dream that I ran away from home and wake up crying. But I never woke up knowing my dream would come true. That the phantasmagoria of my youth would materialize in my waking life, that it already existed beyond my bedroom walls. Since Agent Xidas came into my life I'd slept well, without the aid of booze or scalding showers. The most natural and unnatural sleep of my life, chock full of good old American dreams of principle. The kinds of dreams you didn't want to come true, but you knew that somewhere they already had.

The left lane should only be used when passing vehicles traveling below the speed limit. That's the kind of principle Iggy subscribed to. Thus, we drafted behind a semi, coasting in its wake as Korean grandmas retracing Lewis and Clark's trail to the pacific zipped by in the left lane, simultaneously disproving stereotypes and demonstrating a small scale retrograde orbit. Mom once got me a telescope for my birthday, but wouldn't let me look through the lens until I'd read the accompanying "Beginner's Guide to Understanding Our Place in the Universe." Even after going cover to cover, the most complex philosophical question humanity ever faced remained outside my comprehension, so she donated the telescope to the church. Leave it to Eileen Frogg to bring together science and religion.

"So how's a pretty young thing like you end up working for the Bureau?" I'm guessing she heard me, but the way Iggy looked forward, as though activating her X-Ray vision to see through the sheet metal pull-down door of the semi truck, I wouldn't have been all that shocked if she'd forgotten my presence completely. Maybe she didn't hear me; she'd been up since she dragged me out of the motel almost twenty-four hours earlier. The woman was a machine. She didn't require rest, had no interest in sleep. All she needed was to keep her battery power high enough to maintain operational status. By then I assumed she ran on frustration and I'd kept her tank at capacity since she arrived at the trailer.

A minute passed and still we drove in the shadow of the semi, close enough that I had to pretend not to notice the surprisingly clever yet no less crude mudflap cartoons. If I wanted I could have reached out and knocked on the truck's loading door, just above the 'How Am I Driving?' eight-hundred number, and told the driver in person. Maybe I'd ask him where the best truck stop in Missouri was, seeing as by this point I had a feeling any meal I ate could be my last. Or I could ask him to speed it up or change lanes.

"It's a Batman story." Agent Xidas said, pushing her shades up the bridge of her nose. Could her robot eyes see the road through those things before the sun came up? I returned from my fantasy conversation with the trucker and offered a quizzical head tilt, encouraging her to continue.

"You know how he became a vigilante to get revenge? How all the bad guys in Gotham City would pay the price for the crime of the mugger who killed his parents?" She paused. Sweat appeared on her palms and she wiped them one at a time against her jeans, still dirt-stained from the scuffle at the campsite. "We...I..." She stopped again. "My uncle was killed when I was in high school."

The semi's turn signal flashed ahead of us and the big-rig pulled right into the exit lane, exposing our windshield to the morning light. Agent Xidas retained her posture. I thought I saw her lip quivering.

"I'm sorry about your uncle. Were you close?" Her face turned my way, her jaw set tight. The sedan hopped like a racehorse whipped from trot to gallop. Funny how sleeping with her on our second night of acquaintance didn't feel like moving too fast, but watching her accelerate to five over the speed limit as she eyed me from the driver's seat made me want to sit down and talk about not rushing into things. I grabbed the edges of my armrests and braced for warp speed.

"No. We weren't very close. My cousin and I were though. And he took it pretty hard." She turned back to the road, tapped the brake to bring us back under the legal limit, and took a deep breath. "At the funeral we were a little out of sorts. The whole thing was so unexpected. He was a bystander. Stray bullet kind of deal." She took a deep breath and opened her mouth to continue but didn't say anything. I looked forward and admired the flatness of the road.

"To calm him down, my cousin I mean, I told him I'd make sure nothing like this would happen again. That's when I decided to be a cop. Up until yesterday it was mostly paperwork. Then along came Frogg and..."

"And what?"

158

The highway turned off to the left. I looked across the dashboard into her Aviators.

"And what. Exactly. The rest of my life has become one enormous 'And what?'"

Agent Xidas ran one hand through her hair and sniffed to hold back a tear. *What do you know?* I thought. *So she's a human after all.*

"Did they ever catch him?" I said after a moment's pause. "Your uncle's killer?"

"No. I don't think so. When I was a kid, I had these fantasies about what I'd say to the guy if I ever got the chance. Powerful speeches, imagined conversations in my mind where I always have a good comeback ready." Her grip tightened on the wheel. The stale oxygen from the car's air conditioner tightened the skin of my arms. *How many people thought the same thing about me?* I dropped my chin into my chest as she went on. "Eventually I grew up. The imagined conversations switched to daydreams of exit interviews and telling off my bosses. These days I hardly think about it anymore."

"Batman eventually finds the mugger, right?" I wanted to lift the mood. Miles to go and nothing slows down a road trip like heavy silences and tales of a family demise.

"Yeah. He does. But I'm not Batman."

"No. You're more of a Frog girl."

I smiled. She didn't.

We crossed the border into northeastern Missouri. They don't have a typeset small enough for the cities of the region so looking at our trusty sedan's glove compartment map I pinned us right in the heart of a big green chunk of nothing. Mile markers indicated cities like Edina, but not the Edina you think you might have heard of once. A different, smaller Edina. The one southwest of Kahoka. Looking over the Triple A nonuple folded roadmap didn't help much, but Iggy seemed confident enough chewing up mile after speed limited mile of intrastate routes and one lane highways. Sky eyes repaved every inch of the road.

Before I knew it we passed Mexico. Not that Mexico. A different, smaller Mexico. Mexico, MO, population 12,567, not to be confused with Mexico Mo, the popular Colombian attraction at Mexico, MO's hottest girlie lounge. I've heard tales that she's got a set of Sierra Madres that'd encourage lesser men than Sir Edmund Hilary to try for the summit. Unfortunately I lacked the nerve to request a recreational stop. Agent Xidas developed tunnel vision, with Ed's beacon of white hair acting as the light at the end, beckoning her forward like a marathoner pushing through the pain, oblivious to all distractions and so close to the finish line.

I'm a man of principle. Aren't I? So where in my apothecary's chest of principled potions and moral mixtures could I concoct a brew of ethical codes of conduct to warrant driving towards a nightmarish frog farm in the middle of nowhere? Pondering, I had a fleeting epiphany, like waking from REM sleep and clutching at the memory of a vanished dream, when we pulled off the highway.

What the hell was I doing? I only trusted Iggy because the Solutionist told me to. I wanted answers from Ed, sure, but I didn't see where Iggy fit into this picture. She knew about the Solutionist, but she didn't seem to know anything specific about Ed's work with the FBI or his run in with Bogdan Woland back in Orlando. So what exactly did that porterhouse file on Eddie Mondo contain? A porterhouse? I looked at her, her purposeful posture like a Greek goddess sculpted into a bust of marble, silhouetted against the light of a cloudless sky. Isn't it funny how the heart breaking and the heart wanting are indistinguishable sometimes? I remembered the warmth of her body against mine and wondered if she produced it herself or if it was just my own heat reflecting off her metallic surface.

I needed more answers before taking on the next step. "Iggy, I-"

"We're here."

Uncle Haywood's Fantastic Frog Farm looked anything but. The males croaked in unison, working together in ways far more advanced and utilitarian than their human counterparts. Together their voices rang louder, attracted more females to the area, and gave each of them a better chance of scoring some tailless tail. That's how they'd operate in the ecosystem, forming a platoon, croaking, breaking rank, and reforming platoons from the larger army in another stretch of tall grass later on. Seemed a lot more reliable than waiting for mysterious women to knock on the door of your trailer, but to each frog his own. Different croaks for different folks.

Behind the swamp stood a decrepit old house. A few holes in the upstairs windows, but a light on downstairs meant it hadn't been abandoned. The paint that hadn't stripped off had faded from white to gray on the second story and either had a case of chickenpox downstairs or the yard doubled as a track for dirt bike races, with splotches of mud covering most of the façade. The front door, similarly freckled with brown, stood ajar and a soft, mechanical rumbling whispered through the aperture. Planted in the earth about a hundred yards from the house an equally derelict shed, Ed's shed, called our attention with its silent darkness. Just as I had seen it in the dream, boarded windows, no way in or out, like a Solutionist's luxury suite, complete with easy chair.

"You distract Uncle Haywood. I'll try to draw a bead on Mondo." She went to the trunk as I stretched my arms over my head like I were signaling a biplane. She popped her head around the sedan. "I meant now, Carl."

"Yes, Ma'am." I Walked up to the door as the sun took command of the sky, turning back to find her still three-quarters buried in the trunk. I twisted around and backpedaled as I spoke.

"You may have better luck finding him outside the trunk, babe."

From outside, I peered through the door and saw what appeared to be an office space. Or at least, it had functioned as a front desk at one point. The counter was caked in dust with scratched wainscoting peeling at the corners on its front side. Spider webs covered the register behind the counter, but even the spiders had tired of their landlord's neglect and skipped town. I pushed through to get a better look. "Hello? Anybody in?" A man of principle doesn't fear eight legged arthropods and a bit of bad air quality, so I entered the house. Uncle Haywood's hadn't seen a customer in years. I counted five mismatched chairs sprinkled across the large, open room, with a staircase leading up on the left side and one leading down on the right. The wall to the left housed empty shelves that once displayed plush frogs and encyclopedic guides to the various species. An upright piano decayed in the corner, its keys resembling a British smile, its insides more likely to produce raccoons than Rachmaninoff. Along the base of the wall, I noticed the remains of carpet studs, meaning someone gave the floor a close, straight razor shave that left the wood planks of its face exposed to the elements. Upkeep was kept down. Unlit bulbs dangled three feet from the high ceiling from cords with exposed circuitry. The business might have been robbed, I thought, or abandoned. But the frogs remained, and someone must have saw to that.

The dim light and steady electronic hum from the basement told me I wasn't alone. I followed my ears, "Hey, anyone down there?" Still no response. I hadn't dreamt it, but I felt I had already been here. I found the stairs and peered into the void. Faint light tried to reach up but couldn't make it past the base of the last step. I creaked down the first step, one hand tracing my path down the wall for balance. "Hello? Uncle Haywood?" The sound lightened as I approached, its tone rose an octave, whizzing like a swarm of bees. The windowless lower level beckoned me downwards like a spirited spelunker. I tripped forward over the final few steps, unable to see a wobbling plank on the third stair from the bottom, and landed hard on my knees against the concrete floor of the basement.

"Welcome to the frog farm." He said over the abrasive hum, low and steady like radio static or a small waterfall. Looking up without standing up I saw him, a rail thin man in overalls with no undershirt. He stood with his back to me, leaning over a worktable the size of the entire basement. One enormous piece of plywood supported by a series of strategically placed card tables. A torchiere lamp shone from the corner, casting light onto a model city like an AC/DC compatible sun. The buzzing floated from the city to my ear and lodged in my brain, just behind my eyes. The man stood to the side, faced me, and held a hand out to showcase his hobby. A model train set the size of Edina, Missouri appeared behind him. The buzzing of the train ceased as he set down the controls. Still, I winced as it echoed against the sides of my skull.

"Pretty nice, huh?" His smiled revealed teeth that matched his piano. Balding, but not bald, the area above his forehead resembled a rat's nest after a light rain, a twisted, curled clotting of sparse, sweat stained strands. A man of principle with nineteen kills under his belt knows a killer when he sees one. This man hadn't killed, but his face contained that wild, reckless look that told me he'd thought enough about it to remove the element of hesitation. "We're glad you finally made it, Mr. *Frogg.*"

Over the echoing train, I heard light footsteps behind me.

Did he say "Mr. Frogg?"

I hadn't risen from my knees.

Wait. Did he say "We?"

"Haywood," He leaned back against the scale city, its hillbilly Holy One, "Haywood Hilson."

I hear the bullet enter the chamber beside my ear. *Iggy's a bombtiger and the fuse is lit.*

"I believe you've met my cousin."

Imagined or not, the train whistles blared, everything went dark, and I woke up to find a wide-eyed Ed Mondo peering at me from a broken recliner as though he'd never seen me before. His look conveyed two questions.

1. How could I be stupid enough to wind up there?
2. What the hell took me so long in getting there?

His voice conveyed a different thought. "Rannochio! You look like you got laid." Consciousness lasted all of nine seconds.

Crawfish Brined Solutionism
Wednesday, May 10th, 1989

I came too, still in the shed, slouched against the front entrance without a fat cat on my chest. Woozy, but with it. I had no idea how long I'd been out but Eddie's mouth woke up the instant I did.

"They wanted a trade. The morons," Ed said, sitting in his chair with his ankle elevated atop a stack of milk crates, brandishing a crawfish in his right hand like a drunk sloshing his pint. "If I exploded my last flasher then they'd let you in without killing us."

I said nothing, watching the old man employ his patented vacuum-mouth technique to suck the meat from the shell before tossing the empty husk into a pile. He'd come a long way from the ravioli surgeon I once knew. The shed's windows had been boarded up so my world-renowned circadian rhythms couldn't be trusted. I judged I'd been asleep for a few hours at least based on the cramping in my legs. The stench in the shed brought tears to my eyes. Sour, acrid, and fishy, my nostrils felt like salt-dipped centipedes were crawling up my nose. A mountain range of rotting crawfish carcasses lined the back wall behind Ed's lounger. Scientists claim of all the senses memory associates closest with scent, citing the proximity of the nose and the amygdala. My limbic system, the drama queen of the human brain structures, appears to fall asleep on the job when the body does likewise. Otherwise I'd have sensed the briny musk of the shed when I'd dreamt it. Otherwise I'd suffer sulfuric napalm nightmares and delight in daydreams while pondering potpourri.

"So I tossed the thing. BOOM!" Ed hurled a crawfish at the wall and mimed blocking the glare from his eyes. "They lived up to their word, so I took down the lock and dragged you in." *Has he been talking the whole time I passed out or did he just start as I came to?* My face gave away my confusion. "They want us to stand trial, Rannochio. Together. Insane, if you ask me." He reached into the sack for another crawfish.

I pushed my body up against the door and straightened up to face him, but he continued before I could ask.

"Flash grenades." He looked up briefly to lock me into his gaze, bug-eyed behind the magnification of his glasses. "You'll never believe where I found them, where we found them, I should say. I've been drowning in soluse." Ed twisted another crawfish open. I knew his "we" meant the Solutionist, and that he knew that I knew it. Frog croaks tried to permeate the walls from outside but, despite the oversized producers, got stifled by the distance. The world beyond our shed fell away. A feint bulb hummed, Ed sat in his throne, his pulpit, and I nodded for him to continue.

"It was a good thing I had them, too. If I didn't I'd probably be tied to a chair waiting to be killed."

"Uh, Eddie," I said, taking in the scene in front of me, the one featuring Eddie Mondo, tied to his chair by a busted ankle, waiting for some deranged frog farmer to kill him. "I hate to break it to you, but that doesn't sound too far from the present reality."

The old coot dipped his hand deep into the sack of crawfish and brought it up, letting the dead crustaceans run through his fingers like coins from a pirate's chest. "Here, I'm afforded the simple luxuries of an all you can eat seafood buffet. And nobody, not even Hilson, pesters me. Well, there's you, Rannochio. Maybe now you'll let me finish?"

I smiled. He wasn't the same old Eddie, more like a deranged clone that talked a bit too fast and craved a few too many crawfish. Still, he was the same. Old, and Eddie. Something in his voice sounded off. His movements felt jagged, even by his own rickety standards. I figured he'd finally lost it.

"A permanent soluse had me running all over. Eventually, I was conscious of grappling with our captor. He came at me with a baseball bat and connected hard, like Dimaggio or Rizzuto." Ed mimed the swings of his favorite Italian heritage major leaguers with a crawfish bat. He shook the crawfish at his swollen leg, "He had me crawling for my life. I didn't feel it, thanks to the weight of the soluse, but I knew it'd hurt when I got the place all to myself again." Here, his half-eaten pointer indicated the space between his ears. "Hilson stood over me winding up his home run swing when I realized I held the flasher in my right hand. I covered my eyes in my elbow and set it off an inch away from the bastard's face. Oh, to hear those screams. In the ensuing chaos I made a break for it, but I could only get so far on my ankle. I took the lock from the outside of the shed, set it up on this side of the door, and I've been in here ever since."

Satisfied with his history lesson, Ed treated himself to another crawfish. He took its head in one hand and tail in the other, pinched the ends in his fingertips, twisted, and yanked it apart with practiced efficiency. *Slurp. Slurp.*

"A stroke of good luck that I'd stumbled upon the old recliner," he patted the armrest and sent a flurry of dust mites into the yellow glow of the uncovered bulb. "Not to mention the duct tape for setting the ankle, and of course, my sustenance." The two halves of the shell went over his head into the pile.

"You haven't eaten *every one* of those, have you?" The mountain of crawfish shells, looking like a paint swatch under the heading "red" stood behind him. An impressive mound of pincers rendered harmless and lifeless extending across the entire back wall of the shed, reaching nearly two feet in the air at its peaks. He didn't answer, but did pick up another. "Eddie, that's enough to feed an elephant for God's sake."

"Perhaps. They seem to be keeping me going, I suppose."

I raised a finger to the burlap sack. "Where'd you drag that in from, anyway?"

"Hilson's smarter than he looks."

"While I doubt that. I don't see how it answers my question."

"Rannochio, Rannochio. Wherefore art thou patience?"

Ed picked at the crawfish between his teeth until satisfied with my ability to stay quiet. He eyed me like a school teacher, his silence saying, "I can wait as long as you can, the sooner we get through the material the sooner class will be over." I bit my lower lip in apology.

"Hilson's smarter than he looks," he cleared his throat of maritime phlegm. "And these crawfish are here because of it." He dropped his hand into the sack like an arcade claw crane, pulled one up, and catapulted it at me. I kept my eyes on Eddie and let the slimy bastard collide with my chest and crash onto the floor, where its briny juices turned the pale brown dust around it a deep mahogany. Ed mumbled the next part of his story, his lips moving fast like a man possessed, or maybe a man recently released from possession.

"Eddie, I can't hear a damn word you're saying."

"Huh? Oh. Right. Frogg. Right. Business sense, of course, of course. The crawfish."

"Yeah..." He wasn't right. I kept an eye on his magnums just in case his sanity went AWOL.

"The tourist game is long since over at Uncle Haywood's, but the frogs didn't get the memo. Turns out a man can make a pretty penny shipping the little guys to restaurants and food service companies. Hilson may be a little eccentric, but he recognized he got paid by the pound, not by the frog. Which would be bad news for you," Eddie pointed a set of pincers at my midsection. "He realized that bigger frogs meant bigger frog legs, which meant bigger profits. The lunatic conditioned his frogs to eat crawfish, gave them a taste for the flesh, and after a few generations of breeding he'd achieved those mutants you saw in the dream." Ed bit off another chunk of Hilson's retirement fund. Typically, a man of principle would contest the idea that another man could speak so accurately of his dreams. But at that moment it seemed only fitting that he would. "I wouldn't have made it this long without them." Another shell went end over end, toppling into the side of the mountain and causing an exoskeleton avalanche.

The natty Italian gentlemen I once knew sat in his recliner like a feral beast in its hibernaculum, fattening up for a season long slumber. He munched away with such vigor as to nauseate me. I had to turn my head to avoid looking straight on. A behavioral psychologist PhD student could write a three hundred-page dissertation on what I witnessed from Eddie that night. This new animalistic instinct that grew in him made my skin crawl. I couldn't say what he may have been capable of, but with the pistols resting beneath his arms I couldn't say I'd have liked to find out either.

"Eddie?" When the man said all you can eat, he meant it. "Eddie, where'd you get the guns?" He shifted his weight to acknowledge hearing me and made a demonstrative swallow in the style of a cartoon character ingesting a six-foot submarine sandwich in one gulp.

Eddie waved my question away as though shooing off flies and shook his head. With the amount of crawfish juice in and around him he may have been shooing off flies, too. I looked around the windowless shed and wondered what fate lay in wait for us back at the house.

"You got the briefing, I know," Ed said, "so you have some idea what it means to be solused. But to have it really happen, to enter into another consciousness, Rannochio, you have no idea. Until it happens, you can't explain the awareness. You've felt the warmth crawl through you, perhaps, but not into your soul. Outside looking in. No. Inside looking out. Inside looking in, maybe. There but not there, let's say. Empowered in ways you can't control, but powerless in any way you ever could.

"I was at home with Barolo when I felt it. The second time since the hospital. I had almost convinced myself that it wasn't real, that the whole thing had been a fantasy. Until the morning he arrived outside the trailer, that is. Then I knew it was real. The night I addressed the town, remember? He returned to me that night. His words, mostly, my voice."

I remembered Ed that night. His fiery sermon that felt like a dream even as it happened, shared by the entire town. I looked up at him through narrowed eyes, studying his wrinkled face. I couldn't make out his eyes. He crunched another chunk of crawfish and sent a spattering of juices across his undershirt.

"I left the house feeling the long forgotten warmth of the Solutionist's control. I went to him. We spoke, of what I can't recall. Much of my time since then has been a fog. Memories of my life since leaving the house don't belong entirely to my own mind. Waves, you might say. Flashes here, flashes there. The next thing I remember I had taken the hardware store van for a joyride and wound up at a motel." Ed caught my astonishment without glancing up from his inspection of the crawfish innards. "Yes, the very same. I spoke with the manager, or, *we* spoke with the manager. Hard to say that I had much to do with Solusing the unfortunate man, but together we made arrangements for your future accommodations. It was important you shared the same room as Woland and myself."

"How did you know I'd be there?"

"I didn't. I hardly knew I was there to begin with. But he wanted you there, needed to Soluse you for you to read the briefing." Ed's body shook, an involuntary shiver sending everything from his knuckles to his knees atremble.

"Eddie, are you feeling ok?" He tossed a crawfish shell over his shoulder and coughed, beating at his frail chest beneath the stained undershirt. He took two enormous breaths, holding the oxygen during one prolonged blink, before struggling to right his upper body in the recliner.

"Your mother," Ed said. "She's a sweet, sweet, lady. I can see why you hate yourself so much."

I tried to speak but I had a frog in my throat the size of one of Hilson's pond dwellers.

"Honestly, Rannochio, I've never met such a woman. Surveillance gives you an idea, but to meet her in person was truly wonderful. Although I hardly can say I experienced it in the traditional sense. He did most of the talking." He never looked up from the crawfish, but he waited for me nonetheless. *Surveillance? Mother?* I pulled the skin of my forehead up away from my eyes, trying to massage Ed's words into my mind.

"What did you do to my mother?" I tried to stay calm. Eddie was off the rails, but I couldn't ignore the fact that nothing in my life had been on the rails since the cold steel of Iggy's pistol met my ear in Hilson's basement. And the two days before that weren't necessarily making all the scheduled stops either.

"Standard protocol," the old man said. "Any new operative gets outfitted without their knowledge in several likely locations. The parents' home tops the list."

"Operative?"

"Still don't get it, do you Frogg? Woland knew I once arranged to have weapons stored in your mother's garden shed, so he led me there using the soluse. I may have forgotten but a Solutionist always, always remembers."

"Hold on. Eddie. I'm not getting this. You had pistols and flash grenades stored in my mother's garden shed?"

"For over a decade. Whenever we brought someone in we made sure to cover our bases."

Impossible. I had only known Eddie Mondo for a fraction of that time.

"Frogg," Eddie finally met my stupefied gaze. "Why do you think I'm here right now? Why do you think I came to Chilton of all the places in the world?"

"I..."

"I came to Chilton to get you back." He let the statement dangle in the air between us. I tried to capture its meaning but couldn't grasp it. Whatever Eddie was trying to tell me swayed somewhere in the soft yellow light, amid the dust and the stench of crawfish. I sat on the floor with my back against the door. The pieces were coming together.

"Back to where?"

"Back to work."

"But..."

"That was my signature on those checks." Eddie said it as though asking me to pass him the salt. "My targets in those envelopes. Mark Hilson was my choice. That's why we're here. That's why I'm standing beside you in front of the firing squad. That's why I had weapons stored at your mother's. When I saw what the Agency had turned you into, I knew you were better off in Chilton. I chose to stay, too. When the Solutionist, or Woland, or whoever it was arrived that morning I knew I'd made the right choice. You, Rannochio, were my solution."

The bulb buzzed above us. Ed reached into the sack for another plump specimen. A bombtiger clawed away at my gray matter like a ball of twine while Ed sat sucking the flesh from his crawfish, unconcerned with the revelation. We sat in silence. Silence of dialogue, as the sound waves of Ed's violent slurping reverberated against the walls of the shed.

"You ran the Agency." I heard myself say.

"I did. Very few people knew about us. A small team. I'm actually rather impressed by Hilson and the girl for putting it all together."

"You ran the Agency." In retrospect I'd have sounded a lot better had I been rendered speechless.

"I certainly did. After my experience with Woland, the Bureau discharged me. I was a changed man. I set up my own operation, private investigating at first, but after a few years we became a little more...specialized. We were good. Good enough to take a few jobs from the Feds themselves. I'm surprised they held any information on us that the girl could access.

"You were good, Frogg. We wanted you back. You were our workhorse, six jobs a year can take a toll on the strongest of minds. I don't know how you handled it as well as you did. In fact, one of our clients requested you for each of his jobs. Perhaps you noticed the connection? Do you recall, while solused by Bogdan Woland, a man in Neu Freimann named David Adler?"

Mother.

"Does she know?" Ed, or whoever Ed was in the shed that night, knew what I was getting at but pressed on despite my inability to listen.

"Adler, the crook, came to America and started the business that became Burger Corner. He was a harsh businessman, but who could blame him after what he'd been through. Even as an old man he stayed tough. And we killed for him, for his money."

Ed flicked a crawfish straight into the air and attempted to catch it, shell and all, in his mouth. It landed on his shoulder. He held it out to try again but stopped himself, scrutinized it, and decided it'd be easier to just eat the poor bastard the old fashioned way. *Grip, Rip, Twist, Slurp Slurp.*

"Your last contract, in New York, right?" Ed spit chunks of flesh as he spoke. "Adler heard the guy was going to expose some bad press about the seafood quality standards in his revamped restaurant. You got him in time, but the news broke anyway. Forced Adler to make a big show of using fresh, U.S. products. First and foremost, a new seasonal special on Louisiana frog legs. Adler being Adler, he still lied to his consumers and got his Louisiana product from right here in Missouri. Thanks to you, Haywood Hilson never had to sell the farm."

171

Mother knows.

"What did you say to my mother, Eddie? Please tell me." The irony of Haywood Hilson's financial situation didn't matter much in the face of Eileen Frogg's broken heart.

"We may have mentioned it. But don't worry. She wasn't mad at you. She loves you. Blamed herself, in fact, for driving you away."

I thought about my mother sitting on the edge of the sofa, staring at nothing and wondering how I could have become what I am. Blamed herself? What sort of man let's his own mother take responsibility for his crimes? Not a man of principle, that's for sure.

"We told her how you felt, of course. Apologized, tried to own up to it. We were honest with her. About everything. Not just the violence, but the regret. The shame. The road to recovery."

I must have looked hopeful. Like a kid who'd learned his lesson, about to hear his punishing parent tell him 'I guess you've learned your lesson' just in time for him to still make it to his friend's birthday party.

"We told her how proud we were of you. I did. That moment with your mother, that's the only time I've felt like myself since the fog of the Solutionist's warmth, this damned coating of Soluse came over me. If she were here, she'd forgive you. Frogg. Whatever happens, you shouldn't leave here not knowing that."

He dipped in for another crawfish. Cuts and scratches covered the back of my hands, and as I assessed the damage, the image of my mother stayed with me. Her insistence on holding my hand when we walked through town. Her insistence on not letting go. When was the last time I spoke to her? Hugged her? Been honest with her? With myself?

A crawfish shell flitted down the mountainside. Soft croaks rang out, reminding me of the fate waiting for us beyond the shed.

"Eddie, why'd you keep it a secret? All those nights, you could have told me. Why wouldn't you tell me?" I asked, staring at the ground between us. Ed coughed and I brought my eyes up to him. He beat against his chest, hard, too hard, like his heart was a rundown TV set that had turned to static.

"Don't you remember?" I looked up at the change in tone to see a set of sky eyes narrowed at me. Eddie said, in a voice that sounded an awful lot like Carl Frogg's, "The only solutions I'm after are the ones I come up with on my own."

As soon as the words passed through his lips Eddie Mondo's head slouched forward and hung limp. A crawfish dropped uneaten from his hand and his white hair cast its light on my face as a bead of sweat, or maybe a tear, slid down my cheek.

Night fell over the farm and sent the last glimmer of evening light out on its ass. Booming croaks exploded from the oversized crawfish-fed frogs and the uncovered single bulb dangled in the center of the shed, giving us just enough soft yellow light to see one another. Eddie slept on and off in the recliner and I finally got a chance to think through the entropic chaos that replaced my life. Hilson couldn't get to his crawfish supply, guarded closely and sampled with vigor by Ed Mondo, making his frogs call out in hunger. I listened, wondering what the giant frogs were saying, wishing I could understand the explanations they'd undoubtedly give me if only I spoke my native language. As I tried to make heads and tails of Eddie's big reveal, the heavily sedated former FBI mystery man turned Murder Co. CEO came back to life, a bit. In a silent, shut-eyed stupor he'd gone back to his crawfish consumption at a pace on par with Agent Xidas's driving.

Agent Xidas. Not quite. I knew Agent *Xidas* didn't exist. Everything happened so fast since we got to the farm that I hadn't fully absorbed the notion of *Agent Hilson.* By discovering one truth about her I'd found I knew even less than ever. Did she really work for the Feds? She couldn't.

Ed lulled from side to side, crawfish dangling from the end of a tired upturned arm. He nodded off like a child in the back of a minivan after a New Year's Eve party. What else is that middle portion of life besides a conflicted period wishing you could go back to five or skip ahead to eighty-five. For me, ever since I can remember, I've either dreamt of the glorious period before I could remember, or looked to the future of when I'd have blissfully forgotten. The rest, that period of sexual frustration, newfound aches and pains, and the occasional foray into Solutionist fueled adventures with seductive murderesses and the odor of crawfish, well, you don't have to be a man of principle to know you're better off without it. But that ain't how life goes.

"Ed? You there buddy?"

A nod. I thought. His head drooped forward and bobbed around, as though he dreamt of his boyhood in Italy, protesting against his grandmother's insistence that he finish his antipasta. He went from ranting to reeling in the blink of an eye the way only Eddie Mondo could.

"Part of me knew all along." I said aloud. "She was too damned beautiful to be a Fed." I sat on the ground with my back against the door and my knees up in the air, staring at the top half of an evacuated crawfish exoskeleton. It stared back, but I doubt if either it or Eddie listened to a word. "From the moment I saw her, it didn't make sense. Never made a call to a higher up. No mention of a partner. Hell, she's hardly old enough to finish graduate school let alone make rank all the way to Field Agent."

Ribbit. Ribbit. The frogs stirred in the pond, utterly unaware of how strange their existence was on this planet. They'd never know they were bred for slaughter. Would it be better that way? To live like a king, feasting and mating in a veritable Garden of Eden, growing more powerful than any of your species, living a good life. A short life, but an extraordinary life.

"It adds up, though. The quick temper. I'm really an idiot, I mean, did she really get that frog farm pamphlet at 1:00 a.m. from a tourist rack? She was already heading here. Plus, she didn't exactly hesitate to put my face into the road. The rush. That's what it was. That's what brought me back. Even before Taupe Suit I could feel it rising while she pistol-whipped me on the road. The thrill of the coming kill. But she held back. Maybe because she liked me? Probably not, but no, it felt real. It really did."

Eddie shuddered in his chair, a spasm running through his spine, but he didn't wake. Flies orbited his mass, occasionally

174

breaking through his atmospheric body odor to alight on his brine-soaked undershirt.

"I'm not mad at her." I said to the half shell, which stared back with incredulity. "Really. I wouldn't go back if I could." I thought about her sky eyes outside the trailer, how small she looked in the passenger seat. I remember the way my heart pounded when she came into the kitchen to stop Anne in her tracks. I thought of the sedan by the campfire, where our fractious souls added up, if only for a night, and we were a whole. The warmth of her body. Soft where softness better fit the bill, muscled where it was best to be muscled.

"I have to believe she didn't *have* to do it. I was all in. I'd already come so far, put up with so much uncertainty. Did she fuck me as some sort of twisted power play? One more notch in her belt of confusion and control. Still, I'm glad I did it."

Eddie, while not adding much paternal advice, demonstrated Father of the Year level listening skills.

"If she'd never come to my trailer I'd still be stuck in it. I'd never have found you, Ed. Besides, I've actually gotten some sleep the last few days. And I don't mean the well-oiled sleep we sometimes get after a bottle of the hard stuff. Maybe the Solutionist knows something I don't. Hell, I sure as shit ain't omnipotent. I'm hardly potent at all. He knew she'd come into my life..."

I stopped talking. A man of principle can only wax nostalgic about his kidnapper aloud to a hollowed out shellfish and a shell of an old man for so long. I took a few deep breaths and leaned the crown of my head back against the wooden door. Cobwebs and dust clung to the roof, an abandoned hornet's nest did its best impression of a stalactite. *I should clean my trailer*, I thought, *if I ever go home.*

Ed's busted ankle tipped sideways but stayed on the stack of crates. I stood up to reset his makeshift cast. Any steps he took now may be his last. I located the roll of duct tape and peeled the used strips from his pants. He didn't stir, heavy and lost to another consciousness. *Is he solused?* Whatever that meant. *Or just Eddie being Eddie?* As I tore fresh padding from the recliner and tried not to breath through my nose, I thought about Ed Mondo. Not the Ed Mondo I knew in Chilton, the small farming town celebrity. Not the

Ed Mondo from the Woland briefing, the FBI analyst traveling through time and consciousness. I thought about the Ed Mondo I never knew and was never meant to know. Ed Mondo, Agency Director. Now that I knew if the Agency even had a director, it was tough to swallow that the mound of brine-coated flesh mumbling in his sleep once decided the fate of so many lives. Not exactly the embodiment of evil and amoral sin I'd imagined pulled the strings all those years. I tightened one loop around his foot, another around his calf. He chose Mark Hilson. Not me.

But I pulled the trigger.

I'm the reason we're here.

"I'm not mad at you either, Eddie." I said to the lump, smiling at the pieces of crawfish stuck between his teeth, remembering the olive oil next to his toothpaste. "And Rolo's fine, so no need to worry about him.

"I'm not mad at you, and I'm certainly not mad at Iggy. If it weren't for you, she'd never have come into my life. These last couple days showed me what I was missing. I really fell for her, too. I know I'm a sap. A real sap of principle. She brought me back to life. She may not be the type of girl I'd bring home to meet my mother, but she sure as shit is the type who'd take me home to face my mother. That's a special kind of woman. You might even say she was my solution..." I sucked in my cheeks and shook my head, thinking of what may have been.

"Hmm-fee," Ed snorted and his head straightened up. The twisted tissue of his face loosened and his eyelids fluttered without opening.

"Eddie?" I leaned forward over his ankle.

His wrinkles smoothed out around the corners of his eyes. He looked serene. His chest rose and fell contentedly, like an Olympian poised before his final heat. His voice, again, shifted. "Carl Frogg," the voice said, lips hardly moving. The voice of Bogdan Woland.

"Our mutual friend, Eduardo Mondo, he is not long for this world." Ed's eyes opened and I stared as a wave of warmth shot through me from my feet up through my chest and over my eyes. *I've*

176

felt this before...but when. My sight clouded by a screen of wave-like greens and gold. Sky eyes blaring like twin lighthouses, flooding the shed with a fog of chartreuse light. I couldn't make out his face any longer. I didn't breath but didn't worry, as I felt no need for oxygen. *Dinner. With Ed. I asked about Germany.*

"You did, but it was not yet the time for you." Woland spoke through Ed's body. The warmth, the soluse, settled in my stomach and pumped its way through my limbs and into my extremities. I wanted to sleep but I couldn't close my eyes. *Powerless in any way I'd known.*

"He is alive, for now." Woland's voice returned. "I ask you to trust me, and I appreciate that you will do just that. Eduardo Mondo only lives with my strength, and I will supply him enough to see you through this. Do not ask more of him than he can give. His soul is that of a survivor, but in many ways he is already gone."

I heard the words from somewhere but my senses blended into one massive intake of perception. Sounds, words, temperature, colors, all indistinguishable from one another. I'd have fainted but my body remained entranced by the Solutionist's spell.

"I too, am weakening. The waves, Carl Frogg, are drying up. The firmament is fading into eternal space, and with it I feel my ties to the world evaporating. Omnipotence unlocks many secrets, and immortality provides the time to gain vast knowledge, but for me there is no intersection. I prophesied for you to kill three times in order to feel at peace. I stand by it. I only request you choose wisely. And I thank you."

The bulb in the shed went black. The voice vanished into memory. I stumbled back to life, regaining control of my muscles and finding my vision returned just in time to see Eddie Mondo's face staring into me with big, black eyes. He nodded with such subtlety I knew it wasn't him. Whether I had spoken to the Solutionist, Bogdan Woland, Eddie Mondo or the Devil himself, I couldn't say. Only one thing was certain.

I had been solused. I had been given a solution.

"What's that racket?" Iggy pounded the wall of the hut with the butt of a shovel. *How do I know it's a shovel?* I just knew. I could see without looking. Could hear without listening. It was the butt of a shovel, but the instant the sound waves washed into oblivion my confidence escaped with them. I shook my head. It didn't matter. Weird shit was happening in this shed, no doubt, and the sooner I got out the better.

"Sorry, babe." I called out, coy as a peacock with a capital cock. "Boys will be boys. How are things on your end? Sorry about Uncle Mark. You know what they say about two wrongs, right?" Ed stirred but stayed unconscious, or dead, depending on whether you're a man of principle or a believer in Solutionism. Although by that point the line between the two had thinned from a sumo wrestler to a runway model.

"You've got five minutes," she said. *She turned and took two steps, looked back, and forced a tear back into its duct.* But by the time she turned back to the house I'd covered my face in my hands, convinced I'd imagined the whole thing.

Haywood retrieved the defendants from the shed, a heartbroken man of principle and a comatose half dead Eddie Mondo. Luckily I managed to tuck one of Ed's magnums beneath his shirt in the back of his waistline and helped myself to the other before Haywood finished taunting us from beyond the door. We went quietly. Ed didn't have much of a choice in that regard and I didn't want to create any trouble until I got a chance to speak to Iggy. After removing Ed's body holster and adding it to the top of Mt. Crawfish, I propped his arm over my shoulder and hauled his mangy mass out of the shed. Uncle Haywood, barefoot and likely wearing nothing but his overalls pointed a Civil War era shotgun at us and nodded to the house. A madman's grin splayed across his stubbled cheeks.

"Nice to see you again, Haywood. Sorry about your Dad."

He hocked a loogie, and took his sweet time doing it. I charted it as though in slow motion, following the full vibrato of his internal chambers at work. *The oxygen curdling through his bronchioles, the diaphragm pounding, bubbling through his thorax, into the esophagus, the larynx, bits of phlegm and spittle coagulating into a globule of gross, expelled by the epiglottis, through the mouth, over the tongue, through the lips. To grandmother's house we go.*

It landed square on my shoulder, but I didn't wipe it off, didn't look at it. I couldn't shake the feeling that I'd just seen inside Haywood Hilson's body. He wagged the business end of the shotgun, whipsawing between the house and the two doomed men, and asked the one showing signs of life, "Enjoying yourself?"

I'm a man of principle. I don't go quietly. "Aside from the riveting ribbiting of these amazing amphibians, no, I haven't found the accommodations all that enjoyable." A few of the more drama sensitive frogs came in on cue and croaked for effect. I used the hand that didn't support Eddie's weight as a sound funnel. "Riveting, ain't it?"

He scowled and ordered us to march. I hiked Ed's body up like a pair of oversized button fly jeans worn without a belt and shuffled bowlegged, leaning the old man's (half) dead weight against me, towards the house. *Haywood smiled behind us, guffawing at my struggles but distracted enough not to notice the pistol shaped bulges pressing against our lower backs.* This time, I prayed I was right.

That Warm, Murderous Feeling
Wednesday, May 10, 1989

I pushed through the door, fondly recalling the dust free home of Eddie Mondo as our feet dragged up tiny nebulas of fractured earth from the floor. I set Ed down in a wooden rocking chair and stretched my back before taking in the room. Scanning from side to side, my tongue pressed the top of my mouth, *tut tut tut tut tut.* I had hoped for more. Nothing changed since earlier. The windows were all scratched and caked with dirt. There'd be no surprise witnesses lurking in the night, just a bunch of frogs waiting on the courthouse steps like a mucus covered media mob, only I didn't count on any of them to get the story to the masses. I frowned. No 'Exhibit A' poster board on an easel. No robes and powdered wigs set out for the authorities of this tripped out tribunal. Worst of all, no Iggy.

Haywood's weapon poked my shoulder blades and he grumbled through the side of his mouth that I ought to grab a seat next to Eddie. I obeyed and sat in a small wooden number with no armrests. Eddie slouched sideways, his chair rocking with diminishing force from when I set him down. It didn't look like he was breathing. *Already gone. Waves receding.*

"We know why we're here." Hilson stood ten feet in front of us, keeping his finger on the trigger of the shotgun that pointed my way from beside his hip. The frogs answered from beyond the walls. "I've talked it over with my cousin and the verdict is in. Gentlemen, I'll level with you, you never had much of a chance."

"Haywood," I didn't realize I spoke until I was three words deep into the second sentence. "You seem like a man of principle, and I recognize that you're looking at two dead men. And that may be only half metaphor." A sideways nod to Eddie. "But if it ain't too much trouble, I'd love to have a word with that lovely cousin of yours."

"Oh, I don't doubt that, Mr. Frogg. She played you for a fool, didn't she, Froggy?" I can't hold it against him that he found my name so fascinating. After all, he worked with frogs his whole life, and it was

180

one hell of a coincidence. But still, Hilson was a grown man. He should have gotten past it. "No surprise that a man like you, Mr. Frogg, would take orders from his own tadpole." He snickered and I grimaced at his bare shoulders bobbing up and down beneath the denim overall straps. "No, no, she's seen enough bloodshed in her life and suffered enough on account of you. I'll handle it from here."

The basement steps creaked and Iggy emerged from the subterranean train yard. She'd washed up a bit, her face free of any residual dirt, blood and makeup that'd survived the previous forty-eight hours. Freckles regained property rights on her face and looked to be setting up camp for an extended stay. "It's okay," she said, her cousin never turning his deranged glare from the spot between my eyebrows. For all his backwoods tendencies, I could tell by the way he handled the shotgun that he wouldn't need two shots to hit his mark. Or his Mark, as it seemed I'd soon become. Iggy walked forward a step but stayed behind Hilson. "Let him have his last words." I wanted to believe there was weakness in her voice, but if I'd learned anything the last few days it was that even a man of principle can't get a good read on this broad.

"Hi Iggy." I smiled. She didn't. It was sort of our thing. Hilson's face curled in like the cartoon logo on the package of a sour sucking candy after hearing the pet name. Unfortunately, his shotgun's expression stayed fixed. So did Iggy's. She'd taken up that same rigidity as the first time I'd seen her on my doorstep. Only this time, no Aviators to hide behind. Her eye swelled up from the fireside imbroglio the night before but she still qualified as what Money Mark would call "a tonic for tired eyes."

"I guess I'll do the talking, huh? Fair enough." I cleared my throat and bent forward to stand up but Hilson's shotgun said "*clink*" and I had a change of heart. Sitting would suit me just fine.

"I want to thank you." Her eyebrows rose a quarter inch before her brain reprimanded her forehead muscles and sent them back down like scared puppies. "You saved me. I'd rather have lived these last few days with you then had another forty back in Chilton."

"Yourewelcomeanythingelse?" *Her heart beat too quick, she had to focus to steady her leg shaking.* Another glimpse of truth that

I couldn't possibly know. The warm sensation settled around my feet like winter slippers. *This is it.* Leaning back, I succumbed to the soluse. A man without principles can take the cards he's dealt and hope for the best. The warmth weighed down my ankles and tickled at my knees. I felt the corners of my lips rising.

"Why'd you go through all the trouble? Why not just cuff me and bring me straight here. Or shoot me on sight?"

Her brow furrowed and she breathed through her mouth. With arms crossed over her diaphragm she lowered her head before answering. "We didn't know Ed had lost it so bad. Otherwise, I'd have done just that. I thought you'd help me find him. If I'd known he came here on his own, we'd have driven straight here and you'd have had a bullet hole in each foot for the drive."

"But still," I didn't buy her act. In fact, I *knew* it was just an act. "Why'd you have to cut so deep? Revenge and justice, that's fair play. But you went for the soul. You went for the heart, Iggy."

I thought I heard her croak but it might have been a frog.

"The best way to break the skin," she steadied her voice and lifted her chin a little too proudly, met my gaze, and held her conviction long enough to sputter, "is to go for the bone."

I rubbed my temples, a la Ed Mondo in the trailer, and pondered her action hero punch line and the twists of fate that led to it. *Why would she do this to me? To herself. She's not...*

Without warning, the warmth I'd felt in my feet rocketed up through my body and saturated my mind. *Solused.* I glimpsed the sight of Iggy and Hilson from outside my body, but they vanished. Echoes of distant voices rushed through the back of my mind as though through a tunnel that reached into my past lives. *Woland?* Iggy looked at Hilson. Hilson looked worried and raised his shotgun to his eye. They faded in and out. *Now is the time.* The thoughts, only half mine. The movements, only of my body, not of my control. The voice, my own. The words, shared. The soluse, that mystical warmth, stretched through my arms into my fingers, encased my spine and seeped deep into the recesses of my internal cavities. *Empowered in ways I can't control.* I spoke.

"This is your solution then? To murder an old man? Enough time has passed since Mark Hilson's murder. Fire does not extinguish fire. It fuels it. You won't find what it is you're searching for this way."

Haywood and Iggy glanced at each other, wondering what had changed in my tone. I'd have stood for effect but my legs weren't my own. I could hardly see and felt my head listing to one side. They must have thought I was possessed. They may not have been wrong.

"You've tried to find answers through him, but Solutionism exists independent of the Solutionist. Like any ism, it transcends men and women. It deals not in absolutes, not in rights and wrongs, and most of all not in answers. It deals in solutions. Sometimes the best solution is not to look for answers. Sometimes the most principled man is the one free of principles. Cause and effect are nothing but perspective. Where you think you stand now is not where you'll see yourself standing when you look back tomorrow. You don't realize this, but the death of Mark Hilson set in motion a series of events that would prove to save you from bankruptcy and the Devil only knows what other misfortunes. I am the best thing that ever happened to you."

"Carl...your eyes..." Iggy tried to stop me but I lacked the power to hold back. The soluse pulsed in my core, throbbed in the back of my mind. My shirt clung to my chest, my lungs heaved clouds of dust-laden air in and out. I felt Woland pull the strings and manipulate my head to one side. Through the haze of soluse, my eyes functioned just enough to make out Iggy's form standing at a safe distance, with one foot back and both hands clasped over her mouth.

"And you, Ignatz. You are the best thing that ever happened to me. Perhaps the frog chooses not to jump from the pot of boiling water. Is death not a solution in itself? Maybe even the best solution? Acceptance. Forgiveness. Trust. These are the solutions that bring peace. I thank you because you've shown me that even though the water is boiling, I can still jump out. Who turned on the flame is irrelevant, perspective. Any one of us is as responsible as the next. We make the choices, not the Solutionist. You and me. There's nobody to turn it off. It's done. Iggy, I am a man without principles, and that gives me the strength of all principles. Solutionism, real or imagined, believed or contested, is a part of this. I once said the only solutions I want are the ones I come up with on my own. I amended that principle when you came into my life. It was prophesied that I'd kill for you and I have. And I owe you one more. It was promised. A man of principle keeps his promises. I will kill for you, but I will do it because I want to. Because I believe it is my own solution to do it. That's the solution I've come to on my own."

Hilson brought the gun up to his shoulder and lined up his shot, gripping tighter as I spouted the Solutionist-fueled monologue. I caught bits and pieces of it, but based on Iggy's facial tics I was living a few seconds behind the moment. Ensnared by the heaviness of the Solutionist's control, the heat of the soluse coursed up and down my body in waves. I don't know if I shook in my seat. I don't know if I spoke in English. I had shared the same sensation Eddie experienced with Woland at the hospital years ago, and I chose to let it ride. What else could I do?

"I've made promises to you, Iggy. Promises to Eddie, too. Promises to the man in the box in my yard. Promises to myself. A man of principle keeps his promis-"

In the lost moments of solused life, parts of me handed over the reins. When the Solutionist handed them back, I'd forgotten how to drive. I saw only shadow, felt nothing but cold, and after wavering a moment in the haze, fell forward off the chair. The world dimmed from shadow to black.

I came to in a heap on the floor covered by a cold sweat with Iggy cradling my head in her hands. Tears moved like rollercoaster carts, crawling past the apex of her cheekbones and plummeting down her face. "Carl? Can you hear me?"

"Leave him be." Hilson's muffled voice reached us, pale and thin as though spoken by a ghost.

"Carl?"

I opened my eyes but only saw flashes of light in the periphery.

"Jesus, they're all black...CARL?"

"Just leave him!" The shotgun-toting specter echoed from across a ten foot void that sounded a mile wide.

Her voice trembled and I couldn't make out any words. I tried to smile. I'm guessing she didn't. My body, though slack, felt relaxed. I wasn't paralyzed, just limp. I could still feel the shoes on my feet and the floor beneath me. But I couldn't move. I couldn't see anything but the strange darkness and the streaks of white at the bottom of my sight.

The gun fired.

Iggy dropped my head onto the floor and I heard her gasp and wheeze, her presence left me there, alone on the ground in a darkness all my own.

No. He didn't. How could he? The clarity I'd experienced prior to blacking out vanished. I fought the force weighing me down and tried to lift my arms, my head, my eyes. Nobody spoke. *He'd missed his mark. He'd caught Iggy by mistake.*

I heard soft breathing. Sobbing. *She's alive.*

I needed to break the soluse. My toes twitched. *Yes. Take it. Take it back. It's yours.* The density of the Solutionist's trance diminished and sharp pains popped up over my lifeless body like whack-a-moles. With each aching bruise and welt I gained further control, recognizing another muscle responding to my brain's instructions. I mastered my breathing, and after sucking in a maximum capacity of oxygen I sent a mighty shiver through my body and I flailed my leg into the air. A wave of energy rode through me like a general on horseback galvanizing his troops before battle. My body was mine once more. I bounced to my feet and reached back to pull my magnum on Haywood Hilson.

But why was his shotgun on the ground?

And why was he lying facedown in a pool of blood?

And why were Iggy's sky eyes glowing past me over my shoulder?

For a man labeled "already gone," you had to hand it to Eddie Mondo. He still knew how to make an entrance. He stood in front of the rocking chair, which creaked back and forth like a nodding sycophant at a strategic planning meeting, the only motion breaking the stillness of the room. Eddie held his magnum out at full arm's length. He had one leg bent at the knee and drooped his non-shooting shoulder six inches below his neck. His body looked half dead, whatever life force left in him had rationed itself to only the necessary muscles and veins. He lurched backwards a small step, then swung the same foot forward using the additional momentum. Iggy looked up from her cousin's side, the pair unblinking in their sky eyed staring contest. She cowered backwards on all fours, groping for a weapon, the wall, anything tangible to steady her trembling. Her baseball shirt turned gray with terror sweat.

The only thing between her and a half-dead murderer was a fully dead attempted murderer. Frankenstein Eddie whipped his leg over Hilson's body, his head wobbling atop of his neck like a loose tooth, a newly vestigial lump of gray matter and white hair atop an angry Bogdan Woland's resourceful murder conduit. How much of what happened came from Ed's design and how much could be pinned on the Solutionist didn't matter. *We make our own solutions.*

Ed's pistol wobbled as he made the final zombie lurch towards his prey.

No.

Ed steadied his stance and steadied the magnum. I couldn't see his face.

I'm sorry.

Iggy looked up, her last moment, and met my gaze.

She smiled.

She's smiling?

My heart warmed and pounded in my chest. She loved me, I thought. Even in the face of certain death she had the heart to look past the magnum-wielding monster and give me the gift of a smile. A smile that told me she wished it had ended another way. A smile that said, "I'm sorry."

Then I heard the shot fire. Then I noticed the magnum smoking at the end of my arm and saw Eddie Mondo's body fall to its knees. Then to its side. Then onto its back. The magnum slipped from my palm and landed flat in a single, heavy thud against the floor. Nothing else moved. Thank God I couldn't see his face.

She smiled.

I didn't.

In the calm we heard the croaks of Hilson's frogs vibrating through the still night air.

Ravenous Rannochios
Wednesday, May 10th, 1989

We stood over our loved ones. Iggy sniffed back her tears and rubbed her palms over her forehead and through her hair. She kept her fingers interlocked behind her head, poised to perform a set of standing abdominal crunches to exercise the grief out of her system. Meanwhile, I crouched over Ed's body, wondering how long it'd really been since his soul last took up residence in it. A man of principle knows an acceptable time to shed a tear, and I didn't sniff back a single one. They marched in succession across my scratched and battered face and dripped down onto Ed's pale, lifeless skin.

He'd been more of a father to me than I'd ever known. We shared something closer than DNA, something beyond double recessive genes, a trait outside the confines of a Punnett square. We shared a consciousness. How many men have been under the spell of a Solutionist, had their minds swim in the muddy waters of soluse? Some demonic mystic had spoken to us, acted through us, and left us to pick up the pieces. I had been Eddie Mondo in more ways than one. We shared in the family business of foul play. Solutionism doesn't skip a generation.

His body deflated in front of me. Bereft of its spirit for God only knows how long, it sprawled out across the floor emanating a long awaited tranquility. He didn't wear a countenance of content, but he didn't have the twisted look of a possessed soul either. His glasses had flown off in the fracas. His white hair had taken on the familiar look of the eccentric genius. The Einstein look that came from a brain with an electric output that couldn't be contained by its skull. Had there been a kitchenette in the main room of the house, I'd have deftly located some olive oil and performed one last grooming.

He smelled of crawfish.

The shot cut straight through the heart and broke through his chest. A man of principle doesn't shoot another man in the back, but Eddie Mondo was more crawfish than man, more demon than human by the time my instinct took him out. I slid my palm over his face and closed his eyelids.

"We need to bury them," Iggy said, standing behind me. I looked at her over my shoulder and stood up at full height. With no tissues in sight I used my forearm to wipe my nose. I grabbed the shovel, nodded, and walked to the door.

Ribbit. Ribbit. Ribbit. I dug into the ground, timing each strike of the spade in rhythm with the repetitive ensemble of amphibians. The ground beside the pond made for easy digging, and I had a sizable hole ready within half an hour. Iggy stayed in the house, occasionally I'd hear her blow her nose, but otherwise she held a silent vigil. In the moonlight, my aching hands throbbed with milky pink blisters from grasping the shovel. I stood in the grave, my feet sinking in the murk two feet below the grass, trying to think of anything besides Ed Mondo, but failing. Trying to remember the sensation of the soluse, but even my certainty that it happened wasn't persuasive. *My life has become an enormous "And what?"*

I struck the shovel into the earth as an anchor to hoist myself from the hole. Catching my breath, I admired the product of my labor. A small grave, it didn't take up much space. I squinted into the squishy base of the hole, one more shallow grave in the earth's crust, and considered the type of people who wound up filling them. The straight and narrow path rarely led to a shallow grave. The more normal a lifetime, the deeper one wound up in the ground. Lives with the most depth ended in the shallowest holes. Hilson didn't follow the straight and narrow; he was more of a yellow brick road type. Only instead of yellow bricks, his road was paved with thoughts of vengeance and lined on either side by armies of bullfrogs. Eddie played the role of the wizard; I'd been cast as the wicked witch. Even in burial, there's no place like home.

I wondered if Hilson had been a man of principle. He seemed the type. He'd probably appreciate being laid to rest beside his frogs, in his own little world. Shallow graves stand out, especially once the dirt gets filled in. Hilson's life didn't conform to the ways of the world, as far as I could tell in the blurred hours I'd known him. He liked model trains, frog farming, and obsessive revenge schemes. A simple life that lead to a complicated death. Once laid in the hole

189

he'd find peace, I'd hoped. A thin brown blemish on the green grass of normalcy, Hilson didn't belong in a cemetery. I reaffirmed an old principle: A body should fit its grave, and a grave should fit its body. Meanwhile, Iggy stood leaning against the doorjamb with crossed arms. She'd been watching me. I skulked back to the house with my eyes fixed at her feet. When I reached the door she said, "Ready?"

"Ladies first." I said, and lowered my eyes feeling stupid. I followed her into the house and we lifted Haywood Hilson off the floor. She gripped him by his wrists and I had him by the ankles. Men are not couches. There's no "One Two Three Lift" and no rented truck in the driveway. Picking up a corpse isn't just lifting pounds; it's lifting people. The combined weight of their memories, their souls, their guilt and greed and all their Christmases, and their first kiss, and their fears, and their dreams. In Haywood's case, we carried his grief. A frog farmer looking to avenge his innocent father's death. He'd weighed me down for years, he weighed me down that night, and he'd weigh me down long after I filled in his shallow grave.

We placed him in the ground and I took the shovel out of the earth. "Do you want a minute?" Iggy hadn't said a word, just stood with tired arms drooped low at her sides. Whatever weight I'd shouldered hauling Haywood outside, she'd felt with twice the burden.

"No." She watched the body of her cousin sink into the mud and pond water at the base of the grave without blinking. She'd loved him. Too close to see the maniac's face for what it had become. Too close to recognize the insanity and obsession. I wondered how he'd kept her involved all these years. What did she owe him? I placed the spade in the mound of pond soil and tilted it over Hilson's midsection.

"What about Eddie?" She asked, still watching the corpse. A worm slithered out of the dirt and crawled across Hilson's overalls.

I handed her the shovel, which she accepted without hesitation.

"A man of principle keeps his word," I said, mostly to myself. I wiped the sweat from my forehead with an even sweatier forearm and walked back to the house. *And what am I, if not a man of principle?*

In death, Eddie returned to the same look he had before he shot Hilson, the delirious old man, not the demonic murderer. I wondered whether the bullet actually changed anything. If he'd been this way before, why couldn't he come back again? But I knew. *He's dead. An empty shell. A discarded vessel.* I knew, but I didn't want to believe it. His body felt hollow, and lifting him by the armpits into the rocking chair didn't pose the physical challenge I'd anticipated.

Sighing, I threw him over my shoulder like a limp balloon and kicked the door open. Iggy looked up from her graveyard shift and panted as she leaned against the shovel, watching me haul Ed down to the pond. *Ribbit. Ribbit. Ribbit.* The massive frogs came out from the bushes, their eyes gleaming in the moonlight like billiard table 8-balls, reflecting the deep blue water. I stood at the edge, still with Eddie in tow, and tested the water with the tip of my shoe. Iggy watched from the side in silence. *Ribbit. Ribbit. Ribbit.*

I stepped into the mud and secured my footing. Then moved in deeper. *Ribbit. Ribbit.* My ankles splashed pond scum into the air, producing tiny living sidewinders of perturbed gnats. Frogs circled around us, afraid to move too close, but attracted by the scent of Ed's crawfish-stained skin and clothes. *Ribbit.* One flashed in front from the right as my knees submerged. A streak of green and yellow disappeared among the tall grasses. *Ribbit. Ribbit.* Another jumped from behind me, splashing my stomach with invisible, cool pond water. The water wrapped around my thighs and saturated my jeans, which clung tight and cool against my skin. *Ribbit.* They were so loud I couldn't hear my own words. *Ribbit.*

"Eddie," I said, sliding him carefully off my shoulder and holding him across my chest like a groom carrying his bride across the threshold. "Don't think I'd forgotten my promise." *Ribbit.* Splash. *Ribbit.* Splash. *Ribbit.* "A man of principle is a man of his word." I felt the hind legs of those bowling ball sized frogs crashing against my thighs, spraying silver blue water across my torso in their leaping effort to snatch the decaying flesh in my arms. "I know you wanted wolves,

Eddie. But I think given the circumstances, this'll have to do." I placed him down on the surface of the water. The bravest of the amphibians, or perhaps the hungriest, jumped aboard. I stood for a moment waiting for his body to sink, but it didn't. He floated above the pond until the weight of Uncle Haywood's Amazing Frog Farm's oversized crop proved too much to bear. I stood among the swarm of massive frogs, the ravenous rannochios, as they feasted upon Eddie Mondo's marinated body. Soon after, he disappeared beneath the surface and I stood alone, a pillar among the swaying reeds, staring up at a cloudless violet night.

I turned my back on Eddie Mondo's resting place and trudged out of the pond. There, waiting with tears in her eyes and a shoulder to rest my head was a woman. The only person I had left in the world. I still didn't know her name.

A Man of Principle
Thursday, May 11ᵗʰ, 1989

I saw flashes in the car as I sped along the empty rural Missouri back roads. I chose to ignore them. A spark here, a face there. In all of Eddie's ramblings, he neglected to offer any real advice on how to function as a human with a touch of Solutionism in his blood. I didn't like it, I wanted my old blood back, the blood that ran hot and cold, beat too fast or too slowly, was blue on the inside, red on the outside, had never tasted of soluse and could be counted on to remind me I was only a human.

I let the woman sleep in the back. We hadn't debriefed, in any sense of the word. And to be honest, I didn't know which would have been more satisfying, dropping her panties or dropping her alias. When we left the farm, Iggy handed me the keys and climbed into the back seat. I paused before I got in, deciding that forgiveness is a zero sum game. A wash. You do the right thing but you feel bad afterwards. We'd both lost so much. Could there be any more logical next step than to stick it out a little longer? I got behind the wheel, adjusted the seat and mirror, and opened that engine up for a rare foray beyond the second gear.

Whatever magic brewed in my brain that night stayed my little secret. As I drove, Iggy laid with her back to me and her face in her hands, trying to mourn her cousin's death and realizing the last decade of her life (though it made sense at the time) would be a tough phase to explain to a future shrink. I knew she wasn't sleeping. Just like I knew she worried that her involuntary teeth chattering would give away the fact that she wasn't sleeping. I let her be; a man of principle respects a lady's right to piece it together. She'd come around when she was ready, and until then she could keep on burning holes in the upholstery with the fire stare of her sky eyes.

I took deep breaths, inhaling the aroma of the sedan. I'd spent enough time sleeping in it that its stench resembled the no longer unique scent of my trailer. I felt oddly at home behind the wheel. Hours went by blinking at lane dividers and waiting for the sun to rise.

We crossed into Illinois and I pressed on towards home. Chilton waited no farther than a handful more times over the horizon, where the sun peeked over the horizontal slab of Midwest terra firma. Iggy rose with the sun, her chestnut hair exploding in the style of a post-op electroshock therapy patient as she leaned on one arm and blinked her disbelief in garbled Morse code. I glanced once in the rearview mirror and returned my eyes to the road. She looked small in the backseat.

"Carl." She fished for the right words, but when you dedicate so much of yourself to a cause you no longer believe in, to an evil you regret perpetuating, the well of apologies is shallow and dry. "I..."

I let her dangle even though I knew I shouldn't. I forgave her in the shed. I forgave her in the house. But the world outside the frog farm followed a different order, a set of rules where acts of omnipotence didn't bring about resolution, but instead muddied the means of returning to reality. Back at Hilson's we were kindred souls. Back in the sedan I wondered if we had souls at all.

"I'm sorry I lied to you."

Again I let her sweat it out, tightening my grip on the wheel. Straightening my posture. *If only I had Aviators.*

"You don't have to say anything, but at least hear me out. Okay?"

I didn't say anything. After all, I didn't have to.

"I wasn't lying about why I went into law enforcement. My uncle's murder really shook up our family. Especially Haywood. He wasn't living with Mark at the time, but when he heard about the tragedy at the baseball field he totally lost it. Nobody heard from him for a long time after the funeral. But I still liked the idea of working for the good guys, so I decided to keep my promise to him. When I started at the Bureau, I wasn't out for revenge. I was just a kid who lucked into a job. I had a support role helping investigative specialists and didn't think about Mark or Haywood much at all for years. I just went to work every day like everybody else.

"One night I was looking through storage for something a superior needed. I stumbled upon a folder of redacted documents and caught the name Hilson staring back at me. It had Ed's name too, but not much else that I could make sense out of. I guess the Feds suspected Eddie was linked to Mark's murder.

"For months I kept searching for anything related to Eduardo Mondo. I made up excuses to search through the archives, batted my eyelashes at the storage guards to keep down suspicion, but came up with nothing. I wanted to ask people who'd been there longer about Ed, whether they'd heard of him, worked with him, whatever. But I knew they'd ask me why. And I was smart enough to know not to tell them. Then, one night in the stacks, I uncovered the Solutionist article from the tabloid. That's when I looked up Haywood. I found out about the frog farm and went to visit him, only to find the place was a wreck. But he seemed healthy enough, was making a decent living selling the frogs, and we decided that if either of us could come up with any proof of Ed's involvement, we'd avenge his father.

"Haywood was the type to do it, too. I guess I sort of fed off his energy. Honestly, I didn't think I'd get cold feet or anything. I was the one in law enforcement. I was the one dedicated to justice. So I kept at it, staying late at the office to dig up anything I could on Eddie Mondo and the Solutionist. But there was nothing. A suspicious amount of nothing. After a while, I decided I'd make one last ditch effort. If it didn't work, I'd give it up. That's when I came to Chilton.

"I couldn't get into Ed's house, but I knew about the Solutionist's hut, and I knew that Ed spent a lot of time there, and that someone lived right next door. I asked around town for directions, got your name, found out Eddie and you were close, and to be perfectly honest you filled me in on the rest. Your confession gave me the proof I needed to pin Mark's murder on the Agency, on you, and on Eddie.

"I used a payphone to call Haywood after I dropped you at Ed's house and let him know that I had the shooter but not the one who gave the order. But we had no idea what the Solutionist was capable of. What any of us were capable of."

She stopped and caught her breath. *Blink.* Yellow line. *Blink.* Yellow line. *Blink.*

I couldn't look in the rearview, but I saw her nonetheless. She stared out towards the light blue glow of dawn breaking over the horizon.

"Carl, I don't hold you responsible for Mark's murder. I know you pulled the trigger on all of them. All twenty. I forgive you for all of them. Whether that matters to you or not, I forgive you."

Her sky eyes gleamed with tears as she stared into my profile. I pulled over at the Chilton exit as the sun rose over the distant prairies.

"Carl. I appreciate what you've done for me." I knew what she wanted to say. I knew she was wrong. "I know how hard it was for you, especially with it ending up as Eddie, but..." She drew a deep breath, released it towards the window, and didn't bother returning to her thought.

"Won't you say something?" Her body trembled in the back of the sedan, the distance between us an abyss of silence. I scratched my chin, unshaven, coated with blood and purple scabs.

The trailer came into sight, and beyond it the Solutionist's hut basking in the early dawn light. I parked the sedan between the structures among the remaining vagabonds who rustled in their tents. Turning to the backseat I studied Iggy's face, pleading with me to acknowledge her pain. Not yet.

"Eddie was already dead." I told her. "And I can't say for certain that I'm the one who pulled the trigger that stopped him from finishing you off." I threw the car door open and hauled myself out. Turning, I leaned back and reminded her, "We make our own solutions."

I marched into the unlocked, ransacked trailer and came out with a bottle of lighter fluid, a handful of old books, newspapers, the most recent Victoria's Secret catalogue, and a box of heavy duty single-strike matches. Iggy exited the sedan and watched from between the seat and the door as I approached the front of the hut.

"One more for an even twenty and a clean conscience, right? Wrong. I don't owe you anything. This time I'm doing it for myself." I filled my lungs with oxygen and released it slowly back into the atmosphere, transformed into an elementally new substance. I lined my household kindling along the base of the hut one paperback at a time.

The Solutionist's followers gathered around, some fretful, others lurking, fearful and apprehensive. "Folks. I'm sorry to have to do this." Their tired faces looked to me, eyes locked and unblinking. They waited and listened. For them, this moment meant the end of an era, the beginning of a legend. "He came here for a reason, for a purpose. I believe that purpose has been fulfilled."

I doused the lower section of the hut with lighter fluid and shook the last of the can onto the books and magazines. *You think your soluse was hot?* I smiled at the closed window. Whoever inhabited the hut, if anyone did at all, didn't bother to say goodbye to his loyal supporters. The crowd formed a half circle around me, a safe distance back. Iggy shouldered her way through the disheveled mob, making herself small with her fingers wedged beneath her arms.

I struck a match and held it in front of my face at arm's length as the hut undulated beyond the top of the orange flame.

"Remember the Alamo." I announced to the sky, to Eddie Mondo's ghost, and dropped the flame. It kissed the mound of paper and a corona of orange light burst to life at the base of the hut. I stepped back. The warmth rose fast and violent, as though the red oaken planks housed cotton and newspaper. As the flames climbed up the hut I thought of the soluse, the lifeblood of Solutionism and the way it flowed up through my limbs. Was it real? Did I actually feel it or did I act on my own? Maybe I did kill Eddie Mondo. Iggy made it to my side and took my hand and I realized none of those answers mattered.

We stood together and watched as an amber glow shined through the perimeter of the window. The flames crept up the face of the hut, nearly reaching the height of the window, where the glow pulsated and shook the sliding door. Iggy squeezed my hand and I sensed her fear, but all I could do was squeeze back and stand my ground. Our faces sweat in the heat. The window throbbed and cracked; first at the corners, then across the middle of its face. As the flames crawled over the height of the window, the trembling wooden slab burst open. We covered our eyes at the explosion of light, first amber and gold, then as the flames overtook the opening, the familiar green tinged chartreuse of the Solutionist's sky.

A dense pillar of sky eyed smoke billowed up in a mingling column. Behind us the wanderers and believers cowered, shook, and prayed to their messiah. Iggy and I stood side by side, watching the lime green, yellow streaked cloud spiral upwards as the amber glow faded from the empty void of the hut's window. The followers collapsed to their knees, some genuflecting, some bowing with their foreheads to the earth. Others locked arms and swayed.

The smoke grew thicker and hung above the hut in a cloud. Iggy and I moved to the sedan and stretched out across the hood. We watched as the last semblance of Solutionism burned into vapor. We watched until the final ember sputtered out. Until clouds of soluse, of solutions, filled the morning sky. We stared into that sky, unlike any sky we'd ever seen. Not a dawn sky. Not a morning sky. Not twilight or dusk. A timeless sky covered by a mask of green and yellow clouds.

I can't say how long we stayed on the sedan. As long as it took to realize that our lives would begin anew. As long as it took to understand that we'd destroyed something magical, that what we'd done was irreversible, and that we'd never regret that choice. As long as it took to realize that the choice was my own, right or wrong, and that I'd have to live with it. As long as it took to realize that fulfilling a prophecy only matters to those who believe in it when it's fulfilled. As long as it took to realize that I no longer believed in Solutionism. As long as it took to realize my solution was lying beside me on the hood of the '89 Cadillac Sedan de Ville.

In time, the clouds dissipated, fading into oblivion, revealing a starless black night. A lightless sky hung above a world without a Solutionist. A world left to its own solutions. I led Iggy off the sedan and towards the trailer. Holding the door open, she entered my soup can and mumbled through a smiling yawn, "Thanks, Carl." She turned and kissed my cheek, locking me in with those sky eyes. "For everything."

"My pleasure." I reached an arm around the small of her back and pressed her against me. "A man of principle doesn't let his woman down. And I, my dear, am a man of prin-"

She really was a terrible kisser.

This book would never have been made if not for the help and support of many people. That list includes far more names than I'm able to include here.

I'd like to thank Juan Martinez for his encouragement, Chris Abani for his instruction, and Sandi Wisenberg for everything she does at Northwestern. Also, my thanks to Pete Fagundo for guiding me through a couple of lost years, to John O'connor, and to all the other teachers who have contributed to my education and fostered my love of books. My thanks go out to my friends, to Heine, and to everyone else who encouraged and inspired me during the writing of this book. Thank you to the entire team at EyeScream Media for selecting this manuscript and transforming it into the book you hold in your hands, a dream I never imagined would come true. Lastly, my thanks to my family. I look forward to seeing you at breakfast on Sunday.

www.ingramcontent.com/pod-product-compliance
Lightning Source LLC
Chambersburg PA
CBHW070928250626
47159CB00009B/3163